THE
LAST TO
KNOW

THE
LAST TO
KNOW

JO FURNISS

LAKE UNION
PUBLISHING

Text copyright © 2020 by Joanne Furniss

Published by Lake Union Publishing, Seattle

www.apub.com

Amazon, the Amazon logo, and Lake Union Publishing are trademarks of Amazon.com, Inc., or its affiliates.

ISBN-13: 9781542006538
ISBN-10: 1542006538

Cover design by Zoe Norvell

Printed in the United States of America

To my family near and far

All that I forget, I feel.

—Handwritten note in Gwendoline
Kynaston's journal

CHAPTER 1

As Sergeant Ellie Trevelyan splashed into the floodwater at the end of the road, her boots slid in opposite directions on satin-smooth mud. She grabbed on to an iron gate that marked the approach to Hurtwood House. Flakes of rust punctured her skin, but she clung on. The light was failing now, and a tumble into the freezing water would end in hypothermia.

Ellie knew this landscape, and when the river burst its banks, water could surround you with the silent stealth of wolves. Sirens pealed in the distance. Fire engines would struggle on these narrow, inundated lanes. It might already be too late. In its elevated position, she could see Hurtwood House ablaze, its twin chimneys flaming like devil horns.

Ellie dug into her jacket to find her phone; no calls since the one begging her to come. She pressed redial, listened to the American woman's voice inviting her to leave a message, then hung up, securing the device inside her dry pocket. Pressing the ground one foot at a time, like a firefighter testing if a floor might collapse, Ellie waded through the floodwater.

Beyond the iron gates, the driveway curved upward. After a few yards, her feet found dry land, and she made quicker progress up the steep incline. She passed under a stone arch, and the path leveled off in front of the mansion. Its timbers snapped in the heat of the fire, the sound of a rabid dog biting its own shadow.

"Rose?" Ellie shouted into the night. The only answer was an explosion of glass from a high window. She took cover behind an old Land Rover parked on the gravel. She tried again: "Rose!" Nothing. She tried calling the woman's phone once more: nothing. Ellie's pulse filled her throat.

Rose had said she was at the house. That she was going inside. Dead ivy that clung to the walls like so many wrinkled hands had caught fire, a skin of flame making easy progress across the tinder. Ellie scanned the windows for signs of life, but they were bronzed by the glow. *Is it possible someone is alive in there?* The wind shifted and smoke stung her eyes. There was a side door into the kitchen, Ellie recalled, which she'd first entered twenty years ago as a young officer. Another window popped. *Was that*—Ellie ducked and dived to make out shifting shadows—*was that a face at the window?* She hauled herself up to stand on the front of the Land Rover, to get a better view, to be in view of anyone who might be looking out.

"Rose!" she screamed, long and ragged. In the silence that followed, iced air burned her lungs.

There!

A face at an upstairs window. The far corner. She crouched, intending to jump down from the vehicle but, instead, froze. On the passenger window of the Land Rover, two tiny handprints were revealed by the moonlight. Silvery marks left behind by a child. Rose had said she was looking for her son. Ellie jumped onto the gravel, her boot landing on something soft. She picked up a child's scarf and ran the flame-colored wool through her fingers until its ends lay on her palms. Two wolf faces glared at her: Wolverhampton Wanderers—*Wolves*—the local football team. *If the boy dropped his scarf here, where is he now?* Ellie opened the Land Rover door and dropped the scarf inside for safekeeping. The boy would want it back when they found him.

She looked away from the house to consider her next move. From her vantage point, the extent of the flooding was clear; the farmland below rippled in the moonlight. Hurtwood House was marooned on top of a hill known locally as the Grim's Holm. Legend has it, the Grim's Holm floods when the devil wants a new servant.

Well, the bugger's not getting anyone tonight.

Turning back to Hurtwood House, Ellie saw that the face at the window had gone.

ONE MONTH EARLIER

It is a well-known fact that a squire built a great house on land as had been cursed.

A prosperous well sat upon this land, which gave water to the village—until the squire put a stop to it. Some say he let the peasants come but charged them a ha'penny for what the Lord gives freely. Either way, his avarice pleased the devil, who rewarded the squire with more water, enough to sate all his appetites.

And the prosperous well overflowed.

And the river burst her banks.

And the squire was washed down to serve his grim master.

It is said that e'er the Grim's Holm floods, the devil thirsts for a new servant.

—Torn-out page, pasted into Gwendoline
Kynaston's journal

CHAPTER 2

First time I saw Hurtwood, I was driving home with Dylan. I say *home*, but I'd never been there before, never visited his house or even his country. In the darkness, blurry hills rose and fell like towering waves, breaking with each beat of the windshield wipers. Gray water sluiced my window, and I flinched as if it had slid down my neck.

"And welcome to England," said Dylan. With his torso pitched forward over the wheel, he had the air of a sea captain seeking land. For my part, I was numbed by emotions too overwhelming to articulate. My thoughts settled into the anxious rhythm of the wipers: *end of the earth, end of the earth.*

We sped past a road sign announcing "Shropshire." No welcome, just the fact of the matter. The word itself was ornery—SHROP-shuh—and stuck to my foreign tongue like Dylan's homemade custard. He hid a smile every time I said it, so I knew I hadn't gotten it quite right. But he also said my name must mean we were fated to be together: *Rose.* His American Rose. I glanced at his face lit up by the dashboard, and his eyes flickered to mine, narrowed by concern. He wanted me to be happy, so I smiled. Then yelped as a branch as thick as a woman's arm clawed my window.

"Hold tight, nearly there," he said.

Hurtwood House was his heritage, and it would be his inheritance: his past and his future, even if it hadn't been his present for all the years he'd spent living in London, then Africa, where we had met. Two souls far from home, not lost but wandering. One day, Hurtwood House would pass to our son, and I was poised to throw my heart open to the place, as though the blood I share with my child can flow both ways. I took a quick look at Aled, who'd succumbed to a jetlagged sleep despite being tossed around the back seat.

Dylan negotiated violent bends. Our headlights revealed crippled tree stumps, crooked road signs, and the starlit stare of a fox. I wondered if Hurtwood was ready to accept me, a foreigner, a nomad, an outsider ignorant of its ways. An American. We hurtled down a steep dip into a patch of mist that parted to let us pass, then closed ranks, glaring red in our brake lights.

I slid my palm onto Dylan's thigh. "Can you slow down a little?"

"I know these roads like the veins on my hand." But he eased up on the speed. "Sooner we get there, the sooner Aled will be sat by a roaring fire with his grandmother fussing over him."

A roaring fire did sound good. "You know," I said, "he might be a little overwhelmed, seeing it for the first time. A strange house. His grandmother. I hope Gwendoline won't be disappointed if he doesn't jump right into her lap."

"She knows the score. She reckons Aled might think she's someone from the radio because he's only ever heard her voice."

That made me smile. An only child at almost five years of age, Aled enjoyed *imaginative relationships*, shall we say, with fictional characters. He set places for them at dinner. He chattered to them. When they angered him, he banished them under his bed.

"In any case," Dylan went on in a lower tone, "Gwendoline's not exactly demonstrative. She won't overwhelm him with cuddles." We came to an abrupt halt at an intersection. Dylan palmed the wheel, and we lurched into a narrower lane, high hedgerows enclosing us in a green corridor.

Maybe Gwendoline's reserve was indicative of what I would find here in England. I thought of all those classic novels I'd devoured in college—cruel orphanages, austere aunts, and frigid boarding schools. Dylan said that was all in the past; his mother wasn't uptight or overly traditional—she simply hated technology. She owned no computer or device. Even telephones made her shout, as though she needed to raise her voice for us to hear. By contrast, I could leave Aled chatting with my mom on Skype while I caught up on emails. But the contrast wasn't fair; my mom was used to long-distance relationships after decades as a military wife, raising a family of military brats.

Technically, our move from Kenya to England halved the distance between me and my family in Chicago, but driving deeper into unfamiliar landscape made them seem farther away. Since leaving the dazzle of Heathrow Airport, I'd seen only rain and shadows. The years fell away with the miles, and now our vehicle jerked and rattled like a horse carriage, Dylan hunched forward as though clutching ghostly reins.

Then, just as I thought longingly of Heathrow's hospitable lights, we passed an incongruous modern building set into the side of a hill, its cathedral-high windows burning brightly. Inside, a dinner party in full swing had the air of a theater production. A rangy man in a sports jacket broke the fourth wall to look our way, seemingly disturbed by our headlights on the deserted road. It was the first human life I'd seen since we left London, apart from silhouetted heads in cars.

"Nearly there," muttered Dylan. His voice had a breathless edge that reminded me he was nervous too. All those years without coming home. "We should have spent the night in a hotel," he said. "Driven up in the light."

The worry in his voice, so uncharacteristic, made me squeeze his thigh and echo: "We're nearly there." He took a hand from the wheel to hold mine, and the front tire thudded into a pothole, punching the air from my lungs.

As I got my breath back, the beam of our headlights hit a vast mound of land that lay like a sleeping beast. Dylan brought the car to a halt. "It doesn't seem as bad in the daytime," he said. The hill was surrounded by a dilapidated fence that looked as though a line of spears had been thrown but fallen short.

"Is that it?" I asked.

"That's it."

Dylan jerked the vehicle into gear, and we moved on. The road took a dogleg turn through a set of iron gates. Our engine groused at the steep incline. This place was known as the Grim's Holm, an ancient earthwork raised by long-dead hands. For millennia, souls labored up this hillside to a place of refuge or battle—no one knew which. Now, Hurtwood House and its estate stood on the summit.

Our new home. Our new life. *Finally,* I thought, *somewhere safe.*

CHAPTER 3

Flooded potholes erupted under our tires as we climbed the holm to reach Hurtwood House. The driveway led us under an arch that looked ready to collapse into a pile of stones, then it leveled out onto a graveled area in front of the house.

"Good lord," I said.

Scratch *house*; it was a mansion right off the front of an old-fashioned Christmas card. Our headlights passed over pillars that flanked double front doors, which I could imagine being flung open to reveal a festive tree ablaze with lights. But the doors didn't open and instead fell into darkness as Dylan drove past the house to park at the side. He cut the engine, and within seconds the mansion dissolved in the rain-slick windshield.

"Is this the servants' entrance?" I said, nodding at a smaller door surrounded by ornate ironwork.

"We don't use the front door. Last time I opened it, one of the pillars fell down."

"I knew it was big, Dylan, but this is crazy. It's not a house, it's a manor. It has Doric columns and—" I pointed at a lipstick-shaped tower across the yard.

"That's a dovecote."

Our headlights picked out what looked like a miniature temple beyond the dovecote.

"And that's the old well."

"Is there anything else you haven't told me? Are you lord of the manor?"

"I'll call you Lady Kynaston if you want to play Meghan to my Harry." He grinned and kissed my cheek. "But they're Tuscan columns. Very plain. We're not show-offs." A security light triggered, flooding the yard with shadows and the sound of barking. For the first time I noticed that the windows were dark. Did Gwendoline forget we were coming? A single bulb shone in an upstairs room. It was past midnight by my watch, which I'd reset when the Kenya Airways pilot told us the local time in London.

"It doesn't look like there's a roaring fire to greet us." As Dylan jumped out and slammed the car door, two English springer spaniels weaved around his legs until a sharp whistle brought them slinking back into the house. A woman in a bathrobe stood in a sliver of light on the doorstep.

I recognized Gwendoline—Dylan kept a family photo in a silver frame—but I had to overlay that image with this real woman. She was as lean as one of her pillars and exceptionally tall, the same height as Dylan when he reached her. His hug turned her around on the spot, and I saw that her hair streamed down over her backside. She retained the brunette coloring of Dylan's faded childhood photo, and I thought of one of the old books I'd read in college—*The Picture of Dorian Gray*—and wondered what kind of sorcery kept her looking so young. Whatever Dylan said about his mother being undemonstrative, the cloak-like sleeves of her robe swaddled him. Tears stung my eyes. The longest I'd left Aled was five days, and the yearning had gotten physically painful; it seemed unimaginable that I might not see my son for years. Watching through filmy glass, I had an unwelcome reminder that my greatest blessing was also my greatest fear: gaining a son, losing a son.

Still asleep in the back seat, Aled drew his knees to his chest. Cold seeped inside the vehicle like rising groundwater. I studied the faded grandeur of the house, squinting to see through the only lit window—upstairs, in what must be a hallway—but the rain veiled anything tangible. All I could make out, on one pane of the old sash window, were two handprints the color of moonlight. I was unsure if this vision was real or a pattern of raindrops or even a trick of my tired mind, but the child-sized hands seemed to slide down the glass and drop out of sight. I shivered from head to toe.

Aled stirred again. He needed to be somewhere warm. I pulled my jacket out of the footwell and was about to go meet Gwendoline when the driver's side door opened and Dylan landed heavily in his seat. His door slammed.

"Change of plan," he said, his voice clenched. Outside, the door to the house closed and the security light blinked out, leaving us cocooned in the feeble glow of the car interior. He held up a set of keys. "Apparently, there was a miscommunication. We can't stay in the house because the roof is leaking. She thinks she told me, and I didn't want to let on that she forgot, so . . ."

"Where do we go?" I felt puny and vulnerable, as though the darkness had the physicality of water and we had only minutes before it would flood the car.

"We're in the cottage. She made up the beds and put the heating on." Dylan started the engine. "We'll have more privacy down there anyway."

The car made popgun sounds on the gravel as we crept around the rear of the house. The path took us across the summit and down the far side of the hill until the big house was out of sight behind trees. We reached a squat cottage whose roof sawed the sky. We got out. Rain, greasy as butter, flattened my hair to my head. I waited under the cover of the porch while Dylan inspected the keys.

The cottage was like something from a fairy tale. One of the scary ones. It was hard to see the entire building in the darkness, but the porch was held up by wooden spirals. The door itself was hobbity, with a glass panel that had been boarded up. The windows were also covered by plywood.

"We get vandals," Dylan said, fighting with the lock. The base of the house stood on stones and one had been tagged with graffiti. I pushed aside withered foliage to read -*do* just as Dylan forced the stiff door open. I let the stalks fall back, vowing to scrub off the spray paint. Who would deface an old building?

We stepped inside, and I pulled my jacket tight around my chest. The chill sterilized the air, but it carried a gamey tang. Colorless rooms, one on each side, were so dark with the windows boarded up that I could only make out shapes of furniture. As my eyes adjusted, I saw that one chair stood back from the kitchen table as though someone had risen to greet us.

"She said she put the heating on." Dylan reached out a hand to a skinny radiator but frowned.

"Are the bedrooms upstairs?" I nodded to the dark staircase ahead.

Dylan didn't answer but switched on the hallway light, a bare bulb that made little headway in the gloom. The steps creaked under his weight, and I let him reach the small landing where the stairs turned back on themselves before I dared to follow. At the top, he flicked on another bulb. I took it all in at a glance: two bedrooms with iron bedsteads piled high with blankets, a bathroom with a rolltop tub the color of teeth. Again, we lingered in the hallway like uninvited guests. The murky light added to my sense of drowning.

"Are you hungry?" Dylan asked.

"Just tired."

"Do you think Aled will be hungry?"

"He ate his own bodyweight in chips."

"Then let's go to bed. It'll seem better in the morning."

I bit back my reply. The word *hovel* came to mind.

"I know," Dylan said. "It couldn't look much worse."

He went to get Aled while I ventured into the bedrooms. The radiators were cold hunks of metal. I pulled thin curtains across the windows. There was no way I was putting Aled in a room on his own; the whole house smelled of old bones.

The double bed was wide enough for all of us, and I rolled aside a fistful of comforters and blankets. I was surprised to inhale lavender and crisp cotton. So cold it felt damp, but clean. It gave me fresh energy. As I heard the crack of stairs under Dylan's feet, I lay flat on the bed and scissored my legs, warming the sheet with body heat. When Dylan came in, Aled draped in his arms, he told me it was too early to make snow angels.

"Aled's going to love the snow," I said. Dylan rolled him into the center of the bed, where I knelt to bury our boy in covers. Dylan rested for a moment with his hands flat on the mattress, his head slumped against one elbow. I reached over to rub the indent between his shoulder blades.

"You're a brick, Rose Kynaston," he said.

"Whatever that means, I'll take it as a compliment."

"I mean, instead of complaining about this shitty cold room, you just lay down and make snow angels." He pushed upright, and when I made to follow, he stopped me.

"I'll get the heating going. Why don't you go to bed too?"

Jet lag hit me like the fatigue of early pregnancy, when I would have gratefully lain on pins. I didn't care about the cold, the smell, the inhospitable arrival, or the fact that I was fully dressed and hadn't washed. I dragged off my jeans and, as the weight of the covers overpowered me, nestled into Aled. What felt like moments later, Dylan's shoes hit the floor. The covers shifted as he got in on the far side, his leg encircling

Aled alongside my own. Despite this strange new world, all that I held dear was safe and sound.

"Rosie, are you asleep?" he whispered.

I wanted to kiss him good night, but I didn't have the energy to move. The heavy bedclothes hushed me like a mother's arms.

"I'm sorry," Dylan murmured. His voice was muffled and I was drifting, but I'm sure he said it again. "I'm sorry."

CHAPTER 4

A tiny dog tied up on the pavement prevented Sergeant Ellie Trevelyan from entering the coffee shop. One of those crossbreeds that everyone has nowadays, a cockerpoo or a Maltipoo or a shitzpoo. She hunkered down and let it lick her wrist. Ellie squinted into the low morning sun for the dog's owner. Shoppers advanced into the glare with hands raised in front of their eyes, as though foreign forces had napalmed the high street. A hazard, this winter sun. Sooner or later, there would be a car crash, a driver dazzled, a vehicle in a ditch. It promised a long day for a police officer. Ellie needed a cappuccino with enough froth to bloat a bison. But the poodle looked up with weepy eyes. *Don't let me be a statistic,* it said. A more naive person might have heard a simple whine.

Ellie scrubbed her wet wrist against her trouser leg. Earlier in the year, they'd had a spate of family pets stolen and sold to illegal dogfighters. A truly wicked business devised by some local pinhead—the type who performed the pettiest, most antisocial and contemptible tasks in exchange for pin money. *Pinhead money.* They didn't have the brains or backbone to come up with a scam worth going to hell for. In a way, that's what annoyed Ellie the most about pinheads: their lack of ambition. One of them was out today, she'd heard his car scream past earlier with its muffler removed. Making a nuisance of himself.

Keeping guard over the dog, Ellie peered into the coffee shop, and there, squeezed behind a bistro table like the tiger who came to tea, was Robert Elks. Ellie rapped on the glass, and he lifted his massive orange head. She beckoned, and a moment later Elks joined her on the pavement with two huge cups.

"You're a legend." Ellie let his bulk block the aggressive sunlight. "Got to wait for the owner of this dog."

"Someone'll nick it otherwise," Elks agreed. He fluffed the poodle's ears while Ellie made a start on her coffee. "You summoned me, sergeant? What's new, apart from dogsitting?"

"Much money in that game, do you think? I'm going to need a new job."

Elks lost interest in the dog. "It's official then?"

"As of last night. They voted to sell Hurtwood Police Station to a property developer. You won't get the press release until next week."

"Well, I'm not waiting that long to run the story. Is it as bad as we thought?"

"They selected the biggest balls-up from a carousel of bollocks."

Elks snorted. "Can I quote you on that?"

"We could've had a police counter at the fire station, which wouldn't have been too bad—"

"I thought that was the preferred option?"

"So did I. But no, they're putting us on patrol in 'community vans,' which we'll have to drive back to headquarters every night."

Elks twisted away in disgust, and Ellie was blasted by sunlight until he twisted back again.

"That's an hour round trip," he said.

"At the beginning and end of every shift."

Elks cursed copiously, surprising an elderly gentleman who arrived to collect the poodle. Sergeant Trevelyan tried to warn him not to leave his dog unattended, but he hurried away.

"Don't think he believed me," she said. Man and poodle burned to silhouettes in the glare. "Have I grown cynical? Will it be better to have officers on patrol in vans? Come on, let's walk off these calories." She let the coffee cup warm her hands as they went.

"Feeling your age?" said Elks.

"Feeling my knees."

"You've always been cynical," he said.

"Hard not to be round here."

"It's Hurtwood, not the Bronx."

"That makes it all the more annoying. It should be nice. It *would* be nice if we didn't waste so much time and effort on these pinheads. Some little sod had a go at the pharmacy again last night. Couldn't even manage to break in, so he set fire to the bins. Made a right mess. Lazy sods have no excuse, they're not deprived of anything except brain cells."

"You don't know what goes on behind closed doors—"

"Yes, I do. Their only adversity is the daily struggle against the alarm clock. I grew up on the same streets as these kids. What gives them the right to rebel? That lad who nicked the lead off the church roof"—Ellie gestured at a spire whose pinkish stone flushed in the sunlight—"I know his mum, and she taught him right from wrong. He got six months for robbing the church, but it made no difference; he got out and did it again. If they put half the effort into a proper job as they put into being a nuisance, they wouldn't be such . . . pinheads."

"Anyway."

"Anyway."

They reached a crossing and waited for the drivers heading into the sunlight to see them and stop.

"So is there a timetable on the station closure?"

"It's going to be quick." Ellie rummaged in her pocket in response to a vibration. "Hold on: phone." She answered while they crossed, confirming to the duty officer at the police station that she was in Hurtwood.

19

"It's your dad," the constable told her, quickly following up with, "he's all right, sweet."

Ellie didn't like that *sweet*, not because she objected to the endearment, but because it was deployed to soften whatever was coming next.

"But he's down by the church again. The warden says he's been sitting in the graveyard, won't come inside or go home, and they're worried he'll catch a chill."

Ellie said she'd sort it out and rang off, directing Elks down a side alley. "Me dad's playing silly buggers again."

They had to go single file on the narrow pavement along a cobbled lane called Cheapside that ran parallel to the high street. This was the oldest part of town, in medieval times its marketplace, but now the cramped buildings housed low-rent businesses: a knitting shop called A Stitch in Time, a tarot shop called I've Been Expecting You, and a nail bar called Nail Bar. The latter was so unimaginative, Ellie thought. *I mean, make an effort . . .* Nailed It. Sensationail. High Five. *I could do this all day . . .* She shared her frustration with Elks, who suggested Cute-icles. You've Got Nail. Hand Job! They snickered as they clopped over the cobblestones.

Cheapside was bookended by the Victorian-era police station—soon to be apartments—and the church. Ellie saw her dad from a distance, and her mood plummeted. He sat on a bench between gravestones. He waved a glove. From his vantage point, Jim Trevelyan could see the meager shops and businesses of Cheapside, as well as the gated entrance to a prestigious boys' school, and all the way down the cobbles to Hurtwood Police Station.

"What's he up to?" she asked Elks. "Why does he keep coming here?"

Elks took the questions as rhetorical.

"You'll catch your death," Ellie told her father when they reached him.

"Parky," Jim said.

"Too right it's parky. What are you doing here?"

"Stakeout," he said.

Ellie glanced up at Elks, and Jim took that as an introduction, pushing himself off the bench for a handshake. Elks shook and said: "Inspector Jim Trevelyan, it's been a while."

Ellie turned away and hissed, "Don't encourage him." She looked along the shiny-wet cobbles to the police station, where her father had served thirty years. She would have done the same if it hadn't been sold off. Truth dawned. Jim was watching his former police station. His old life. Poor, purposeless old bugger.

"Come on, Dad. Let's get you home where it's warm."

Jim picked up his newspaper, obedient as a poodle. Then he spun around and pointed a finger at Elks: "Robert Elks. Editor of the *Midland Post*?"

Elks beamed. "Never made editor, but yes, I'm with the *Post*. I interviewed you a few times in my cub days."

"I remember, I remember," said Jim, but Ellie doubted that very much. He'd taken two showers that morning and used up all the hot water. Good as gold now, though, Jim trotted past the posh-boys' school in the direction of home. It was only a five-minute walk, and Ellie figured she should make sure he got home safely.

"Have to go," she said to Elks. "That's all I've got on the station closure. I'll leave it in your capable hands."

"I'll give the cage a rattle, watch the turds fall out. Any more on that place?" Elks nodded across the street to the Nail Bar.

"Robert, if I go in there one more time, they'll do me for police harassment. We've checked their documents, the immigration papers are in order, and no one has made a complaint. Not the customers, nor the workers."

"Only because they don't speak English."

"They almost certainly don't pay their taxes, I'll give you that, but tax is not my job."

"There are two Vietnamese lads and one young girl living above the shop. She's no more than a teenager. And yet I never see them in town. I wonder if they're allowed out?" Elks rubbed his bristles and hummed. "Even if it's not illegal, it's no way to live."

Jim stopped, turning to follow Elks's gaze to the Nail Bar. "Hottie," he said. "Hottie."

"Oh Christ!" Ellie grabbed her father's sleeve. She towed him away from the Nail Bar and its *"exotic"* teenage girl. "All I need is a senile sex pest on my hands."

CHAPTER 5

On the first morning at Hurtwood, I woke to find the space next to me empty. I sat up and took the covers with me, making Dylan groan. Low-slung sunlight hit my face.

"Where's Aled?"

My son wasn't in the bathroom or the second bedroom. Dylan got up to feel the radiator: "Heating's working." That much was obvious; the room was as stuffy as a pocket.

"But where's Aled?" I said, pulling on my jeans.

Dylan whipped aside handkerchief-thin curtains. He wrinkled his nose at the dust burning off the radiators while he peered out of the window. "He's outside with my mum. I can see them in the field. He'll be fine."

That seemed questionable. Gwendoline must have let herself into the cottage and taken Aled outside. I hurried downstairs. All the kitchen chairs stood back from the table as though startled by my arrival. The room was dingy and primitive. Brass taps with a running leak whispered into a butler's sink. I found the back door unlocked but had to shoulder it open.

There was Aled in the field, a little bird against a perpetual sky, stroking a rust-colored pony. He threw his head back in laughter, throat exposed, when it nipped his coat looking for treats. The spindly figure of Gwendoline put down the wheelbarrow she was pushing and looked our way. I waved. She picked up the load and kept moving. On the far side of the pasture, a manure pile steamed.

Aled came running over, followed by the pony. Freezing air made his breath glisten. Under my clumsy tread, ice puddles shattered into the pattern of Tiffany lamps. It was one of those rare mornings that made it hard to believe nature was a lucky accident.

"He's a horsey, Mommy." I lifted Aled over the dilapidated fence and kissed him. When the horse raised its nose to smell the fog of my breath, I kissed it too. Dylan came up behind me and draped my jacket over my shoulders.

"Should we go help your mom?" I asked.

He sucked air through his teeth. "She's very particular."

I knew the type; my much-older sister always interpreted any offer of assistance as a passive-aggressive form of criticism. So we stroked the pony until I was shivering, even in my jacket. And I figured that Gwendoline was not coming to greet us. Dylan seemed unfazed by the slight, so I decided I would be too and, instead, tried to get my bearings. I could see the slate roof of Hurtwood House on the summit, rising above a stand of trees. Our cottage and the stables faced off across a lower pasture. The fields of Shropshire rippled from the foot of the hill like the folds of a skirt.

I was about to take Aled inside for a bath when he shouted, "Gwen-ma!" and I turned to see her reach over the fence to tug his zipper up to his chin.

"This young man is the apple of my eye," she said. Dylan put a hand on each of their shoulders, closing the circle, and it occurred to me that this was a seminal moment, when a father steps up as the conduit between generations. The wind carried the sigh of a lone buzzard on the wing.

Gwendoline broke the loop to look at me: "I find it hard to concentrate when I have things to do. Hello, Rose, dear." We shared a hug over the wire, her chin pressing into my forehead. "I have you to thank," she whispered, bending closer to my ear, "for letting my boys come home."

I hadn't been the one keeping them away. I didn't know how to respond, so I smiled. "You two have already met . . ."

"Well, I come sneaking in at eight o'clock"—Gwendoline squatted in front of Aled and made her hand into a creeping animal—"with a pint of milk and some eggs, and I hear a little mouse on the stairs."

"That's me!" Aled joined in.

"And the little mouse has breakfast and plays card games until nine o'clock when it is time to come outside and wake the ponies. And then chores. And now here we are." She stood up again, and considered the long view where predatory cloud shadows roamed the fields. "I'm sorry the big house isn't fit for you." I jumped in to say the cottage was fine, but she plunged on: "It's good to hear young voices."

"It must get quiet up here," I said.

"Well, we all inhabit an island of the mind. I have my dogs. And Guinevere"—Gwendoline patted the pony's neck, then pointed to another horse skulking inside a field shelter—"and that's Morgana."

"She's mean," Aled whispered.

"She's old. And the cold makes her leg hurt. That's why she forgets her manners. Speaking of manners, I'm holding you up. Come for supper, six o'clock." Suddenly businesslike, Gwendoline gave Guinevere's mane a tug, and the pony trailed after her.

After a beat, Dylan said: "So that's my mother. She hasn't changed." We picked our way over snapping ice to the cottage. While Aled and I bathed, Dylan wrenched the boards off the downstairs windows. "Let there be light!" he yelled from outside, making us laugh. The kitchen was indeed transformed. I cleaned up the Aga, a metal oven the size of a pony. I found china plates and washed them in the butler's sink. It had two separate brass taps, and I discovered that one produced water hot enough to cook a lobster and the other water cold enough to freeze it again. As there was no plug that let me fill the sink, I watched my hands turn from red to blue as I washed each dish. When Dylan cleaned up for breakfast, he shuffled his hands between the two extremes without complaint, apparently accustomed to having no happy medium.

After breakfast, he took us for a walk to see the lay of the land.

When we lived in Africa, I'd exercised my linguistic muscles. But I didn't realize Shropshire would pose a new language challenge. I looked sideways at Dylan as the wind became *nesh*, a distant hill a *mynd*, and the raised mound of land we stood upon a *holm*. This old part of him was new to me; he'd reacclimated as easily as putting an adapter on a plug. By contrast, I would need rewiring. For the first time in a life of traveling, I felt daunted.

As we walked, Dylan explained the strange formation of the *holm*. The entire hill we stood on had been raised by hand thousands of years ago, when Iron Age workers piled up the earth to form a mound in the shape of a vast hamburger bun. Centuries later, Hurtwood House had been built on its flattened top. Our cottage nestled into one of its sides. We strolled along a footpath that circled the rim. It was easy to see how the ancient people had exploited the natural terrain, building upon a ridge to form a steep-sided fortress. Even so, it looked surreal, a landscape altered on such a scale that it didn't feel man-made, but it didn't feel natural either.

The wind buffeted in all directions as though it too had lost its bearings. As the path skirted the holm, Aled ran after a red-breasted robin, its belly sucked in like an old soldier.

"So why the *Grim's* Holm?" I said.

"*Grim* is an Old English word for devil." Dylan pointed to the glass house we'd seen the previous night on the opposite side of the holm. "That's Low Farm." I'd been so tired that I was almost surprised to find the modern building really existed. Now I could see that the glass dining room was attached to the front of an older building.

"Monstrosity," Dylan muttered.

Most of the homes we'd passed on the way here had squinted windows, as though the buildings were suspicious of their neighbors. By contrast, Low Farm appeared open and hospitable. But I wondered if its occupants felt exposed at night, eye to eye through the glass with the devil.

The footpath joined the driveway we'd taken the previous night, and we passed under the stone arch again. Dylan pointed at more buildings scattered off to one side. "So what's the oldest part of the holm, d'you think?"

"The rocks," shouted Aled.

"Clever boy!" Dylan laughed in delight. "I should have been more precise: Which building is the oldest?"

The obvious answer was Hurtwood House, but I could tell from Dylan's face that he had a trick up his sleeve. His expression reminded me of our first date. Voluntary date, that is, not the terrifying days and nights we were forced to spend together after we first met. Once that ordeal was over and we'd arrived back in Nairobi, he took me out. He made me guess what was inside a brown paper bag that he dangled as bait. I got it right away: a Hershey bar. During our captivity, we'd talked endlessly about food and the simple pleasures we'd never again take for granted. The gift of a Hershey bar told me he was a keeper.

Now, on the holm, he was playing games once more.

"The dovecote," I said. "It's a ruin."

"The dovecote has always been a ruin; it's a folly."

The wind grabbed my hair and threw it over my eyes. A fake—it was obvious now that he said it. A journalist shouldn't fall for the obvious. *But how am I supposed to know, I don't come from around here . . .* Suddenly, Dylan wasn't the man from our first date at all; instead of two strangers helping each other in a foreign land, he made me feel like a stranger in his land. I raised both palms in exasperation.

"Sorry, I'm a history bore." He took my arm as we set off across the gravel: "It's the old flint barn, it was a lazar house."

Despite myself, the phrase piqued my interest. "Lazar, as in lepers?"

"The holm was a leper colony in the Middle Ages."

"So *holm* is the Old English word for *home*?" I said. "As in *sanctuary*?"

"No, *holm* means an island in a river. I'll show you." We veered off into the trees. Aled scampered ahead, looking for his robin.

"How does your mom manage this place?" I asked.

"I'm not sure she does manage. She can't get anyone to work here." I hurried to catch up with Aled, until I saw him standing safely in a grassy area beyond the trees. My mind flicked back to the conversation.

"Why won't anyone work here?" I asked.

"Because of my father."

Stanley Kynaston. The man who died of shame. All I knew was that Stanley had been a soccer coach, and one of his players had passed away. I was about to ask Dylan why people had blamed his father for the tragedy, but at that exact moment Aled stepped onto the rocks, slipped onto his backside, and plummeted from view.

CHAPTER 6

Sergeant Ellie Trevelyan picked up a package of adult diapers and pretended to read the description. In the aisle beyond the shelf, an elderly lady wearing a biker's jacket studied a row of pregnancy tests. Her crisp white bob contrasted elegantly with the black leather. The pharmacy was no larger than Ellie's kitchen. Not a lot of privacy for customers, although quite convenient for spying. Ellie put down the diapers and picked up a foot pumice.

Now, the old woman held a different pregnancy test in each hand. Her head snapped up, aware she was being watched. The sergeant side-stepped behind a display of joint-support products just as the woman looked at the exact spot where Ellie had been standing. Selecting a brace for her dodgy left knee, Ellie went to the counter. Out of the corner of her eye, she noticed the elderly lady select another brand of pregnancy test.

The cramped retail area left plenty of room behind the counter for Mr. Samwel's exhaustive stockpile of medication. Ellie imagined that, in a previous life, Mr. Samwel had been a Victorian gentleman of the kind who would pin butterflies and beetles onto boards and keep them in mahogany displays in his library. His pharmaceuticals were arranged in color-coded pigeonholes stretching from floor to ceiling. In this life, Mr. Samwel came from Tanzania and had arrived in Hurtwood ten years ago when his eldest son secured a place at the prestigious boys' school in town. Now all three sons and a daughter were destined for the medical profession. His children, their school, this town—according to Mr. Samwel, everything was "wonderful." In addition to the contents of his well-organized shelves, Mr. Samwel's levelheaded enthusiasm for life provided Ellie with a much-needed tonic.

When she came in for bandages after slicing her hand open on broken beer bottles at the children's playground, Mr. Samwel assured her that the job she did for the community was "wonderful." When one of the pinheads smashed his rear shopwindow in an attempt to steal opioids from the safe, Mr. Samwel sighed that God's mercy would be "wonderful." When Ellie's father was diagnosed with Alzheimer's and she cried at Mr. Samwel's counter, he said dementia was not "wonderful," but the medication would help to manage it.

She handed her father's repeat prescription slip to Mr. Samwel along with the knee brace.

"Are you fighting the good fight, Sergeant Trevelyan?" he asked.

"Like yourself, Mr. Samwel. They should give both of us a cape."

"And how is your father?"

"He's convinced he's twenty-five, so he's happy as Larry." Ellie felt the wooden floorboards give as the old woman with the pregnancy tests stood in line behind her. "Would you like to serve this customer first, Mr. Samwel, so she doesn't have to wait for you to deal with my prescription?"

"That would be wonderful," agreed the pharmacist.

The little old lady nodded at Ellie. She wore half-moon glasses that—combined with the sharp haircut and leather jacket—gave her an ironic air, as though age was yet another fad. Ellie had met this lady before, at the Nail Bar on Cheapside. She was the manager. In the salon, where she had been wearing a uniform, Ellie merely noted her as "well preserved." Hardly surprising, given her line of business. But out in the world, she seemed formidable. The woman recognized the police officer—they exchanged how-are-yous—and then she paid for two pregnancy tests, leaving the pharmacy with a paper bag and a jangle of the door. Ellie noticed that Mr. Samwel's eyebrows were up near his hairline.

"Maybe she's also convinced she's still twenty-five," Ellie said.

"I couldn't say," said Mr. Samwel. He took her prescription and went to locate Jim's medication.

Oister. The old woman's name was Lillian Oister. Strange name. Memorable. Could be a star of the silent screen. Ellie had spoken to her at the Nail Bar about a month ago. Lillian Oister didn't speak Vietnamese, and two of the three nail technicians didn't speak English, so it wasn't clear how they communicated. Robert Elks said the staff weren't allowed to leave the premises. Correction, Elks *speculated* that the staff weren't allowed to leave. And here she was, Lillian Oister, who must have been in her late sixties if she was a day, buying pregnancy tests.

"Your order came in the delivery one hour ago," said Mr. Samwel, snapping Ellie out of it. "You must have a sixth sense." He folded a neat box inside a neat bag and sealed it with a neat label. Clinical and organized, far removed from the messy reality of her father's mind. Who knew the messy reality of Lillian Oister's mind? The pregnancy tests could be for a relative or a neighbor or—

"That woman." Mr. Samwel pitched his voice as low as the winter sun. "Do you know her?"

"She runs a nail bar. Are pregnancy tests an unusual purchase for an older lady?"

"She is a regular customer."

"Of pregnancy tests?"

"I cannot discuss her medical requirements. There is confidentiality to consider."

"Mr. Samwel, you look after all your customers wonderfully."

"I hope so." He put through the payment for the prescription and the knee brace, then went to peer through a door at the back of the

31

shop. He returned to the counter. "My son was here earlier, but he is gone now. I don't want him to overhear, he might not approve."

"Approve of what?"

"I am not a gossip, but if a pharmacist has concerns about the welfare of a patient, then it is appropriate—no, it is a duty—to inform the authorities, is it not?"

"Yes, we're all responsible for safeguarding."

"I have not been able to alert that woman's GP because she is not registered with a doctor. So maybe I should alert the police instead? What do you think?"

"You're concerned for her health?"

Mr. Samwel leaned over the counter. "I googled her, and she is sixty-six. Every week, she comes in here to buy condoms."

Ellie smiled. "Older people have sex too—"

"And that is wonderful, but she has also bought the morning-after pill twice. Now, pregnancy tests. Who is using them? She told me they are for her daughter, but I see on Facebook that her daughter lives in London, so I think she's not telling the truth. If she asks for a morning-after pill again, I will have to speak to the daughter. But what if someone who needs a morning-after pill doesn't get it because I have refused? And then there could be an unwanted pregnancy. I thought maybe you know more about her, if there is another daughter who lives in Hurtwood?"

Ellie reassured Mr. Samwel that he was right to be cautious. She promised to find out more about Lillian Oister and her dependents. She suspected that Robert Elks might be the man for the job.

CHAPTER 7

U nbeknownst to me as we casually explored our new surroundings, one tip of the holm ended in a sandstone cliff. If the mound was shaped like a vast hamburger bun, as I'd imagined it, then it was a hamburger bun with a bite taken out. Unbeknownst to Dylan, a landslide the previous winter had brought the cliff edge closer to Hurtwood House. This is where Aled fell.

A river curving around the base of the holm had formed the cliff over time, and it was this river that Dylan wanted to show me that first day. On rare occasions it burst its banks and inundated the surrounding farmland. This left the man-made mound isolated in the flood. An island in a river. A holm.

The recent slump altered a landscape that Dylan had known since boyhood, but I wondered if his memory had also been eroded by time. By luck, Aled landed on a rocky lip and suffered only a barcode of scratches on his forehead. If we'd taken a different path through the trees, he might have plunged down a sheer section of the cliff and—

I fell through the days following the accident, jetlagged and plagued by images of his body flip-flopping over rocks. In the middle of a task— we had so much to do—a memory of his lucky escape would hit me like a fist. I couldn't dodge the cruelty of my own imagination. I couldn't shake off a sense of threat closing in on all sides of the exposed holm. The wind sounded an ever-present drumroll.

When Dylan found me one evening, close to tears while watching Aled in his bedtime bath, he held me and whispered: "This isn't like you, Rosie." He tipped my face up to his. "I've seen you stare down a terrorist."

"He wasn't a real terrorist; he was a douchebag with a gun, and anyway, look how that ended." Outside, the weight of darkness made the afternoon feel as ominous as night. As winter closed in, every day grew shorter as though time was running out. Dylan tried to help me settle. For Thanksgiving, he ordered a can of pumpkin puree online when I couldn't find any in the store in Hurtwood. How could I tell him that no matter how many boxes I unpacked, how many curtains I fixed up, how many pies I baked, I couldn't make his home feel like my home?

I drove every day into the town of Hurtwood, compelled by some kind of nesting instinct to purchase knickknacks that might improve the cottage. Gwendoline never left the holm—"I shop wholesale twice a year, and that's all I need"—but I always dropped in to the great house to invite her to come into town with me.

Aled already had a favorite chair in her kitchen. Routines took root quickly. The first time we ever came into the house—right after his fall—Aled had been shivering, and Gwendoline fetched a blanket that instantly became *his* blanket. Maybe he would have forgotten about the accident—maybe I would have forgotten too—if we hadn't made such a furor, if Gwendoline hadn't kept clutching his shoulders and muttering, "I keep seeing you disappear over the cliff" or "Thank goodness we found you in time" or "Luck of the devil, you." I'd also sat there shivering, not from cold or shock, but from anger. She paused, hand on hip, as though she were an illustration that had stepped out of the pages of a Roald Dahl book: tall, angular, scratchy at the edges. And she let slip that the cliff had a name: the Long Drop. Its danger was well-known, and yet both of them, Dylan and Gwendoline, had let Aled go bounding around like a spring lamb.

All the portentous words that tagged their landscape—the Grim's this and the Devil's that and the Long Drop—and yet they acted oblivious to its dangers. There were times when I felt like the only wide-awake person among sleepwalkers.

As usual, when Aled and I stopped at the great house, he wrapped himself in the blanket that was draped over one of the kitchen chairs. Deep inside the house, a clock struck the hour. She offered him cake, even though it was barely past breakfast time. I said we were on our way to Hurtwood, Dylan was coming, would she like to join us? She tightened Aled's new scarf around his neck. It was orange and decorated with stylized wolf faces—for the local soccer team. Aled loved it. The bright color reassured me that I'd be able to spot him if he wandered off into the trees.

"Nothing I need in town," said Gwendoline.

"You can show us around," I pressed.

"Show you up, more like. No, Dylan!" She snatched out of Aled's hands a hard-backed notepad with an elephant on the cover. Her temper was so unexpected, I didn't notice until later that she'd mixed up the boys' names. She put the book in her corner cupboard, moving stuff around with the intensity of a chess player. Aled slid from his chair as though he'd melted and appeared a moment later from under the table, burrowing onto my lap. I stroked his hair and whispered that it was okay; Gwen-ma wasn't angry. He buried his face in my woolen shawl.

In the shocked hush that followed, a door that led into the rest of the house clicked, its brass knob turned, and it swung open. Wider and wider, as though being steadily pushed, it revealed a somber hallway. No one there. Only a wooden staircase with faded paint. The flesh on my back crept, as though fingers had straddled my spine and gathered up the skin. Gwendoline muttered something, and the other door—the one behind me that led outside—rattled in its frame. She took slipper-soft steps to press the hallway door shut with a snick. I felt Aled's limbs soften, and only then did I realize that his whole body had gone rigid when the door opened.

I stood up with Aled in my arms. We said goodbye and left. I didn't want to mention it in front of the boy, but as I picked up Dylan and drove off the holm, I bit back words of relief that we weren't staying at Hurtwood House after all.

Ten minutes later, we parked and walked along Hurtwood's main street. Dylan looked left and right, amazed by the bustling traffic and pedestrians. The town had grown, he said, and was swollen by new houses. He pointed to a hipster café, complaining that they'd only had instant coffee when he lived here. We ducked into a housewares store where we bought a rug from a clerk who acted like the transaction was a major imposition. Her tattooed eyebrows arched as she trudged to the stockroom. Dylan slapped his wallet on his palm.

"Why don't you head to the bank while I wait?" I said. The ATM functioned in the way he preferred: methodical, reliable, courteous. Everything this store clerk was not. The door jangled on his way out. When the clerk returned and wrote my name on the receipt, I said, "It's Rose Ky—"

"Kynaston." Her eyes didn't leave the pink chit.

"How did you—"

"He won't remember me, I don't suppose." She ripped off the top sheet and pushed it across the counter, eyeballing Aled, who lay on the rolled-up carpet as though it was a log on a swollen river. The clerk snatched her cell and started tapping out a message. I wondered if it concerned Dylan. Or all of us. We set off down the sidewalk as fast as the rug would allow.

Dylan appeared by my side. "Let me take that."

I shrugged the load onto his shoulder. "Did you know that woman in the shop?" I asked.

"The one with the eyebrows? What's happened to women's eyebrows since I've been away?" He ducked down an alleyway, and we emerged on a cobbled street with a police station at one end and a church at the other. A car thrummed past, and I held Aled's hand on the narrow sidewalk.

When we could walk together again, I said, "She knew you. Were you at school together?"

"Don't think so; I went to the boys' school. Over there." He pointed the end of the rug at a brass sign engraved with "Hurtwood Boys' School est. 1556." The plaque exuded understated confidence. Dylan strode by with barely a glance at the ivy-covered building. "Maybe she was someone's sister. Pretty sure I never slept with her." He pulled his mouth down into a cheeky face, but I rolled my eyes.

"You knew her well enough to piss her off. She did not like you."

"People in small towns"—Dylan shifted the rug to the other shoulder—"carry a grudge like a genetic condition. You kick one person in the shin, and half the town limps."

Is that true? I'd grown up a military brat, moving between tight-knit communities. Life on a base gets intense, but camaraderie makes up for the fishbowl effect. What made the community in Hurtwood so dysfunctional?

"What kind of grudge?" I said.

"My father. Stanley. Dead nearly twenty years—you'd think they'd have got over it by now." Without looking, he crossed the cobbles. I caught Aled's hand and made him check both ways. He ran to catch up with his father, who led us down another alley. The sound of our footsteps was discordant against the old brickwork. *Stanley. The man who died of shame.* Dylan rarely talked about his father. Maybe that would change now that we were here? His father never forgave himself after a young soccer player died in his care. The police got involved, but Stanley himself passed away soon afterward; he didn't live long enough to clear his name. Dylan believed his innocence, and I believed Dylan's sincerity.

Except . . .

Except shame is the seed of many a secret. My mother believed that everyone had a right to tell what she called "cosmetic lies," as though our minor misdeeds are blemishes that we cover up with powder. As a reporter, I'd seen more of the ugly kind. The paper trail of corruption. The fraudster's offshore accounts. The emails revealing sexual harassment. The human capacity to keep secrets is limited only by the size of the available hiding place.

A shrink might suggest that my journalistic curiosity came from growing up with my father. One autumn day, a year after he retired from the US military and settled us all in his hometown outside Chicago, his secret emerged from its hiding place in our neighbor's womb. My mother's subsequent investigations unearthed affairs on every base we'd ever inhabited. My mother dignified his deceit with a divorce, he moved away, and we got left in his hometown like luggage forgotten on a station platform. Some might say I have a suspicious nature, but I'm pretty sure it's mostly nurture.

From my absent father to Dylan's: Stanley Kynaston, *the man who died of shame.* How did a soccer player die in his care? I recalled Dylan saying the boy "fell"—I guessed he hit his head. The kind of tragedy that causes a tight-knit community to strangle itself with recriminations. And the last straw for Stanley, who was already battling an illness. But it'd happened twenty years ago, so did these people really hold a grudge, or was there more to it? Maybe Dylan was right, and his father had done nothing wrong. Or maybe the human mind offers limitless storage space, and there a man could hide all the secrets he desired.

CHAPTER 8

Whenever the wind dropped, mist snuck up around the base of the holm, and we drifted in a gray sea. Each morning, I tugged on a smile for Aled in the same way a depressed person might wear colorful clothes. I could no more blow off my funk than I could blow away the fog.

The Kynastons' pariah status left me more alienated than ever. I woke before sunrise; even my body clock was out of kilter. I took to prowling around without switching on the lights, wading through insomnia. One day, I realized that daybreak in Hurtwood was late evening in Chicago and called my mother, who'd always been a night owl.

"Rosetta!" Her voice was as reassuring as a Pyrex warming in the oven.

"Mama," I said, toggling the volume on my laptop so she didn't wake the boys.

"Why are you up so late?" Despite having lived on four continents, my mom had never nailed time zones. There was a spike of laughter in the background.

"Who's there, Mama?"

Her book group had taken up poker. She put me on speakerphone, but I failed to find a gap in their dovetailed chatter. I reassured my mom—and her friends—that everything was perfect in England and let her get back to her game.

I made a pot of coffee, wishing it was whatever she was having.

The sun appeared on the horizon at the height of a peephole. I thought of an eye watching me through a slot in a metal door. The eye of a terrorist. *Don't think about that now.* I spilled some coffee, splashes sizzling on the hot plate of the Aga. It smelled like the acrid heat in our cell, where the eye had appeared at the door morning and evening. The eye had always lingered on me longer than on Dylan. *Don't think about Mogadishu.*

I took myself outside to clear my head. The air reeked of fox musk. Logs were stacked by the door, and I thought it would be a good distraction to start a fire to make the living room cozier. I swept aside dead foliage, revealing the graffiti daubed on the sandstone: *Pedo.*

Charming. Why would vandals come all the way up here? I pushed the nettles back to cover the word and carried an armful of logs inside. But as soon as my kindling curled into flame, a velvet tongue of smoke rolled out to lap the walls. *Dumb to light a fire without checking the chimney. Get a grip.* I doused it with the dregs of my coffee. *You've coped with worse than this, much worse.*

I tried not to think about Mogadishu, but it was too late.

A barbecue smoking in a rooftop restaurant. Flare of fat dripping on embers. Sizzling, laughter, a distant crack from a car or a gun. Mogadishu, Somalia. I've been in the country for three hours. My only contact—a fellow American journalist—tells me I'm an idiot. *Get some security, or get back to Kenya.* He calls over a lone figure from the bar to talk sense into me.

The Englishman introduces himself as a correspondent. I'd noticed him when I first walked in—broad, cute, nose in a book—but took him for ex-military—lean, clean, back like a flagpole. But journalist, okay. We shake hands over the candle, making the flame quiver. Our mutual friend squints: "Don't look at her like that, man, I'm trying to keep her safe." Dylan pulls up a chair, and we ignore the comment.

"And why do you *boys* think I need protection?"

"It's Somalia. Everyone needs protection." Dylan nods at a neighboring table packed with local men. "There's my driver, my fixer, my security detail. Background checked and well paid, with the promise of a bonus if they keep me alive."

"I have a fixer—"

"And how do you know he won't sell you to the first Al-Shabaab lowlife who offers more than you're paying? You're freelance—you've got no backup. Why would you come to a place like this?"

The barbecue guy puts a plate of glistening meat on the table. I'm so hungry I feel hollow. "I'm a nobody, like you say, and I want to make a name for myself. I figured I wouldn't have much competition here."

Dylan offers me the last of his beer. "Didn't say you were a nobody." Then he offers me the last seat in a secure vehicle on a press trip the following day. I accept both. Looking back, it's only in the game of life that you can roll a winning and losing dice at the same time.

While my boys slept, I went for a run. Coming back up the holm on the steep path alongside the pasture, I stopped to catch my breath and heard stones scatter behind me.

"This is private property." The man's voice was too high for his size. Wide at the shoulder and hip, he carried little weight and appeared flat, as though he'd stepped out of a playing card. It was the man from the glass house. Guinevere trotted up to the fence and pushed her nose into my pocket. "If we have to call the vet because of whatever you're feeding those ponies," he said, "I'll be sure to forward his invoice."

I pushed Guinevere aside, along with his empty threat. His tone stiffened my spine. The assumption that he could size me up just by looking at me had been typical at my first "proper" job, a television network run by pale males cut from his cotton. With the predictability of the hourly news, they'd condescend to young women who were considered as transient and insubstantial as pixels on a screen. I said, "This is Kynaston land."

He cocked his head. "Have we met?"

"No, you'd remember. I'm Rose. I live here."

"The son's wife." He shifted his weight. "The wanderer returns. I wasn't sure if he was really coming home or if it was one of Gwendoline's ideas." His eyes widened, inviting me to join him in laughing at an old woman. He held out a hand, which I shook after a beat. "Tony Thorn. From the so-called Low Farm. I'm sure you spotted it on the hill."

"The glass house."

"I snapped it up when it was a wreck. I don't think many people could have recognized its potential, but I saw a vision. Like the Iron Age people who erected the holm. Only I have underfloor heating." He smiled at his own wit while I sighed inwardly. I'd relocated often enough to know that settling into a new community is like dating. You have to put yourself out there with energy, humility, a hopeful heart. If I was going to make this place home, I'd need all the allies I could get. Even this clown.

Tony Thorn was on his way to see Gwendoline, so we walked together. He announced he was a television producer. I breathed warm air onto my cupped hands to cover a smile. *I must have smelled it.* He owned a production company that made a show called *The Quest.* I'd never heard of it but understood from his tone that I should be impressed. I told him I also worked in television; I'd been a documentary-maker in Chicago, then a freelancer in Africa. I left out the personal reason I resigned from the network; only two people in the world knew that story, and neither of those was Dylan.

"So what do you plan to do here?" Tony Thorn asked.

"We're setting up a production company to cover rural news."

He walked into the kitchen of the great house without knocking. Dylan and Aled were sitting at the table.

"It's you, Thorn." Gwendoline stood sentry behind her table. She dribbled tea into a cup and pushed it into his hand. "You're in a hurry. Tell me what it is you want, while I make a fresh pot for Rose."

Thorn trailed her around the kitchen relating a long anecdote about a celebrity named Lindy Berg. When he reached his punch line and stood back to receive Gwendoline's approval, she narrowed her eyes, swirling the teapot over the sink: "Isn't Lindy Berg the one who's dead?"

"What?" Thorn recoiled. "I met her yesterday. Lindy Berg is the presenter of *The Quest*. She's coming here for filming." Even though Thorn must have been in his late forties, I wondered if Gwendoline functioned as a mother figure. In response to his scolding, her shoulders hunched. Whether she was out of touch or becoming forgetful with age, Thorn's tone seemed cruel. Dylan put himself between them.

"What's this about filming?" he asked.

Thorn explained that Lindy Berg's next quest would be to uncover the history of the holm by leading an archaeological dig on television. Gwendoline's face told me this was not the first time the subject had been aired. The only sound came from one of the English springer spaniels licking itself.

"What do you think, Mum?" Dylan said gently. "The holm on television."

"Over my dead body." After a beat, she turned to me. "Are you hungry, Rose? I made scones."

Thorn stepped forward. "Now, Gwendoline—"

"Jam!" Aled yelled, and the spaniels leaped up, barking. While Gwendoline flapped her tea towel at the dogs, the men exited through the side door. The spaniels slunk to their beds, circled, and collapsed with a sigh. Outside the window, I could hear the rumble of male voices.

"The gelatinous Tony Thorn." Gwendoline said *gelatinous* with such relish, her tongue slapped.

"Tony Torn," echoed Aled, and dolloped jam onto the table.

Gwendoline passed him a plate. "Lindy Berg! She's on the radio all the time. Flogging her book about aging. Silly moo makes it sound like she invented it."

"You knew she was alive." I laughed.

Gwendoline wrinkled her nose. "He comes in here, eyes everywhere, like he's measuring up. We're not for sale." The wrinkle deepened, pulling her features into a scowl. She seemed to lose her posture and shrink into a smaller person. "What's he going to find on this quest?"

"There's plenty of history on the holm."

"Let it rest in peace." She put one hand to her hair as though preventing a hat from blowing away. "This country is cluttered with more relics than an old woman's mantelpiece—"

She stopped when the door on the far side of the kitchen clicked, the handle made a quarter turn, and it swung open. The maudlin hallway exposed itself. The skin around my spine shrank to the bone. Gwendoline muttered something, and Aled spat crumbs as he echoed her. Behind us, the outside door rattled in its frame.

"What did you say?" I whispered to him.

He looked me in the eye. "Make yourself at home." Under the table, his small hand gripped my fingers.

"Why does that door—" My skin lifted when the outside door opened, but it was only Dylan coming back inside. He trailed a hand over my shoulder as he passed, en route to warm up by the Aga.

"Why does the door open by itself?" I asked again.

"It's the wind," Dylan said. I noticed he didn't ask, "Which door?" He carried on: "You'll never guess what. Thorn offered me a job on *The Quest*."

"You don't work in television."

"It's only for the episode being filmed here, but he'll give me a credit."

I grated my tongue over the back of my teeth. There was no way I wanted to work for a baby-man like Thorn, so I wasn't sure why I felt bent out of shape. But he should have offered me that job; I was the one in broadcasting. Dylan worked in print, and yet he got handed a job like an invitation to boys' poker night.

"Rosie," Dylan said, "he needs someone with local influence."

But everyone in Hurtwood hates you because of your father! I took a bite of scone to stop myself from saying such a bitter thought aloud. *But, still. How typical.* I washed the crumbs down with tea. "What about setting up our business?" I asked.

Dylan looked around, and I realized Gwendoline had made herself scarce. He sat next to me.

"Thorn needs me to persuade Mum to let them film in the barn—the leper house, you remember? She won't sign the release forms. Maybe I can calm her down. The pay's not bad, and I'll spend a couple of days in Manchester making contacts that might be useful to us later—"

"Manchester? But that's far."

"It's a two-hour drive. I'll have to stay overnight—"

My chair skidded over the flagstones as I stood up.

"You angry, Mommy?" Aled said, and then to Dylan: "Mommy's angry."

Through the window, a solitary hill blocked the horizon like a fist slammed down onto the land.

CHAPTER 9

My attempt to blow off steam on the road to Hurtwood was hampered by fat pigeons strewn along the road like rocks. They waited until I braked—making me the chicken—before flapping to safety.

I parked in town and found the butcher's. The air inside smelled as clean and sharp as a blade. While I stood in line, my mind slid back to the pigeons. Would I also fail to react until it was too late? The new start Dylan and I had planned included the flexibility to share childcare so we could both thrive. Maybe, once we were established, we'd have a second child. But how could I work if Dylan was in Manchester? We'd hoped Gwendoline might help with childcare, but she hadn't offered to babysit; she complained about being busy, and I had no idea what she did all day.

Plus, there was a question mark over her capability. Dylan insisted she was just a little forgetful, but it felt like more than that . . . From a display shelf, I picked up a jar of pickled walnuts that looked like shrunken little brains. Gwendoline looked after herself and her animals, but a child was more demanding. More fragile. More precious. It was great that Dylan had been offered a job so soon, but he'd trampled my toes in his rush to get ahead.

"Harsh, isn't it?" The butcher glanced outside so I guessed he was talking about the weather.

"It's freezing, but this blue sky is beautiful."

"You're not from Shropshire, are you?" His accent curled off his tongue like the ham he rolled up and passed over the counter on a cocktail stick. "This one's local born and bred, from a farm on the far side of the Wrekin."

I recognized the name of the solitary hill I'd seen from Gwendoline's kitchen. Its distinctive summit followed me like a portrait with watchful eyes. I told him I was from Chicago and lots of other places.

"Hope you settle in, duck. What can I get you?"

I ordered, thinking, *Did he just call me* duck? and left the store loaded with meat, cheese, and the jar of pickled walnuts. But as soon as I got outside, the cold wind prodded me and I remembered Dylan wanted bacon. I ducked back through the closing door just as the old woman who'd been in line behind me bellowed "—married to that Kynaston boy." The door shut as quietly as a person slipping into the shadows. The woman pressed her chest against the counter, elbows planted at chin height, addressing the butcher's back as he bent over a noisy slicing machine.

"From Chicago," he called over his shoulder without turning. "She'll be used to this wind!"

"She'll have more than the weather to worry about if she's living on the holm. I heard they've got a boy. Who'd take a child up there?"

The butcher leaned his weight on the slicer.

"Everyone knows what went on at Hurtwood House," she pressed.

The air smelled of blood that hadn't quite been washed away. I had to hear more. I stepped behind the shelf of pickle jars.

The butcher held the meat aloft so the old woman could see. "Enough?"

"Add a few slices for the grandbabbies. Now, my babbies know there are lines that won't be crossed, or, never mind the law, they'd have me to answer to. But what happened up on that hill happened right under that woman's nose, and she never did nothing about it. Never trust a six-foot woman, my mother told me, they're as uppity as men. Present company excepted. You best give me some gammon for the grandbabbies; they'd live on bananas if it was left to their mother."

She must be referring to the soccer player who died. I was trapped behind the shelf, unable to move without drawing attention to myself; as soon as the butcher was done cutting thick slabs of ham and turned around, he'd see me. "Old lady Kynaston has her own cross to bear," he muttered as he drew the knife. "Haven't seen her for a long while; I wonder if she hasn't gone into a home."

"My boys collect scrap from the lady of the manor. Leaves their money on the doorstep, she does. Won't give them the time of day. Convenient, isn't it, her *illness*? Awful young for dementia. Can't be more'n sixty-something. My mother didn't go senile until her eighties."

"It affects people all ways."

"Easy to fake. That's what my daughter-in-law says, and she's a doctor's receptionist. Easy to pretend, shut away in that big house and emerging once in a blue moon to make a show of being scatty. Maybe living like a recluse has driven her round the bend, but my daughter-in-law reckons old lady Kynaston knows what she's playing at. You can't prosecute someone who's senile. That's the law. It'll get the police off her back if they ever solve the case."

The case? Like police case? A cold blast hit the back of my legs as the door opened. *I should go while I have the chance.* I caught the closing door, but I couldn't quite leave in case there was more. The man who'd come in, slapping fish-pink hands together to warm up, gave me a questioning look. The butcher turned to greet the new customer—"Just a moment"—his face going slack when he saw me in the doorway. I fled onto the sidewalk, hurrying away so fast I left my own breath behind in thought clouds.

When I reached the car, I threw the meat in the back and scooted down in my seat until I hid behind the steering wheel. When we lived in Africa, I'd always been conspicuous, a curiosity. Not a problem, but after five years I'd grown weary of being the outsider. It must be how a celebrity feels, only I endured the fame without the fortune. But it was no different here; in fact, it was worse. Now, I had notoriety. Every time I opened my mouth, people would know I was the American who married into the most hated family in town. I started the engine to go home.

Home!

As if Hurtwood House—or even our cottage—felt like home. I should demand we move somewhere we might be welcome. I felt the tug of the engine against the brakes, the car ready to respond. The voice of the old woman sliced through my head: *Convenient, isn't it, her illness?* People could be cruel. Gwendoline had endured such bitterness. If it had gotten to me after a few weeks, what effect had it had on her after nearly twenty years?

I felt a rush of longing for the life we left behind, our little garden in Nairobi with red-leafed trees and tortoises who ruined my lettuce patch. Weird thing to miss, but it came in a wave, like the sorrow after my father passed. The person who had died this time, though, was me: the old me. My home, my friends, my work, the mundane routine that formed the predictably safe walls of my day; these four pillars had been knocked from under me like a rickety stool. And now I sat here, wide-eyed and winded, under a sky as gray as grief.

I shut off the engine and got out of the car. Exhaust fumes had gathered like a mob. *Bitter old crone. She can't run me out of town.* Weaving through alleyways to the main street, I forced myself to be positive. The sky was blue. The air was clean. Aled was happy. A church bell tolled, and I noticed its spire reflected in a Georgian window. I took out my cell to get a shot for Instagram. Caption: *Living in a chocolate box!* An upbeat approach was the best way to get a few likes. Right then I'd have taken any kind of boost, even an Insta-high.

Across the street, I saw a sign reading "Western News." I walked over to check out the window display. The daily newspaper was called the *Midland Post*. Today's headline: "Police Defend Station Closure." This office was a far cry from the cut-and-thrust of African politics or the gloss of network television in Chicago, but I felt a sense of kinship, like recognizing the shape of your own nose on the face of a distant cousin. On a whim, I went in.

The door had to be persuaded to leave its frame. The air inside carried a tang of unwashed coffee mugs and the carbon smell of ink. I rubbed my fingertips together as though they were already stained. I called hello. An orange beard appeared from behind a screen: "Looking for the post office? It's two doors down." An inflatable crocodile suspended from the ceiling skulked through the gloom.

"I'm looking for the *Midland Post*."

"Goodness me, a visitor from afar." The man got up and moved with grace despite the fact that he looked like a closet wearing a suit. "Robert Elks. Contributor to every section of the *Midland Post* except the obituaries, but I'll get there eventually."

"I'm Rose." I decided to be myself for a moment, without the Kynaston name lurking over my shoulder like a gangster's heavy. I explained I'd just moved to the area and I was a journalist. He invited me to sit down while he made coffee. I took a closer look around the office, noting a filing cabinet marked *Archive*. It was nosy, ghoulish even, but I wondered if he'd written about the events at Hurtwood House. That woman in the butcher shop mentioned a case. Had Stanley been questioned after the youngster died? Had Gwendoline? And what about the boy's family—were they still in the area? I preferred to be forewarned if I was likely to run into them in the butcher's shop. My fingers itched to creep into the archive, but Elks came back with two mugs.

We discussed the state of modern journalism and sighed wistfully about Africa, where he'd worked as a cub reporter, and he talked about expanding their social media presence to reach people in remote areas.

I could help with that . . . I realized I had said it out loud.

"You're looking for a job?" he asked.

I thought of the partnership I'd planned with Dylan. That dream had dissipated like breath in the cold Shropshire air. "I'd love to find work," I said. "I think it'll be crucial to settling down here. But I'm a documentary-maker. I don't work in print."

"We're not looking for another old hack. Our online presence is pitiful. If we had someone with multimedia skills . . ." Elks stood up, and I was struck by his apt name as his bulk filled the space. "I'll need to speak to head office. But someone with your experience doesn't just walk in off the street . . ." He went in search of a business card. Once upon a time, this must have been a thriving news hub; there was space for a handful of reporters. Outside, people rushed past, looking at their phones rather than the headlines in the window. I'd spoken without thinking it through, but what I said was true: if Elks wanted to engage with the community, I could help with that.

When he returned, I asked about the police station closure and discovered he'd been campaigning against it. Elks bemoaned a lack of interest from the townsfolk, who didn't attend meetings but complained about decisions made in their absence.

"Maybe," I thought aloud, "if people could see for themselves how much local officers do in the community . . ." A storyboard took shape on the canvas of my mind; a day in the life of a Hurtwood cop. Elks nodded, but his eyes flitted to the clock.

"On a deadline?" I asked.

"Always. But hold that thought, I'll be in touch."

As I bent to write my contact details on his notepad, my pen lifted off the paper after *Rose* . . . Then I scrawled the rest of my name and number, and handed it to him.

"Rose Falcone," he read aloud. From his questioning look, I wondered if he already knew my real name, that I was a Kynaston. "Did I pronounce it right: Fal-CONE-ay?" he asked. I confirmed that he had, it was Italian. And I chided myself for being paranoid.

I left the *Midland Post* on a high, both about the job and the archive that might answer a lot of pertinent questions. But, as I hurried along the main street, I also wondered how I would explain to Dylan that I'd felt the need to forsake his name.

CHAPTER 10

Sergeant Ellie Trevelyan wrestled with the sash window of the station's storeroom, cursing as the effort to cool down only made her hotter. When the pane finally shot up, she planted both hands on the lintel and leaned into the wind, scrutinizing the high street while her heat wave passed. The church bells pealed: praise be for lunchtime. The air chimed with competing smells from the chip shop and the curry house. *Lead us not into temptation,* Ellie thought, *deliver us from evil, the carbs and the spices, for ever and ever, amen-opause.* Instead of chips or chapatis, her lunch would be salad and a pint of evening primrose oil.

Shifting her gaze beyond the high street, beyond the town, beyond several miles of countryside, she spotted the distinctive summit of the Wrekin, smoky against the blue sky. *If you can't see the Wrekin, it's raining; if you can see the Wrekin, it's going to rain soon.* Her dad's approach to weather forecasting. Heaven knows, she hadn't seen much of that hill lately.

Down on the high street, some guy was so busy chatting up a leggy woman that his young son was about to wander into the road. "Hey," Ellie called, but the man was too far away. *What is wrong with people?* She was about to yell again when the kid spotted a puddle on the pavement and sat in it. Safe, for the time being. Ellie let the window drop with a glass-rattling crack. People would have to manage by themselves.

If they didn't like it, they should have switched off their televisions long enough to go to the meeting and vote to save their police station.

Twenty-five years of memories swirled around the room, along with dust motes. Each bundle of dried-out paperwork Ellie shifted into packing boxes spoke of lies and fuckwittery and everyday horrors. She closed her eyes and tried to focus for a moment on the good work she'd done in the community. Light shadows flickered on the inside of her eyelids as positive thoughts scattered to the dark edges of her mind, like pigeons pounced on by a cat. She couldn't recall a single day when she'd won at the game of life. There must have been a few. One? She'd have to WhatsApp her sister, who would dole out a pep talk like a spoonful of sugar.

Overall, Hurtwood had been a tolerable town to police; she wasn't troubled by flashbacks to kids left to starve in drug dens, or the hollow faces of trafficked women, or filthy pedophile rings. She'd never been involved in the hunt for a serial killer or a missing child (apart from the odd teenage girl soon found in bed with the odd teenage boy). But still, people were inalienably human. Behind closed doors—even doors surrounded by roses—all sorts of things could happen.

Ellie didn't need to open the bundles to check which case notes should be transferred to the head office; they echoed in her mind. She fought the urge to throw the paperwork out the window and watch the sheets scatter over Hurtwood like ticker tape. Then these passive residents, who'd barely protested the closure of their police station, might notice the work she did. And Ellie could watch the smiles slide off their faces as they read her notes and saw all that she had seen. They'd change their tune when they glimpsed the lies and fuckwittery and everyday horrors that are kept from them *like the children that they are*. Ellie spat a little and realized she was mouthing the words going through her head. Not a good sign.

She hunkered down on her haunches and squeezed her nose between two fingers. Her skin slid over her bones. *I've got to get a grip,* she thought, *on the fury*. She stood up, wondering if it was a menopausal symptom; everyone knew about hot flashes, but what about hot furies? *Is that a thing?*

Ever since the station closure had been confirmed, anger had eaten her from the inside out. For weeks she'd wanted to rage, but she had to think of her pension. And, in any case, the young constables wanted to work out of headquarters. It was better in the city. Better for the majority. Better if she kept her fury under her hat as though the end of her career was no more than a bad hair day.

Ellie moved along the row, stopping as heat rose from navel to chest again, like sunburn on the inside. As she flapped the collar of her white shirt, her eyes came to rest on a large box on the top shelf. She reached up to bring down the container.

Of all the voices in the storeroom, this case whispered the loudest. It was a voice she'd never heard in the flesh, though his words were scored in her memory. A boy found at the foot of the cliffs near Hurtwood House. Kenny Bale. The memory of seeing Kenny's small body on the rocks was enough to cool her blood even twenty years later. The coroner had recorded a verdict of "death by misadventure." Ellie thought of some misadventure cases as "death by silly buggers"—people whose risky behavior turned out exactly as their mothers could have predicted. Kenny Bale was different. Ellie had expected a verdict of suicide. But maybe the coroner wanted to spare his family from a stigma that still existed even today?

I can't take no more, Kenny Bale wrote in his diary. *I can't see no way out*. The rest of his journal was kept private, except from the coroner and the police. It made harrowing reading, although the boy never explicitly said he intended to kill himself—maybe that put a seed of doubt in the coroner's mind. Nonetheless, Ellie had wanted justice for a child who'd been so badly treated he'd—probably—taken his own life. She'd tried to find out who drove him to despair. The whole force tried. But justice eluded her and young Kenny Bale.

She went back to the window, thrusting it up with one hand. Someone in this town had as good as killed Kenny; bullying and abuse had wounded that child as deeply as sticks and stones. If he'd been the victim of a knife crime, his case wouldn't have been sidelined. If he'd been strangled, headquarters would have sent detectives. It didn't seem fair. Ellie scanned the figures on the street, scuttling along in coats of charcoal, russet, mustard—all the phases of a bruise. Someone in Hurtwood damaged that boy, and now, with her twenty-five-year career setting too early, like the winter sun, she'd never find out what—or who—sent Kenny Bale over that cliff.

A screech of tires snatched her attention to the road below. As predicted, the guy with the child was involved, and he was now standing in the road clutching the boy to his chest. The man looked up for a moment, right in Ellie's direction, and her heart faltered: *Stanley Kynaston.* She shook her head. *Not possible.* He'd been dead twenty years. Stan died soon after Kenny Bale. *How bizarre,* Ellie thought, *to see a look-alike at this very moment.* That's why his face came to mind, she reasoned; her brain was making connections that weren't there. She squinted down at the man, who was frozen in shock. He really did look like Stanley Kynaston, though. And Stan had had a son. *Could it be . . . ?* The look-alike jolted as though he'd come to, running toward the other side of the street, where Ellie realized someone had been injured. She grabbed her coat and went to help, leaving the window open and the breeze sifting through Kenny Bale's case file.

CHAPTER 11

The street outside the *Midland Post* felt like an act of aggression. The traffic was surprisingly intense for a small town. I wanted to know what had happened at Hurtwood House. Anyone fighting their way along this sidewalk would have an opinion, but I wanted facts, not rumors. The newspaper archive might answer my questions, and I wondered how long until I could get back in the office. Soon, if Elks offered me work.

I walked past the library and doubled back to go inside. "Microfiche?" I asked the librarian. She frowned like I'd asked for the pornography section. "Never mind." I took a seat beneath a notice board, where a *Save Our Police Station* poster had been half covered by a flyer for Argentine tango classes. It takes two to tango, I thought, which makes it twice as popular as Elks's solo *Save Our Police Station* performance.

I pulled out my phone and spent some time googling newspaper archives. Elks hadn't been exaggerating when he said their online services sucked. As I got up to leave, my cell pinged a notification. Instagram. I tapped my Hurtwood photo to see who'd liked it.

Victor Carlson.

Instinctively, I sheltered my cell from prying eyes.

Vic? It was only a like, but after all this time . . . He would have considered the impact of a simple like. The man once compared office politics to diamond cutting: check twice, he said, strike once. This like, I knew, was a message.

His profile picture was the logo of the television network we'd both called home once. I tapped to see his page. Location: London. *Vic is in England?* I scrolled through a few pictures: it seemed he'd been here a while. There was no sign of his wife and the child. So that was his message: *Here I am,* he was saying. *I'm here, and you owe me.*

I took a deep breath and blew out the hot air of panic. *No one here knows who he is; no one is going to tell Dylan what happened in Chicago or, even worse, in Somalia.* Even if Vic was trying to make contact, I could choose not to respond. And that would send a message in return. *I don't need you in my life, not again.*

Leaving the library, I tried to distract myself by window-shopping. My heart still rattled around my chest as I studied one tasteful window filled with jewelry alongside another selling vape cartridges. It reminded me of the pleasing contradictions of Africa: a goat herder on a smartphone, benga music blasting from a Land Cruiser, and—a less pleasing contrast—the scrupulous courtesy of a terrorist while he threatened your life. *Don't think about Mogadishu.* I focused on the cinnamon glow of a bakery. *You're safe, go buy a Danish.* But my fingers, clutching my phone, looked incongruously tanned in the pale light. Like a sunburn, it would take time for that experience to fade.

I take up Dylan's offer of a ride in his secure car. We travel to a displaced persons camp on the outskirts of Mogadishu. I'd planned to visit a different camp, had it lined up with an NGO, but Dylan's security consultant deemed the route unsafe. Instead, we navigate labyrinthine streets to a smaller site. Better, the fixer tells us—no other journalists. I don't question the wisdom. I don't have money to pay for protection. I agree to go with them, and for that I can't blame anyone but myself.

Our outward journey has a hysterical kind of jollity—a sense of danger combined with our unconcealed mutual attraction making a heady mix—but the return is somber. The camp is shocking and I try to maintain my detachment by filming all the while, but children know no barriers, and I end the visit on the verge of tears, reproaching myself, as we set off back to the city, because I hadn't brought sweets. "Real journalists don't cry," I whisper to Dylan. He squeezes my shoulder and confesses that he gave all his pens to the kids and now has nothing to write with. We sit in silence, bumping shoulders as we bounce over potholes. As a military brat, I've spent my whole life moving, but Mogadishu is the first place I've ever felt lost.

I stare out of the window, trying to orientate myself. Even glancing at Dylan triggers a flash of interest in his tanned nape or muscled forearm. It feels crass and, somehow, tainted. When Dylan's hand slides across the seat and covers my own, it offers only comfort. Our attraction will return—we seem to have settled into a placid acceptance of the fact—but today won't end in romance.

Then, ahead, a small flashlight glints from an alleyway. The two men up front break into rapid discussion.

"What?" Dylan asks. "What is it?"

The security guy in the passenger seat shouts, and I hear panic: "Go. Drive." Maybe: "Don't stop!" It's the last instruction he gives.

Our vehicle follows the flashlight into a narrow street between concrete buildings. Before the car comes to a halt, the passenger door opens, and the security guy is wrenched out, still in the act of pulling his gun from his holster. A single gunshot. No exchange of fire. Our security guy isn't shooting back. In the rearview mirror I make eye contact with Dylan's fixer. "They took my daughter," he says. "It was her or you."

My door flies open, and before I have the chance to scream, I'm on the ground. Hands dig into my flesh. A jute bag is pulled over my head. I leave the ground and moments later land—hard. A door slams:

I'm in another vehicle. A jerk and something, someone, rolls against me. *Dylan.* Already, I recognize his shape.

It hasn't yet occurred to me that I shouldn't have been in that car, on that road, with Dylan and his compromised fixer. That I've been mansplained into this predicament. That resentment surfaces later like a bruise. But it must have occurred to Dylan because he clings to me as we roll around the trunk and says, "I'm sorry."

Mommy!

The word entered my consciousness while I was five years in the past. "Mommy." I heard it again. It snapped me out of Mogadishu and back to Hurtwood.

Aled? I'd heard Aled.

"Mommy, over here!"

I scanned the street. There he was! On the other side of the road, standing between two parked cars, his head no higher than their brake lights. Waving his hands to get my attention. I remembered the handprints I'd seen in the window of the great house on the day we arrived. Hands sliding down the glass. I had a crazy thought that this vision had been a warning. I moved toward Aled, but he turned away to the sidewalk where he pointed at a puddle, showing it to me, and then sat down in the water. Grinning. *Okay, not ideal, but at least he's out of the road.*

Farther up the sidewalk, Dylan had his back to Aled and me. He was facing a woman, a beautiful woman, and they were laughing. I snatched my phone from my pocket and called his number. Touching the bicep of the beautiful woman with one hand, he lifted his phone with the other, checked the screen, and slid it back into his pocket.

Over the growl of traffic, I listened to his cell ring and go to voice mail.

"Mommy!"

Aled stood between the parked cars again. In the road, vehicles came from both directions. He might as well be standing on a cliff edge.

"Go to Daddy!" I screamed. The traffic was so dense, I couldn't cross. I stepped forward, holding my palms up to force a car to stop, but its driver swerved and sounded the horn. Still, I inched forward, waving my arms. "Watch out! There's a child!" The cars kept coming. A bus blasted my hair off my face. "Get back, Aled!" I screamed after it passed, and if I scared him, then *good*, because one more step and he'd be under someone's wheels. And Dylan was right there, oblivious!

A small crowd had formed on the sidewalk behind me. "My son!" I pointed at Aled. An elderly man set off in a limping half run toward the crosswalk down the street, but there wasn't time. I saw a gap in the traffic. "Stay there!" I shouted at Aled. I didn't want him to run to me. I stepped in front of the oncoming car. Time slowed. It was an SUV, a Range Rover, shiny and black. There wasn't space to cross unless the driver braked. He would brake. I took another step, trying to communicate in a moment of eye contact: *You'll brake now, and when I have my son in my arms, you'll understand.*

You need to brake.

Brake!

But I couldn't make eye contact because the driver was staring out of the side window. Not staring, *glaring*. At Dylan and the woman on the sidewalk. The driver snarled. And he was so distracted by Dylan that he didn't see my palms out in supplication. He didn't see me. He didn't brake. I folded my arms over my head and waited for impact.

CHAPTER 12

My bandages turned the color of weak tea as I limped through puddles from the hospital to the car.

Someone had hauled me out of the path of the Range Rover. My savior muttered, "No harm done," even though he'd ripped his pants when we crash-landed on the sidewalk. Strange hands returned my belongings. Dylan and Aled arrived; a policewoman appeared from nowhere. She sent the Range Rover on its way. Its driver glared at Dylan before cruising off through the traffic like a shark.

When I stood up, pain hit me with the force of a truck—ironically— and tears froze on the woolen fibers of my gloves. "A twist'll be more painful than a break," said the officer. Her accent gave a downward lilt to every sentence so that she sounded disappointed. She lectured Dylan and handed me her business card with a last glance at my husband that suggested I might need it. Trying to redeem himself, Dylan insisted on taking me to the hospital, where we spent three hours surrounded by patients whose continual tutting sounded like blood dripping on linoleum.

I'd tried to resist getting into an argument. It could wait until we got home. But three hours was too long. Three hours when my only entertainment was the memory of Dylan seeing my number on his screen and *ignoring it*—slipping me into his pocket to deal with later as he might a snotty tissue. My resistance crumbled, and I jerked my head to indicate that Dylan should join me in a corner behind a vending machine while Aled played on my iPhone.

"Who's the woman you were so interested in?"

"An old friend. I'm not interested in her."

"Well, she was more interesting than your son."

The effort to keep my voice low made my words sharp, as though pressed to a point between tight lips. Aled found us and started firing off questions about who was angry with whom. So we returned to the plastic seats that creaked under our collective weight and sat it out in silence.

Now, as we drove home, the pressure inside the car swelled with unaired words. My ankle ached. An argument loomed like a horror movie monster; we knew it was there but didn't dare face it. Outside, the hedgerow blurred into the movement of the Range Rover that had borne down on me.

"That driver . . ." In my mind, I saw the man's face again, his jaw tensing to support a snarl. "D'you know him?"

"I didn't see him. And anyway, I don't know everyone in Hurtwood. The town has grown since I left—"

"I'm not interested in demographics. I'm interested in that driver. He was staring at you. That's why he didn't see me. His face was contorted, like in disgust or"—I noticed Dylan's jaw flex under his skin—"fury."

"I told you, I—" He adjusted the rearview mirror to check on Aled, who had fallen asleep with his chin held up by the seat belt. "I look a lot like my father."

"And why is that so terrible?" His father again. This tragedy that hung over the family. The soccer player who died, the shame that killed Stanley. Dylan told me about it early in our relationship, but only in vague terms. Naturally, it pained him to talk about it, so I'd let it go. Bygones went with the territory for a military kid. Each move was an opportunity to dispose of your clutter, not just unwanted belongings but undesirable parts of yourself, the mistakes and bad habits. When someone didn't want to talk about the past, well, that was their prerogative. In fact, knowing when to shut up made me a good interviewer. But now I wondered if I should have pressed Dylan for more details.

None of what he'd told me accounted for the reactions I'd seen in Hurtwood. The look on that driver's face. The woman in the butcher's. Gwendoline's refusal to set foot in town. His family wasn't unpopular, they were *hated*.

"Dylan, what did your father do that was so bad?"

He shifted his hands on the steering wheel.

"So you know Dad was all about the football?"

I did; soccer had been his father's life. First as a professional player, then as a coach, then as an agent for talented youngsters.

"He represented several boys who got signed by big clubs." Dylan named players and teams that I would have known if I'd watched one single soccer match in my whole life. I nodded—I got the point—and Dylan carried on. "But then one of his boys fell—or more likely jumped—off the Long Drop."

That punched the air out of my lungs, as though we'd hit a pothole. I'd assumed the boy's death had been something health related or an accident. But suicide . . .

"I'd just got an offer to study at Cambridge—"

"But you didn't go to Cambridge." Dylan had taken the long route into journalism, starting in the mail room at a newspaper and working up to a role as a foreign correspondent.

"Cambridge never happened." Dylan licked his lips as though parched. "Which was a shame because the footballing gene skipped a generation—I play like a fish with a trumpet—and my dad never did a great job of hiding his disappointment. I was into books, digging around the holm, outside with a metal detector. A geek. Good job I'm so handsome, or I'd still be a virgin." He attempted to flash me a grin, but it failed to ignite and fizzled out. "When I got a place to study history at Cambridge, I made him proud." He glanced at my face. "I'm making him sound bad. He was a great dad, but sport was everything to him . . ."

"He gave more time to those talented young players than to you?"

Dylan gave a surprised laugh. "Razor-sharp analysis, as ever. I guess that is what happened. I went off the rails for a while. Maybe I was attention seeking. Or maybe that's my excuse for being a little shit."

"And the boy who died . . ."

"Yeah. So this boy had been signed to a local team, but my dad had bigger ambitions for him. His parents did too. He used to come up to the holm for extra training, and my dad would film him going through drills to show other talent scouts. That's commonplace now—videos of young players are shared on scouting websites—but not so much back then. He was ahead of his time, my dad—" Dylan's voice broke, and he coughed to cover it, checking the rearview mirror again to ensure Aled wasn't listening. "When the boy died, we went into shock. Why did he wander to the Long Drop? The football field was on the other side of the holm. It made no sense . . ."

"But he might have jumped?"

"At first, we assumed he'd fallen. I mean, no one expects a twelve-year-old to commit suicide, do they? Especially one who's talented, world at his feet." He paused, and I heard the shush of wet tires. "But then they found his diary." Dylan was driving fast and smooth, as if on rails. "He wrote that he was being abused. Filmed and abused. He'd been threatened that if he told anyone, his football career would be over. He couldn't see any other way out . . ."

The car dipped into the cold mist that haunted this particular valley. It whited out the road as though the boy's confused logic filled the air.

"What was his name?"

"His name was Kenny Bale."

I couldn't help but glance at Aled, safe in the back seat. The lights of Low Farm glowed on the hillside as we came around the holm. "Did Kenny Bale name his abuser?"

"He didn't name names. But people put two and two together—the football, the location of his suicide, the filming—and made five." We turned sharply between the iron gates.

"Everyone in this town thinks your father abused a boy and drove him to suicide."

"The police interviewed the other players, who said Stanley Kynaston never touched them. Never so much as looked at them. They took his filming equipment, and there was nothing except goals and free kicks. But the other players, every single one of them, described Kenny Bale as my dad's favorite—which he was. Kenny was the best player Dad had ever seen. Coached him since he was a toddler. The police couldn't get past it; *Kenny Bale was Stanley's favorite.* But I can tell you, any favoritism came from pride, not perversion." Dylan's final phrase rolled out with the ease of one that has been aired many times before. If I were interviewing him for a documentary, I'd think he sounded rehearsed.

We drove into the imperious glare of Hurtwood House. Gravel scattered from our wheels, and I had an urge to grab a handful and pepper the warped windows with it. Just like Dylan and Gwendoline, I'd used my vantage point up on the holm to look down on the people of Hurtwood; I'd judged them as small-minded, unforgiving muckrakers. Well, the ground had shifted. My certainty had eroded. A community standing firm against a pedophile—whole different story. Who was going to argue with that? Not this mother. I dug my fingers into my seat.

How dare he?

My nails caught a seam, and I pulled my skin to a breaking point. *A crumbling house that isn't a home. A town that hates us. Where our child is the grandson of a criminal. The worst sort of criminal, one who preys on children.*

Whether Stanley did it or not wasn't even the issue; people believed he'd done it. His reputation was a yoke that Dylan placed around our necks. We stopped outside the cottage, and I was out of the car before the engine stopped running. I dragged my injured foot up the creaking stairs to Aled's bedroom and collapsed onto his narrow bed. It would be impossible to look at my husband right now without saying something I might regret.

The front door slammed. I heard Dylan prompt a sleepy Aled into the kitchen, to lay his head on the table while Daddy fixed him a drink. I could hear Dylan's reassurances rumble like the sound of a kettle warming to make tea. Then my phone buzzed in my pocket, and I plucked it out to see Robert Elks was calling. *Thank goodness I gave him my maiden name so he doesn't know I'm a Kynaston.* I took the call, and he explained that his editor had approved our day in the life of a Hurtwood cop idea. He'd arranged for me to film with an officer tomorrow, as news of the station closure would break this week. The pay was meager, but I accepted without hesitation. After what I'd learned about Dylan's father, I needed to stay in the game. A local paper was a far cry from a television network in Chicago or filming documentaries in Africa, but at least I'd get press accreditation and access to the archive, which might answer some pressing personal questions . . . Plus, it was better than sitting home and wondering what people were saying about me.

I rolled onto my side. What happened twenty years ago wasn't Dylan's fault. But his secrecy had made it harder, and moving my family from one continent to another had been hard enough. Our suitcases stood in the corner. I read the white airline label hanging off my rolling bag: *NBO-LHR*. Nairobi to London Heathrow. If only there was a simplified code for what had come next. LHR-WTF, perhaps?

I scanned the white barcode stickers from my travels. ORD for Chicago. NBO, where Aled was born. MGQ: Mogadishu, Somalia.

The town where Dylan put my life in danger. And where he believed he'd saved it again.

Our cell is stifling. Like having my face pressed into someone's crotch. Time skips beats. I'm dizzy with dehydration. Our kidnapper is in the cell, and I didn't realize the door had opened. It's the first time we've seen him since we were taken. We're guarded by a teenager who looks more scared than us. "You can follow me now," the kidnapper says. His voice is polite. We waver to our feet. "You can stay," he says to Dylan, and kicks the guard, who passes me a bottle of water with an apology.

Dylan starts talking, his voice as wobbly as his legs: "Don't touch her . . . bad for you if you touch her . . ."

The teenager waves at him, whispering, "Haram, haram." Forbidden. I'm not sure if the kid means it's forbidden to rape me or that Dylan is forbidden to speak to the kidnapper. *Shut up,* I want to say to Dylan. *Stop putting ideas into his head.*

But Dylan doesn't shut up. "Don't touch her, bad for you, don't touch her." He earns a flat-handed slap that comes so hard and fast Dylan doesn't have time to duck.

"Calm down," the kidnapper says. "I'm here to discuss your options."

Dylan's employer has insurance, and the hotel has instructions to contact his embassy if he fails to return. As a freelancer, I have nothing. No one knows I'm missing.

"Take me first," says Dylan. "My company will pay big dollars."

"'Big dollars,'" mimics the kidnapper. "Which one of us doesn't speak proper English?"

"They'll pay a ransom. You can let her go."

Dylan begs for my life. "Go on," he says to me, "run if you get the chance." Later, when the kidnapper receives the money, I'm released while Dylan stays in the cell. *Go on, run,* Dylan had said, and to my shame I do.

Only three people knew who paid that ransom: me, the kidnapper, and Victor Carlson. What Dylan didn't know wouldn't hurt him. It's not like one missing chapter changed a whole story.

On Aled's bed, I pushed myself up so my legs dangled over the side. *Even with Vic in London, my secret is safe; he's got as much to lose as I have.* But I should forgive Dylan his secrecy. I may have been a liar by omission, but I wouldn't be a hypocrite too.

CHAPTER 13

Sergeant Ellie Trevelyan stumbled over her own name when it came to speak. Her voice had the cadence of a wasp dying in a jar. The reporter, Rose Falcone, adjusted the microphone clipped to Ellie's jacket and tinkered with the camera.

Ellie noted that Rose didn't use her husband's name. Probably for the best. Distaste for that name hardened people's bones along with the minerals in the water supply. In the same way a murderer might be identified by the soil on his boots, a Hurtwoodian would be picked out by their hatred of the Kynastons.

If Rose was aware of it, she put on a ballsy show. Even on this steely morning, she seemed to have a sunbeam lighting her face, though it was probably the remains of her African tan. "Thank you for agreeing to do this," the journalist said, happy at last with the camera settings. "I hope it might make a difference."

"It's probably too late to make a difference, whatever Elks has told you. He can't save the station now. What's he planning to do with this documentary?"

"It's an experiment, to be honest, for the online service."

"A day in the life of a dinosaur?"

"We thought if we show people a typical day in the life of a police officer, they'll realize what they're going to lose."

"Well, then. My shift starts in an hour, let's crack on." Standing in the alley beside the station, the officer glanced over her shoulder, distracted by the thought that her body language mirrored that of the petty criminals who occupied the town's car parks and canal towpath after dark. Ellie took a baby step closer to understanding the mentality of those pinheads; doing this interview, she felt a thrill of the illicit, an anxious rush of adrenaline and even a self-righteous belief in *sticking it to the man*. Ellie could have asked her boss to authorize this interview with the *Midland Post*. But she didn't. Like her glue-sniffing nemeses, her jobless future offered a nihilistic sense of freedom. What did she have to lose?

Rose shifted the camera onto her shoulder. Slowly, the sergeant relaxed into her favorite topic, her work in her town. Ellie felt heat creep up her face, only this time it wasn't hormones, it was injustice.

"Can you have the same impact when your job moves to headquarters?" Rose asked.

Ellie hesitated for a moment before plunging on. "I'm not going to headquarters."

"Because you oppose the closure?"

"Because I care for my elderly father. I wouldn't be able to visit him twice a day if I had to travel to the city. So"—Ellie was distracted by the warning whoop of a siren as a police vehicle left the compound—"my career ends here." Her lips didn't fit back together properly, giving away her emotions as clearly as if they'd carried on speaking. The camera would pick that up.

"And how do you feel about that?" Rose must have also picked it up.

To her horror, Ellie's throat constricted. Her father had been a police officer. A shared history gave them something solid to cling to, even as Alzheimer's dragged him into a perpetual present tense. Jim Trevelyan would never blacken the name of the force, not even to criticize a dumb cost-cutting decision. She'd agreed to do this day-in-the-life interview because she wanted to say her piece. But she wouldn't bitch and moan about the force. "Sometimes change is hard."

The camera dropped from Rose's shoulder. The younger woman gave Ellie a long look and then nodded. "Shall we take a walk?"

They filmed on the high street and then took a shortcut to a playground, where Ellie picked up a handful of discarded nitrous oxide canisters from beneath the swings. "Legal highs," she explained to the camera, "because I wouldn't want anyone at home to underestimate the hard work and creativity that pinheads put into getting wasted. Work, not so much, but addling their brains on laughing gas from soda siphons—unwavering commitment." She threw a canister, in a cool arc of several yards, into the bin.

Rose asked what made Hurtwood special to Ellie. Squatting on her haunches in the wood chips, the camera largely forgotten, Ellie thought about it. "Small towns like Hurtwood might as well be invisible," she said. "They're like middle-aged women. People assume they're frumpy and boring; they take them for granted." Ellie licked her cold lips. "But these communities have depths and complexities. Buried problems that push to the surface." She picked up another canister of laughing gas.

"What sort of problems?"

The metal vial rotated at satisfying speed through the officer's fingers. "All the original sins. But people get invested in an idea of innocence. That the countryside is immune to the kind of crime found in the city. They don't want to accept that their town—their little slice of middle England—isn't a picture postcard of perfection. So they won't acknowledge that one of their own is capable of inflicting harm. There's a sense of collective guilt, almost. A pointed finger could turn on any one of us. It's hard to get to the truth when everyone comes over all see no evil, hear no evil. The biggest problem is when they speak no evil."

"Have you encountered evil, sergeant?"

Ellie's thighs had gone numb from squatting, and she had to pull herself up by the metal chain of the swings. When she let go, its unoiled bracket squeaked from high to low like a boy's breaking voice. *I can't take it no more.* Ellie heard the voice in her head. *I can't see no way out.* She tried to shake it away. "I don't know what you mean by evil. That sounds a bit . . . out there. I've seen plenty of suffering. People who inflict pain."

"I guess I'm asking if you've ever had a case that got under your skin."

"I don't really see what this has got to do with everyday policing." Sergeant Trevelyan couldn't stop her gaze from flitting to the pupil of the camera, even though Rose had asked her not to look into the lens. It was instinct and training that compelled Ellie to check someone's eyes for a sign of what they were holding back. Was Rose digging? The connection was obvious—Rose to Dylan, Dylan to Stanley, Stanley to Kenny Bale. The journalist must be aware of the case. *What was her question again? Was there a case that got under your skin? Yes, Kenny Bale, so deep it itches.* But Rose's question had been general enough. Maybe the links were all in Ellie's imagination; Kenny Bale was certainly on her mind. The previous night, her sleeping self saw a boy falling, and as she ran to catch him, his feet kicked her in the face—crack, crack. As she woke, panting and checking her mouth for blood, she recognized the explosive crack of a modified car engine racing by on the street outside. Pinheads steaming home in the wee hours. Probably from this playground, where Ellie cleaned up their mess every morning before any kids arrived.

"Maybe an unresolved case?" Rose said. "Because your local knowledge will be lost when the police service is centralized, won't it?"

"Open cases will continue to be investigated," Ellie said.

Rose lowered the camera and suggested they take a break. The American looked disappointed. Ellie took a breath and let out a silent sigh. Unless she spoke her mind, she was wasting everyone's time—she knew that. Both women stood for a moment, fighting the wind for control over their hair.

"There was one case," Ellie said, tucking strands behind her ear. "I can't talk about it on camera."

"An unsolved case?"

"Officially, there wasn't a case to solve. A boy died, and we had reason to believe he'd been driven to suicide." Ellie felt the reporter's attention pique, even while her gaze remained on a cable she was untangling; the aperture of her eyes narrowed a fraction. *She does know what the Kynaston name means round here. I was right—she's ballsy.*

"Online bullying?" the younger woman asked.

"It happened long before social media."

"Is it the case with the soccer player?"

"That's the one. I suppose you know what happened."

"Of course, my husband told me," Rose said. "Must have rocked the community."

"Like I said, people don't like to think that one of their own is responsible for . . . well, for want of a better word, evil. I think we can all agree that, in common parlance, child abuse is evil."

"I think we can." The reporter's voice was hushed.

Sergeant Trevelyan told herself to shut up. *Stop talking before you say something you regret.*

"So what do you think happened to Kenny Bale?" Rose asked.

Ellie cleared her throat, and the air between the women froze into a cloud. "He was abused by someone in Hurtwood."

"And everyone believes it was Stanley Kynaston?"

"The lack of evidence points that way." Ellie pushed her hands into her pockets.

Rose pressed: "But Stanley's death wasn't connected to the case?"

Clearly, your husband hasn't told you everything. Or you don't believe him. "He had a heart condition."

"Were there any other cases of abuse linked to Stanley?"

Ellie shook her head. "I don't know why I mentioned the Kenny Bale case; it's got nothing to do with the police station closure. It's just been on my mind, I suppose."

The journalist zipped up her bag. "Back in the day, I made documentaries. True-crime style. Have you heard of *Serial*? *Making a Murderer*?"

Ellie nodded; she'd been rapt by these real-time investigations of cold cases.

"Mine wasn't high-profile, but it was popular around Chicago. We won an award. It was called *Burden of Proof* and then the name of the place."

"So you're thinking of doing *Burden of Proof: Hurtwood*?" said Ellie.

"Maybe it could work. I guess I'm curious if there are any loose ends . . ."

"There's one loose end as thick as a noose: we don't know who abused Kenny Bale. There were no other accusations against Stanley. But also no further cases after he died."

"Except?"

Ellie huffed, her breath thick as vape smoke. "I knew Stanley Kynaston at school. He was older than me, in my sister's class. And I just don't—" The police officer dropped her head back and gritted her teeth at the sky before making eye contact with Rose again. "As I said before, people don't like to think of one of their own being responsible for evil."

"You don't think it was Stanley?"

Ellie shrugged.

"So who abused Kenny Bale? And why did he fall from the Long Drop?"

Ellie looked away to where the dorsal fin of the Wrekin surfaced on the horizon. The solitary hill never failed to orientate her, its varied flanks as sure as a signpost. A constant companion in the background, as this case had been for the past twenty years. And, like the Wrekin, Sergeant Ellie Trevelyan felt that the Kenny Bale case was bigger than it looked from a distance.

CHAPTER 14

As I drove toward the holm, the distant hills were as hazy as promises. The policewoman's voice echoed in my mind, talking about an abrupt end to her career. Before I could get maudlin about the identity that had sunk in my wake, a text pinged: Dylan had left Aled with Gwendoline.

I sped up the slope to the Grim's Holm. The settlement had developed over centuries, like a microcivilization that flourished and died and rose again. Between the forlorn outbuildings, the skeletal goalposts of Stanley's soccer field, and the abandoned dreams, the view carried a Soviet air that had nothing to do with the Siberian wind blowing in the trees.

I stopped on the gravel outside the great house, relieved to see Aled through the kitchen window. My anxiety faded. Last night in bed, I'd asked Dylan what it was like growing up in a haunted house. He scoffed. "I was more worried about the boys. Dad's boys, I mean. If I left my stuff outside or in the kitchen, they'd wreck it. Nothing was sacred. I found this windowless room behind a panel in the wall and kept everything hidden. Didn't realize at the time, but it was a priest's hole. I don't think my parents knew it was there, and it was right in their room. Years later, I found the priest's hole of Hurtwood House mentioned in a book." He talked about Catholics and persecuted clergymen.

After Dylan fell asleep, I'd lain in the dark, tearful for a little boy hiding between the walls.

I got out of the car and looked up at the house. The facade had been remodeled over the centuries, each era offering its refinement. It made me think again of past lives. Was I still the child who grew up a nomad or the fool who believed a married man's excuses or the reckless reporter who nearly got herself killed in Mogadishu? Were these mistakes or facets of my character? Did it matter? Even a diamond has flaws.

I thought about the priest's hole, a secret hidden inside the edifice of Hurtwood House. Are people the same, a framework that remains intact over time while the facade changes? Is Dylan still good at hiding? Maybe a need for secrecy was bricked up inside him.

Then I noticed something about the Georgian precision of the house; it was flawed. The windows above the kitchen—one of which I knew was Gwendoline's bedroom—were slightly wider spaced than the rest. It was just a matter of a few bricks, but it was obvious if you studied the proportions. I wondered if this accounted for Dylan's hidden room between the walls?

I was distracted by a shout. Behind me across the yard, the double-height doors of the flint barn were open. A green car was parked in the doorway, an old-style Land Rover of a type I'd often seen in Africa. The rail-thin figure of Gwendoline was addressing someone I couldn't see but who must have been standing inside the barn. She'd warned us not to let Aled go into the former leper home because she'd seen chunks of masonry crash down and solid-looking floorboards disintegrate into dust.

If it was unsafe, why was a Land Rover parked inside? And why was Gwendoline thumping its hood and shouting? Most importantly, if she was in the barn, who was looking after Aled in the kitchen? The treetops flapped and hissed like disgruntled geese. Gwendoline's voice blew into meaningless fragments. I left her to her argument and went inside, where I found Aled drawing.

"Are you on your own?"

"Gwen-ma told me to stay and draw so I stayed and drewed."

I hugged him to my chest until he wriggled to get down. I left a note for Gwendoline and took Aled back to the cottage. He was fine. Was I overreacting? He was almost five years old. Sometimes I left him in front of the television to take a shower. But I never left him when I went out of the house . . . where he might follow me and wander off. Who knew how long Gwendoline had been gone? Long enough to get into a fight with someone in the barn. Dylan and I had always been on the same page with childcare. In Kenya, we'd sat down together with our nanny and agreed upon the rules. But our rules had departed with the paid nanny. Dylan, understandably, didn't want to think of his mother getting old. That woman at the butcher's thought Gwendoline was faking. Other people chalked it up to eccentricity. To me, a fresh pair of eyes, it looked like plain old dementia. Early stages, maybe, but a problem nonetheless.

I must have sighed, because Aled's soft hand slid into mine.

"Don't worry, baby," I told him. "I'm just thinking about work."

As soon as I mentioned work, Aled clamped onto my legs. In Africa, Dylan and I had taken turns covering stories around a busy region. We'd tried to ensure Aled never felt like he was being handed between us like a baton, but the fact was our situation had been born of necessity. We knew the risks associated with our jobs, but we needed both incomes. Even then we never had enough spare money to make trips home. My father died without meeting his grandson. I knotted that guilt into a cattail of my own shortcomings. And after Aled's birth I got scared of work for the first time. People told me it was natural after what had happened in Mogadishu—maybe I had PTSD?—but I knew better. Motherhood changed me more than the kidnapping. Death was now the penultimate price; the ultimate would be any harm to my son. So when Dylan was offered a severance package, we fled to England.

To safety. Stability.

Or so I thought.

"I'm not going away, Aled," I said, a shudder of relief in my voice.

"Good." He pushed out his bottom lip to show he wasn't joking. "I don't like it when you go to work."

Dylan walked in on that statement. "Maybe we can find someone for you to play with when Mummy goes to work?" he said. I peeled Aled from my legs and placed him in his father's arms. Dylan attached childcare to my working life, not his, as though my job was a motorcycle with a sidecar containing a kid, while his was a go-anywhere superbike.

I picked a dead bug off the table. "Daddy can research day care while I edit my interview." I dropped the tiny corpse in the trash. "I found Aled alone in the great house"—Dylan mouthed a cuss word—"so we're going to need a day care for when we're both working." I may have put an emphasis on *both* because Dylan led Aled by the hand to go get his laptop.

Every day care center in Hurtwood had a waitlist, but Dylan got us an appointment at a "forest school." I was unfamiliar with the concept, and he said he was too, but forest schools were Scandinavian, and we all want to be more *hygge*, so, I figured, why not check it out?

He navigated to the remote location by instinct. We passed a tree where someone called Brains totaled his car an hour after taking his driving test. This was the arcane knowledge I got handed instead of a map. We parked and followed a trail into the woods. A young woman emerged from a white dome in the trees. She made a beeline for Aled and led him away to explore the camp.

Dylan took me under a shelter to stand by the firepit. I grabbed his lapels and pulled him against me, feeling his arms fold across my back. "What if he gets cold?" I said into his chest.

"The kids can sit by the fire. Or go into the dome."

"What if he gets lost in the forest?"

"There's a fence around the camp."

"What if he—"

"Rose."

"I know." The embers sputtered in the grate. "It's like day camp for little kids."

"It's heaven, isn't it? This is how I grew up, totally free. Only he'll be safe here and have mates."

We stood for a moment, breathing in pine and kicked-up earth and the maple tang of burnt marshmallows. "Dylan, what if he falls in the fire?"

He gave a low growl of exasperation. I pushed myself off his chest and went to check on Aled. He was covered in mud and totally happy, so I left him with the assistant. Through the trees, I heard Dylan's laughter. He'd been joined by a woman I recognized, the one he'd been speaking to in Hurtwood when Aled nearly walked into the road and I nearly went under a car. I slipped behind a tree. She wore no makeup, and her skin was flushed from the cold, but she had a natural beauty. Hair braided like a Viking's and a smudge of soot that accentuated her cheekbones gave her a warrior edge. I wondered if she'd put it there on purpose.

"Do me a favor and put Aled at the top of the waiting list," Dylan was saying. "I need to keep her sweet."

Does he mean me? I sound like a royal pain in his butt.

"Do *you* a favor! You owe me, Nasty Boy." Her mouth pouted like she was sucking a cherry. Her accent sounded like that too.

"Lower your voice, Meredith . . ." Dylan used a warning tone I rarely heard. "And please don't call me that name—you know I hate it."

"Sorry!" She didn't sound sorry, she sounded mocking, like a teenager. "I'll take Aled, but I can't do full-time; there are regulations, you know."

"Thank you, Merry Fiddler."

She groaned. "And you know I hate that name!"

I decided to come out from behind my tree before their froideur thawed any further. "Rose!" said Dylan, unusually jolly while he introduced us.

Meredith asked after my ankle, but she was more interested in Dylan. "Did you hear what happened to Smartie?" An old friend had lost her money after building a house on a floodplain. Smartie sounded about as smart as Brains who'd crashed his car into a tree. Smartie, Brains, and—what had she called Dylan? Nasty Boy? There wasn't a person in Hurtwood known by the name their mother gave them. I wondered if people went by these nicknames in the outside world or whether they were only used in Hurtwood, like a handshake for the initiated.

And I wondered if the names defined the people. Did every sardonic utterance of *Brains* snip away shoots of growth until the boy and then the man was diminished, bonsai-style, by a teenage mistake that no one would let him outgrow?

I filled out paperwork while Meredith and Dylan reminisced. She touched Dylan on the forearm to prompt a recollection: the name of the place where the thing happened. They laughed at the memory and didn't explain.

I scored our family name in block letters on official forms while rain licked the leaves. The clouds raced at time-lapse speed, and I had the sense that life was on rewind. The present was a drop in the ocean. The shared childhood of Dylan and Meredith, a deep well of experience. This man—this Nasty Boy—didn't belong to me anymore; he belonged to Hurtwood.

CHAPTER 15

Walking back to the parking lot at the forest school, I laid my hand against the trunk of a fir tree, the bark as wiry as bear's fur. It took me to another wooded trail, one I'd visited regularly in the months before I left Chicago. *Somewhere I never should have been.* The treetops swayed in unison. *With someone who wasn't mine.* On my cell, I checked Instagram and saw that Victor Carlson had liked another one of my posts. I jogged to catch up with my boys.

Dylan and Aled chattered about the day camp. "So you liked it, mate?" Dylan said.

Mate.

This was a new endearment, one Dylan hadn't used before we arrived in England. Now he said it all the time. It didn't suit him, as though he'd purchased a whole new wardrobe in a too-young style. Or maybe I was the one who'd changed, from someone who knew all I needed to know about my husband, to an insecure woman who couldn't resist plundering his past.

Everyone has a history. *God knows I do.* What I had with Dylan made Vic seem like ancient history. Like something that happened to another person. Rose Falcone was gone, I was Rose Kynaston now. I felt sure the same held true for Dylan. He lifted our son into the car, checked and rechecked the straps. This move was starting to change us, which was fine; we'd wanted change, we'd wanted safety. If only I felt secure.

"Ready to go, mate?" Dylan slammed the door, and it rattled my teeth.

On the way home, it became clear that Meredith Fiddler was Dylan's ex. I got the feeling they'd been serious, or as serious as you get at an age when life is all giggles. Dylan chose his words carefully. I could feel the tiny delay as he edited his thoughts before he spoke.

"Never thought she'd end up back in Hurtwood. Alone." The white lines on the road swept under our hood. "Meredith Fiddler. Merry Fiddler, the boys called her. If she was merry, you might fiddle 'er." He snickered like Beavis and Butthead.

"Teenage boys are crass," I said.

"Especially when they want something they can't have."

"So she was your girlfriend?"

"Most of the time—" He froze like a child who was about to curse in front of an adult. "Sometimes she was Giles Hotchen's."

"Ouch."

"He came from money and liked to flash the cash. In the pub, he used to buy a whole bottle of wine for the girls." Dylan shook his head in mock wonder. "The rest of us bought it by the glass in case they left. So anyway she'd run with him for a bit, then he'd do something crude that upset her, and she'd come back to me. And in the meantime, he tried to be my best mate because of my dad, the footballing legend."

A love triangle. I guess that summed up small-town life. It hadn't been so different on the military base. And what did teenage hijinks matter? Dylan and I had been through experiences no one else could understand. An outsider could never grasp the delicate balance of trust, power, and need that forms the foundation of a relationship. Or breaks it.

I wouldn't expect Dylan to understand why I'd gotten involved with a married man. I found it hard enough to understand myself, and so I'd never told another person. Except a terrorist in Mogadishu.

Our car passed over the river that carved into the base of the Long Drop. I changed the subject and asked Dylan if he knew who'd come to visit Gwendoline the day before. I remembered how she'd given the green Land Rover a beating while talking to someone. But Dylan only shrugged.

"Gwen-ma has a friend." Aled's voice from the back seat.

I twisted around. "Oh yeah?"

"Her friend comes to say hello."

"That's nice. What's her friend's name, Aled?"

"Dunno." He looked out the window until we reached the top of the holm, where he spotted a robin redbreast near the dovecote so we got out. Dylan drove home to make some calls. The little bird sang an energetic song, flitting from branch to branch as though luring us into the trees. I held Aled back by the sleeve.

"A boy cut off his finger," Aled said.

"Who?"

"Rhys."

"At forest school?"

"No." Aled's lips pursed as he tried to concentrate. "His mommy is Gwen-ma's friend."

"Oh no. What happened to his finger?"

"A chicken cut it off."

"I don't think so."

"It did! The chickens go along and flap their wings 'cause they don't like it, and it cuts their head off. But it chopped the boy's finger."

"So this boy, Rhys, caught his finger in the machinery?"

"He went to the hos-dipal."

"He had to go to the hospital? Oh no. Does Gwendoline's friend have a chicken farm?"

"Yes. It cut off his finger." Aled pinched the nail of his pinkie with the other hand.

"The tip of his finger?"

Aled nodded solemnly, still holding his finger. I steered him to the side door of the great house. Maybe Gwendoline hadn't been yelling in the barn. Maybe she'd been upset? I decided to make sure she was okay. She soon had Aled wrapped in his blanket and occupied with coloring. When I asked about Rhys, she launched into a lecture about how Aled shouldn't play in the barn . . .

Aled's purple crayon circled the paper, drumming over the uneven surface of the table, leaving dark flakes when it hit whorls in the wood. I wondered if that's how Gwendoline's mind felt when she lost track: slivers left behind, making it worse the harder she pressed for the truth. I'd been stupid to ask a direct question that involved her short-term memory. But it was so difficult to gauge her ability when some of the time she seemed fine. And, of course, I hadn't known her for long; it was hard to detach what seemed like confusion from her general belligerence. Who else would know if she'd always been this way? Thorn, maybe? Meredith? I didn't fancy going to either of them for help. And the words of the woman in the butcher shop lurked in my head: *Convenient, isn't it, her illness?* Aled's crayon thrummed louder and louder until I put out a hand to make him stop. He held up his drawing, and Gwendoline prompted Aled to tell a detailed story that she lapped up. They were on the same untethered wavelength, two minds drawing freehand.

I gave up on finding out more about Rhys. Instead, I mentioned Meredith. I may have been digging for information. Gwendoline's head shook once, as though the name gave her an involuntary twitch: "Don't believe a word that girl says." She turned away to pin Aled's picture over the Aga. It had gotten dark outside so we shrugged on our coats. When I was halfway out the door, Aled racing ahead with the spaniels, Gwendoline whispered: "The boy shouldn't be allowed in the shed."

"Aled?"

"Rhys. It's too dangerous for a child in a chicken shed."

Okay, so her pendulum had swung back to my earlier question. "Is his mom okay? She's your friend, right?"

"Shawna?" Gwendoline waved the tea towel in front of her face. "She shouldn't tell stories. I'm sorry if he's frightened about the finger."

"Aled's fine."

"Shawna should know better. She's lackadaisical. Always leaves us to clear up her mess." Gwendoline's head shook with distress. "Such a . . . flibbertigibbet!"

The strange word lightened the atmosphere, and I stifled a smile. "Aled was entertained by the whole thing. He's fascinated by anything macabre." A thought popped up: *Is it normal for a child to be unaffected—amused, almost—by something as horrific as a lost finger?* "Aled can be quite ghoulish."

Gwendoline chuckled. "Dylan's the same. I remember a dead sheep. Dylan and Rhys poking around in the maggots. Dreadful smell! Such good fun to scare themselves."

"Bravado," I said.

"That's boys for you."

So Aled *was* normal. He flung a stick, and the dogs raced into the darkness. I said goodbye and was about to pull the door closed when a thought hit me. I reversed into the kitchen. If Rhys and Dylan had found this sheep together . . . "Gwendoline, when did Rhys cut off his finger?"

"Years ago. I don't know why Shawna is thinking about that all of a sudden. I'll give her what for next time I see her!"

"Is she the one with the green Land Rover?"

"That car is her pride and joy. At least Aled will stay away from the barn if he thinks he's going to get his fingers taken off by chickens!"

Aled and I walked home hand in hand. A wraith of smoke twisted over the roof of the cottage in the shape of a silken nightgown. Aled ran inside, leaving the front door open. Golden light spilled out, until

Dylan slammed it shut. My ungloved hands stung as the wind nibbled my edges. From inside, my boys called my name, and the front door swung open again; the night released me, and I rushed into the warmth.

"I thought you were inside!" Dylan greeted me with a kiss.

I felt lost on the holm. Dylan, Gwendoline, Aled: unreliable guides, all. I had to find my own way. Starting with Stanley. Sergeant Trevelyan had doubts about his guilt. What if I kept picking at that knotty secret? Was there a loose end that might unravel and free the Kynaston name from its noose?

CHAPTER 16

Sergeant Ellie Trevelyan got home to find the house in darkness, both taps running into the kitchen sink (all the hot water gone again), and a catalogue of surveillance equipment on the table. But no elderly father. She picked up an apple and halved it with one bite. The low-carb diet left her hungry as a horse. In fact, it was best suited to a horse. *What has the world come to when a woman can't enjoy a potato?* Flipping open the catalogue, she noted a security camera worth £5,000. A light bulb that transmitted audio. A car tracker the size of a two-pence coin. Serious gear. The discarded envelope showed that the catalogue had been ordered by Jim Trevelyan. She lodged the remainder of the apple between her teeth while she pulled her coat back on. Then she retraced her route past the police station onto the cobbles of Cheapside. At the church graveyard, Jim Trevelyan was also eating an apple.

"All right, Dad?" She lowered herself onto the bench beside him.

"Parky." He flicked the apple core behind a gravestone.

"Yep, it's cold all right. Don't you think you should call it a night?"

"Waiting."

"For what?"

"Don't want to miss 'em."

"Miss who, Dad?"

"Hottie."

Ellie snapped to her feet, picking up a discarded bag and punching into it all the trash he'd strewn around in the hours he'd sat there: a bottle of water, chocolate wrappers, a skinny notepad, and a stub of pencil.

"Not that," Jim said, snatching the book.

"This is getting beyond a joke."

Jim pulled up to his full height—Ellie had a flash of how invincible he'd seemed as a younger man, her father the policeman, a detective no less—and looked down at his daughter. His unfocused gaze cleared for a moment. "Indeed, Eleanor, I'm deadly serious. I've got all the time in the world for this Hottie."

Not if I push you in the canal. Instead, she pushed him away from the Nail Bar, which was still open for business, its fluorescent lights staining the cobbles. Ellie walked on, but Jim stopped at the gates of the boys' school.

"Nasty Boy," said Jim.

"I'm sure they're all angels, apples of their mothers' eyes. Come on, Dad, home. I'm Hank Marvin."

"The Shadows."

"That's right. Hank Marvin was a guitarist in the Shadows. I mean I'm starving. I haven't had my dinner."

"Sorry, sweet."

"That's all right, Dad."

They moved on, and the school disappeared behind a high wall. After a few minutes they turned onto a road that ran alongside its playing fields, rugby posts white against the suburban streetlights. Jim walked quickly once he got going, and he strode along, muttering the odd word. Ellie heard *nasty boy* again. It made Ellie wonder who he was thinking about.

"Dad . . ."

He slowed a fraction, enough to suggest he was listening.

"Did you ever work the Kenny Bale case?" She knew very well he had, but wanted to offer him an out in case that memory had gone to the great filing cabinet in the sky.

"Went to this school." Jim bobbed his head toward the playing fields.

Bingo. He remembered. Ellie didn't need to prompt any more.

"Football. He was good. Very good. Tragic." Okay, she'd been hoping for a bit more. But Jim stopped walking again and looked across the field. Ellie followed his gaze over the rugby pitch, over the sports complex and the old dormitory, to the backs of the Georgian shops that lined the cobbled street they'd followed. The church spire was lit up. Jim pointed vaguely in that direction.

"Nasty Boy."

"Who? Kenny Bale?"

"No, no, no. Good lad. Great footballer."

"Then who are you talking about?"

Jim took a deep breath. "Turd on the headmaster's car. Massive thing it was."

"Someone put a dog turd on the headmaster's car?"

"Real turd."

"One of the boys did a turd on the headmaster's car?"

"Never caught 'em." Jim shook his head and walked on.

"That is nasty."

But Jim wasn't up to full speed, and he slowed to a halt again. There was more.

"What was his name again?" He turned to Ellie, mouth agape, as though she should pop in the answer like a pacifier. "Oh, you know. Nasty . . ."

"Before my time, Dad."

"Not before your time. You know." Jim stamped his foot, a petulant child. "Nasty . . . Nasty. Come on, Eleanor!"

Ellie put her hand over her mouth and felt a prickle of tears. She hated seeing him distressed. And she'd brought it on with her questions. "Does the name sound like *nasty*? Is that it?"

"You know the name. Everyone knows the fucking name!" His voice cannoned up the street, and Ellie glanced over her shoulder at the houses where everyone would be tutting about the hoodlum disturbing their supper.

"Nasty . . . ," she tried, prompting him like a mother with a baby. "Nast . . ."

"Nast . . . Naston. Kynaston!" He blew out a breath, and the rage dissipated. "Kynaston. Dylan Kynaston. Nasty Boy they called him. Afterward."

Ellie and Jim walked. *That name again.*

"What about him, Dad? What about Dylan Kynaston? It was his father, Stanley, who was implicated in the death of Kenny Bale, not the son."

"Guilty as a dog sitting next to a pile of poo." Jim chuckled at that.

"But you think he was involved with Kenny Bale?"

"What?" Jim frowned and pinched his forehead, a sign that he was growing frustrated again.

"What did Dylan do, Dad?"

"Turd."

"Dylan did the turd?"

"Giles Hotchen."

"Giles Hotchen did the turd?" Everyone knew the name Giles Hotchen. Second to Stanley Kynaston, it was the most whispered name in Hurtwood.

"No! Giles Hotchen blamed Dylan Kynaston. Told the headmaster. About the turd. And that night Giles Hotchen nearly died." Jim walked on, full speed ahead. Mic drop. He was out of here. Ellie trotted to keep up.

Jim was right, she had been in the force then, but she didn't work the Giles Hotchen case. Like everyone else in Hurtwood, she knew about it. Hotchen was in his final year at Hurtwood Boys' School when he rode his bike under the wheels of a truck. He survived, but with significant head injuries. Took years to recover. Luckily, his father had fingers in many pies, and so Giles Hotchen, once he was well enough, took over one of the family businesses and turned it into an empire. He lived in a swanky pad behind a big wall a few miles outside town. People said he was a recluse because he couldn't speak properly. People said he never married because he lost a vital part in the accident. Other people said, on the contrary, he was rich and single and ran swinger parties. People said all kinds of drivel about a bloke who was too wealthy to care.

But people never said Dylan Kynaston had something to do with his accident. Jim strode ahead at top speed, apparently liberated of a secret that had weighed so heavily it slowed him down.

CHAPTER 17

The sun was slumped on the horizon like a daytime drunk. I drove to the forest school with one hand raised against the glare, and the thought that Meredith Fiddler and all the other mothers believed Aled's grandfather was a pedophile, his grandmother and father apologists for a pedophile. Everyone in Hurtwood knew about it, including the Range Rover driver who'd been so infuriated by the sight of Dylan that he nearly ran me down.

"Aled's mum!" a voice called from the dome. I found Meredith Fiddler holding aside the entrance flap to let my son race out into my arms. With his head pressed against my belly, my fingers felt wet cheeks. I tipped his pink-rimmed eyes up to mine.

"He looks like Dylan, doesn't he?" Meredith said this in a tone of mild surprise. And then: "We had an incident."

Aled's arms clamped my thighs. "Did he get hurt?"

"Unfortunately, I've had complaints."

"Complaints from who?"

"From parents who pick up before lunch. A mum called after she got home."

"I don't understand . . ." Aled's grip tightened.

"Aled frightened the children. He told them a horror story. I'm sure he was only trying to get their attention—first-day nerves—but I do wonder if he's watching age-appropriate movies . . . ?"

"He watches *Dora* and *Peppa Pig.*"

Meredith's face buckled into a skeptical expression. She had the flattering soot-smudge on her cheekbone again. "He told a story about someone's mother being thrown in the cellar and her ghost haunting the house. One of the mums thought it might be from a movie, but I forgot the name she said . . . *Horror House* something?"

"No clue. I haven't seen a movie like that, and neither has Aled."

"Maybe on YouTube?"

"He doesn't have access to YouTube. He doesn't watch scary movies; he's too sensitive. I . . ." I stopped, angry at myself for engaging in this pointless autopsy. I took a breath and started afresh. "Did you hear Aled tell this story?"

"It happened while the kids were playing."

"Unattended?"

"Our aim at forest school is to encourage independence—"

"You didn't actually hear Aled tell the story?"

"The other mums—"

"You said one mum—one mum called."

"But that mum phoned another mum, who asked her child, and she gave the same account."

"Prompted by her mother? Do you think they're credible witnesses at five years old?"

Meredith held my gaze, and I held it right back. *I'm a journalist, I'm a mama bear, and I'm your ex-boyfriend's wife. Do you really think I'm going to back the fuck down?* Meredith broke eye contact and huffed with impatience. "They're not the sort of kids who lie," she said.

I let that comment flap around the trees for a moment, loud and ungainly as a pigeon. If I had been recording her for an interview, I would have time-stamped the tape right there: exhibit A, the moment of truth. "So you've assumed my son *is* the sort of kid who lies? Because he's a Kynaston? How about you get to know him before you label him?"

I swung Aled onto my hip and carried him away from the forest school. My footsteps pounded the path on the way back to the car. I dropped my weight behind the wheel, hauling the door shut. Silence squashed in with us. Aled clambered into the back. Outside, a breeze flipped the last leaves to their silver side. Then, from the back seat, a lowing sound. I adjusted the mirror to see Aled with his lips drawn into a wide grimace. The noise continued—a colorless drone—as he pushed breath through his teeth.

"What are you doing, baby? Is that the sound of the wind?"

Aled's eyes snapped to mine. "Mommy, I'm the ghost."

When we got back to the cottage, Aled settled down with his shows—*Dora* and *Peppa Pig*—and I stirred my tea until the spoon got too hot to hold. I thought of the weird kitchen door in the great house and Aled whispering, *Make yourself at home.* Surely a mansion like that had a cellar, and maybe he saw it and his imagination put the two together and came up with this crazy story. Or maybe that story about the boy having his finger cut off had scared Aled more than I realized.

Another thought scored my mind: Maybe Hurtwood House had brought out a dark side in Aled. *Maybe it's in his blood.* If what they said about Stanley Kynaston was true, there could be darkness in the genes. Dylan said the talent for soccer had skipped a generation from Stanley to Aled . . . Maybe soccer wasn't his only inheritance—

Enough!

In that moment, I felt a flash of spite for Meredith—not petty jealousy, but something as dark and rich as blood, a genuine hatred for making me question the goodness of my son.

I picked up my cell and called Dylan in Manchester. His response when I explained what had happened at the forest school came in grunts. Voices in the background told me he was in the office.

"I don't want him to go back there," I said. "But I have to work too. When are you home?"

"Can Gwendoline watch him?"

"She left him alone last time!"

"It was only for a few minutes. And he was in the house. He was fine."

"It's not just Gwendoline, it's"—I heard a woman calling Dylan's name—"it's that house. I hate the thought of him being alone in there."

Dylan told someone he'd be two minutes. "I grew up in that house. It's fine."

"That door in the kitchen. Your mother mutters a *spell* every time it opens."

"Spell!" Dylan scoffed.

I wished I hadn't said *spell*—that wasn't what I meant. An incantation? A charm? "Aled said it too, something about *make yourself at home*—"

"Mistress Payne! Oh my God, it's an old wives' tale. I told you, that door opens because of the air flow between the two chimneys, it's a vortex—"

"What is Mistress Pa—?"

"Mistress Payne. *P-A-Y-N-E.* She sours the milk. She makes mares lose their foals. She steals your most precious belongings. Google it, she's famous. A famous ghost. Except, of course, she's not. Can we talk about this when I get home? Let Gwendoline watch Aled while you work, and I'll sort everything out when I get there."

"I don't need you to *sort everything out!*" But I was talking to the ether, Dylan had gone. From the other room, I heard Aled chatting to the television. Like him, I'd lost all sense of what was real. I googled "Mistress *P-A-Y-N-E* Shropshire."

The Tale of Mistress Payne

Mistress Payne is a local ghost in the market town of Hurtwood, Shropshire. It is said that Squire Payne, a resident of a medieval settlement on an ancient site known as the Grim's Holm, much abused all the young women in his household until one became with child. Knowing her master to be hard-hearted, the scullery maid hid her newborn in a secret hole inside the house, but it was soon discovered. The squire ejected the girl and his bastard child from the house and instructed the surrounding farming folk not to offer shelter, at the risk of falling out of his favor. It was deep winter when Miss Payne found herself in this predicament, whereupon she hid in the undercroft of an old lazar house, but a cold snap turned the night so bitter that she perished. Her bones and those of her child were found the following spring. (Editorial note: it seems unlikely that a body could have decomposed so quickly during the winter months.)

Legacy

It is said that the restless spirit of Mistress Payne haunts the holm and the surrounding flatlands, where the ghost seeks shelter for her child. The Shropshire historian Brother Whyte of Oswestry described how families who did not welcome Mistress Payne would be cursed; she takes whatever they love the most. Her wrath has been blamed for the untimely deaths of local children, the souring of milk, and the loss of livestock. Credulous townsfolk went as far as bidding her welcome and even laying an extra place setting at the dinner table. On moonlit winter nights, she can be sighted as a wisp of smoke floating above houses.

In the 1920s, a photographer claimed to have secured a picture of Mistress Payne, though this was later shown to be a hoax (see also: Cottingley Fairies).

I read the entry once again. So that's what Gwendoline had been muttering: *Make yourself at home.* Had she told Aled to say it too? Or could he sense a presence himself? My hand went to my mouth: *I hadn't welcomed Mistress Payne. Would she take what I loved most? Would she take Aled?*

Stupid! I closed down the internet browser and wished I could shut off the creepy feeling as easily. Dusk was sniffing around outside, making me want to bolt the doors. The last thing I wanted to do was walk up to the great house with our laundry. But I figured it would be best to confront the fear head-on, prove to myself that it was nonsense. So we pulled on our coats and boots, and set off.

As we trudged up the path, I saw a wisp of smoke over the big house, coming from the chimney, obviously, on a winter night. As Dylan said, it was ridiculous! Aled ran to pick up his soccer ball, and a moment later it arched through the air and Gwendoline opened the side door in time for it to bounce right inside.

"Good shot, Aled," she said.

Inside, he got into the basket with the dogs, while Gwendoline and I tussled over the laundry, which she always insisted on doing. She kept saying her machine was too old, too cantankerous. I sighed as she disappeared through the spooky door, closing it tight behind her. I still hadn't been beyond the kitchen since we arrived. Maybe she was a private person, which was her prerogative, but I didn't want to create more work by dumping my laundry on her kitchen table every time I needed fresh underwear. The dogs' water bowl was empty, so I filled it and the pipes jackhammered.

Looking around the kitchen was like unearthing a time capsule. In one corner sat a television with a built-it VCR, like I'd had as a teen. Gwendoline's house phone was a stubby cordless model with a stumpy antenna, similar to the one my mom bought when they first came out. She wowed herself by taking calls *while walking around*! Still smiling at that memory, I picked up a Central Perk mug from the drainer. Everything here was dated but familiar, like reruns of *Friends*. I could be back in my grandmother's house watching our favorite show as we had the last evening I ever saw her. She would have been around Gwendoline's age then.

I'd stayed with her for almost a month while my mother and father separated. His extramarital baby arrived with all the usual screaming and tearing of flesh, except that the pain had started a month ahead of labor, when my mother found out. It had been a relief to get out of that war zone, and my memories of the time I spent with my grandmother were colored in the pastel hue of postcards. I'd enjoyed the heady freedom of a vacation. But, like spring break, it had to end.

My mother came to collect me one evening. My grandmother gathered my belongings, placing them on the table in a pile that slumped sideways. My small bag contained a packet of homemade buttermilk scones. My mother's car ground to a halt outside, one tire wincing as it glanced off the curb. I clung to my grandmother, knowing I was upsetting my mother, who also needed a hug after weeks apart, but the feeling of dread was strong. I could sense it the way children hear sounds too high for the adult ear. Rather like sitting in Gwendoline's kitchen, waiting for that door to open by itself, I felt an apprehension so overwhelming I almost wanted something to happen, just to get it over. I glanced at that door now before the Central Perk mug took me back to my grandmother urging me to get in the car.

"Don't be silly," my grandmother said.

"Don't be silly," my mother said.

But I wasn't silly. I left, and my grandmother passed before her scones went stale.

In the kitchen of the great house, the door swung open and my head snapped up, but it was only Gwendoline coming back from the laundry. I placed the Central Perk mug back on the drainer. She handed me my scarf, which I must have left behind. I buried my hands in the wool and found that an old loose thread had been repaired.

"Shawna is good with sewing," Gwendoline said.

My fingernail traced stitches that overlapped like bad teeth. "That was kind of her. Can you please thank her?"

"When she turns up again. She's a flibbertigibbet."

"Does she live in Hurtwood?"

"Shawna? She lives at Low Farm. I must introduce you!" Gwendoline pouted at her own bad manners. I was torn; I wanted to reassure Gwendoline that she hadn't been impolite but couldn't do that without drawing attention to the fact that Shawna left Low Farm some twenty years ago. Another memory lapse.

"I'll meet her next time she comes," I said. "There's no rush."

"She pops in on Tuesdays after the farmer's market."

"Perfect."

Gwendoline bustled off to check the wash, even though the machine had only been running for five minutes. She seemed bad tonight. Maybe the forgetfulness got worse when she was tired? Aled got bored of the dogs and sidled onto my lap. I stroked his hair back from his face. No more forest school. We'd come back from Africa thinking this would be a simpler life, and safer too. I was no longer worried about flights on dubious airlines or carjackings or Al-Shabaab terrorists, but other dangers felt just as pressing—Gwendoline could forget about Aled and let him wander to the Long Drop. I didn't know enough about dementia to make a call. I eyed Gwendoline's house phone. I gave Aled some crayons and went to the spooky door, the closest I'd gotten to the rest of the house. All quiet. I picked up the handset and pressed the memory button to access contacts. I wasn't sure what I was looking for, maybe a number for a doctor? Someone who could give me a second opinion on the extent of her illness?

Shawna . . . Dylan . . . Rose . . . Vet . . . back to Shawna again. That was it. Four numbers. I copied Shawna's and placed the handset back in its base just as Gwendoline came through the door.

"That machine's slow," she complained. "I'll get someone to take a look at it."

"It's probably on an economy cycle," I said.

"That'll be it. You are good with technology."

Outside the window, the Wrekin sat alone on the horizon, its back hunched against the wind. My relief at being indoors had a primal intensity. Deep inside the house, a clock chimed the hour, and Gwendoline went to her corner cupboard.

"Six o'clock." She turned to Aled. "Suppertime. Wash your hands, Dylan, after petting the dogs."

I'd planned to get him to bed early. Work on my edit so I could hit my deadline. But despite the tug of obligations, my own loneliness rising like floodwater, I couldn't abandon Gwendoline to her solitude.

CHAPTER 18

Submerged in the bath, I listened to the pipes grumble as though the cottage was digesting. I could be in the womb. I was regressing. Or maybe PTSD was kicking in. They say growing up as a military brat fosters a spine of steel, but the experiences of the past five years had weakened me: leaving Vic, leaving my job, leaving Chicago. Mogadishu. Always running. Leaving Africa. Dylan was the first person who'd made me feel I might one day stop running.

My pregnancy after six weeks with Dylan hit us like breaking news. We absorbed it with the aplomb of journalists; we were happy, but good news doesn't warrant the same coverage as bad news. We made a good team as journalists and new parents; we approached the two roles in much the same way, playing to our individual talents, sharing the load, reveling in the challenge. Our home became an oasis from the chaos, crises, and combat that defined our work.

But the move to England was sending tremors through my once-solid marriage. I wondered if the war zone had shifted from outside to inside. I thought of the landslide that had eroded one end of the holm, bringing the cliff edge closer to Hurtwood House. One day, it would fall.

I got out of the bath and toweled my hair while looking over the holm, trying to distract myself from bleak thoughts. The filigree oak trees were beautiful, but they had a subtly different shape than the ones in Chicago. My decade there was the longest I'd ever spent in one place. These English oaks were tall rather than wide. Maybe that was it? I didn't know enough to identify why they felt wrong, but they did. Sometimes similarity was more confusing than difference.

I turned away to select my warmest clothes. I'd be outdoors for most of the day, filming the making of *The Quest*.

My day-in-the-life documentary on Sergeant Ellie Trevelyan had scored a home run. Robert Elks had published it on the *Midland Post* website. Nothing much happened until I clipped the interview into bite-sized morsels for the social media feed. A twelve-second snippet of Sergeant Trevelyan talking about small towns—*They're like middle-aged women*—got retweeted and picked up by a national paper, went viral, and an outtake was used to introduce a televised debate about rural crime. Now I was on the radar of editors who might give me more freelance work. I couldn't have hoped for a more promising start.

But I didn't know if the same could be said about Ellie. While her police chief was being grilled on national television—asked if officers like Sergeant Trevelyan were more in touch with the community than their deskbound bosses—he paid tight-lipped tribute to her "single-minded dedication." I wondered what words he used to describe Sergeant Trevelyan off-screen.

Elks wanted a follow-up, and I'd suggested a behind-the-scenes film about the making of *The Quest*. It wasn't hard news, but it had local interest, and the Grim's Holm was infamous. Dylan got me access, but now that we were both working on the same day, I had a childcare problem. I bit my lip as the thought crossed my mind; I hated myself for thinking of Aled as a problem. Back in Africa, where Dylan and I had shared the cost of a nanny, there'd been no problem.

I confronted him over breakfast. "We both have a job today, Dylan."

"What job?" He carried on texting while answering. "With respect, Rose—"

"Why is it when you say 'with respect' it's followed by something disrespectful?"

He finished his text and then raised his eyes to mine. "It's an English thing."

"It's shit is what it is."

"Aled can hear you."

"Aled is watching television. We both have a job, we both have a child."

Dylan sighed. "Leave him with Gwendoline. She's refusing to leave the house anyway while the show is being filmed." He blew his cheeks out and then spoke in a rush. "The team needs to film inside the barn, the leper house. She still won't sign the release forms."

"She's probably afraid they'll mention your father. She's had a bum rap over the years; I'm not surprised she's nervous."

"It's not that. She's got the idea that Thorn wants Hurtwood House. That the program is part of a grand scheme to get rid of her."

"Whatever. I'm not comfortable leaving Aled with Gwendoline—"

"I know she's a little forgetful—"

"A little!"

"Yeah, a little. She's getting old, it's normal."

"She's only sixty-something."

"I know she uses the wrong name now and then, like calling Aled 'Dylan,' but she always did that. Back in the day, every girlfriend got called by the name of the one before; it used to piss them off. She's always been . . . caught up in her own business. And now she spends way too much time on her own, inside her own head. She thinks Thorn wants to buy Hurtwood House, but she's also pissed off because he gets in her face. He bought her a journal, some book to help her remember things, and she took umbrage. It's insulting to a woman who's always been organized."

"He's a dick, but he may have a point. You should persuade her to go see a doctor. They can do an assessment . . ."

"I'll speak to her when *The Quest* is over. Look, Rose"—Dylan took my shoulders in both hands—"I'm sorry this hasn't started well for you. After today, we can talk about where we want to be. You'd like Manchester, it's buzzing. It'd be better for us."

Dylan's about-turns threatened to give me whiplash. "What about Gwendoline? We just leave her?"

"Maybe she'll come with us?"

"To the city? She won't even leave the house!"

He started pushing stuff in his pockets: cell, keys, wallet. I slipped my hands around his waist and felt him sag. He pulled my hand to his mouth and kissed my palm, then headed out the door toward Low Farm. In the television room, Aled snickered as Peppa Pig's daddy fell down a hill that looked like a childish rendition of the holm.

CHAPTER 19

M y office, Sergeant Kardashian." The chief super's words when he spotted Ellie. The desk clerk winced and said it was because Ellie was a social media sensation. But one of the young constables said it was because she'd been "a massive arse."

Ellie dragged herself into the chief super's office to be told she was on traffic duty. A television show was being filmed near Hurtwood House.

"That's a constable's job," Ellie pointed out.

"As you're so committed to rural policing, you'll enjoy standing in a field."

A half hour later, she parked the patrol car and stepped into a frigid morning. Mist hung over the river. Bulrushes resembled the limp wings of tiny birds caught in the reeds. Ellie's boots sounded hollow as she walked the narrow lane. She heard the rasp of an engine, pressing her back into the hedge to let a truck pass, its roof trembling under antennae and a satellite dish.

The last time she'd visited Low Farm, it had been so run-down it was hard to believe someone was living there. A young mother, buxom, unusual name. It would be in Kenny Bale's case file. There was a son too, a boy around the same age as Dylan Kynaston. One of those kids who glances at his mother before speaking. Too-long neck. No husband; the woman inherited Low Farm and raised the son alone. Ellie thought it was weird how she could remember an entire life story and yet no name. In her mind, an image emerged like a card from a pack, a woman in a floral dress that was at odds with the decay. Shawna—*that was it: unusual*—Shawna Dourish. She'd been a streak of color against the drab farm, bright as a circus poster in a dead-end town.

Shawna had been adamant there was no abuse at the sports camp. The son shook his head in agreement. Stanley Kynaston, salt of the earth. How many times had Ellie heard that?

Ellie hoped Shawna and her spiny son had fared as well as Low Farm, with its rebirth into an architectural wonder. As the path circled the holm, Ellie saw again the farmhouse that had been transformed into a glass cathedral. Everyone knew it was owned by the television producer who devised *The Quest*. It was one of those ubiquitous shows you had to actively avoid if you didn't want to catch it, the influenza of television programs. As well as being on all the time, its presenter's shouty face beamed from magazine racks, selling face cream or a diet or a book, all of which made Ellie hate herself and Lindy Berg in equal measure.

Ellie entered the yard where the crew gathered around a catering truck in a fug of tea steam and bacon fumes. She glanced around, hoping to catch sight of Lindy Berg up close and detect if her "youthful glow" was the result of yoga and spirulina, or if she had one of those Botox death masks, all dense and gray and shiny like fresh-laid cement. But the presenter was nowhere to be seen.

Tony Thorn strode around in a summer-colored coat. His energy and patter and wild eyes made Ellie think of Willy Wonka. She wondered if he was on drugs. She wondered who trusted him with a huge budget. Ellie couldn't get a few hundred pounds to install CCTV at the children's playground where drug dealers hung out, never mind the many thousands it must have cost to dig up a hill on television.

As the line for tea and bacon was so long, she walked to the summit of the holm. It had been almost twenty years since she accompanied a senior officer there to interview Stanley Kynaston. A month later, she returned for his memorial service. Ellie had wanted to leave a bouquet on behalf of her sister, Cassie, who'd grown up with Stanley but lived in Australia. Gwendoline Kynaston told her to take the "guilty" flowers and leave. It wasn't easy to help that woman.

Ellie passed a cottage—charmingly daubed with the word *pedo*—and wondered if this was where Cassie had been deflowered by Stanley's cousin during the long, hot summer of 1976. Ellie snapped a photo and WhatsApped it to her sister alongside an eggplant emoji and a question mark. As the path approached Hurtwood House, she pocketed the phone and stopped, not wanting to startle a small boy who was performing an extraordinary number of keepie-uppies with a ball on the front lawn.

Age had withered the grand house. *That happens to the best of us,* Ellie thought. Just like her own body, the building had faded, sagged, and sprouted: wrinkled paintwork around the windows, gray streaks of bird poop on the roof, an unplucked rosebush around the door. A wisp of smoke escaped from the chimney. It was a shame, as Stanley had been house proud; on the day they came to question him about Kenny Bale, he'd been building a fence.

The side door opened, and Ellie shrank back, but not before she glimpsed Rose Falcone. Seeing Rose brought a flush to Ellie's cheeks. She suspected that the fallout from their film had yet to reach peak mortification. The Kardashian comment was only the start. Principles were all very well—Ellie stood by the comments she'd made on camera—but it was sad to spend her final few weeks as a police officer out in the cold.

Rose stopped to pull on a pair of gloves. Ellie felt no animosity toward the reporter. After all, she'd been doing a job. Rose had expertly poked and prodded and coaxed Ellie until she dragged a real emotion from the police officer like a clod of hair from the shower. Cassie said that was why the interview went viral—Ellie spoke from the heart, at odds with the doublespeak that people hear all the time on the news.

In a way, she admired Rose. Ellie herself had a knack for getting people to open up. Some officers dug into witnesses with the subtlety of a spade. But Ellie saw it as a process of erosion, sometimes requiring blunt force, other times a persistent friction, but often a slow creep into their nooks and crevices. Is that what Rose had been doing during the interview, finding her way in? She checked her watch; she'd better get back to *The Quest*. Gravel scattered as she spun on her heel. With a chill that had nothing to do with the north wind, Ellie realized that the reporter could have secretly recorded her talking about the Kenny Bale case. Maybe Rose would use it in the true-crime documentary she mentioned. Of course, she'd want to shift the blame away from the Kynastons. And it would look as though Ellie was complicit.

CHAPTER 20

Aled ran outside, glad to be freed from the confines of Gwendoline's kitchen. She kept force-feeding him because it was "snack time," according to her arbitrary timetable. I'd asked her to please not leave him on his own, and she insisted she would never do that. I mentioned the time she left him to go speak to Shawna in the barn, and she said, "I'll make sure Shawna doesn't show her face today." I bit back my irritation that she'd missed the point. *Just take him with you if you go outside, that's all I ask.* But none of this was her fault; I was taking it out on the wrong person. I went out and pulled on my gloves, taking a moment to regroup.

My eyes darted up to a window on the second floor. The one where I'd imagined a child's hands sliding down the pane and out of sight. I saw no handprints today. Only glass reflecting the clouds like the surface of a pond. Nothing to worry about. Maybe Dylan was right and Gwendoline was perfectly normal. Even so, I'd only leave Aled with her for an hour, then come back—

My attention was snatched away by a scrunch of gravel on the path. Sergeant Ellie Trevelyan walking away toward Low Farm.

Why is she here? Too senior for crowd control, surely? Is she here to speak to me? Is she mad about the documentary? My hands were all fingers and thumbs, snagging the wool. I persuaded Aled back into the house. By the time I was able to leave, Sergeant Trevelyan had gone.

On the lower side of the holm, Tony Thorn strutted around in a peacock-blue coat with the presenter, Lindy Berg. The one who wasn't dead. The crew and onlookers orbited her star. Because I was a foreigner who'd never heard of Lindy Berg until a week ago, her magnetism was lost on me. The only shine came from her yellow jumpsuit.

I established that the filming would move between three sites: an excavation to date the original earthworks, an exploration of a natural spring that was used for sacrifices, and a dig near the river. I figured that Lindy Berg would cover the most exciting discoveries, so I'd stick close to her.

Two archaeologists functioned as co-presenters, both household names from daytime shows. The younger one, Ross, was photogenic with tousled hair and a Mister Darcy complex: a reputation for getting his shirt unnecessarily wet. He backed Thorn's claim that the holm was a prehistoric site of national significance. His senior colleague, Morwenna, was an oak of a woman with legs as thick as Lindy Berg's waist. She rolled her eyes right into my camera when I filmed Ross and Thorn's excited discussion.

A hush descended as everyone found their places. I kept back beside the Outside Broadcast vehicle while Lindy Berg found her spot, hopping from foot to foot like an athlete as she waited for her cue. Behind her, the sculptured glass of the house framed a long view over the Shropshire hills. One of the technicians whispered that the show could be an expensive real estate listing for Thorn's home.

The director counted down: "Going live in five, four . . ." Bombastic music played, and Lindy Berg bounced on her toes. "Cue Lindy in two, one—"

And she lifted on invisible wires like a marionette: "Is this one of the most important historical sites in Britain? Undiscovered until today! Welcome to a special edition of *The Quest* with me, Lindy Berg, at the Grim's Holm." Music played and Lindy deflated as though unplugged.

The director and Lindy Berg hopped onto quad bikes that roared down to the first excavation site. I scooped up my camera bag and ran in their wake. By the time I arrived, Ross the archaeologist was standing in a waterlogged trench pointing his trowel at muddy stonework under peeled-back earth. "So much archaeology, it's like shooting fish in a barrel."

Lindy splashed down into the ditch. "What are you seeing? And what would you like to find today?"

"I'm seeing Iron Age stonework. And what would I *like* to find? Well, I'm dreaming of ironwork, Lindy—rare in this part of the world, even though Shropshire has the most Iron Age hill forts in the country."

Behind me, the director's walkie-talkie buzzed. He gave Lindy a hand signal to wrap up.

"Exciting developments, and we're only a few minutes into our quest!" She pressed a finger to her earpiece. "I'm told there's a find at the natural spring. No rest on the quest!"

They straddled their bikes, Lindy's backside bobbing like a balloon. I followed them to the "spring"—a disappointing mud wallow beside a pile of rocks—where the party atmosphere had evaporated, leaving a salty tension. Morwenna straddled her trench, the width of a grave but only a few inches deep. Lindy and the cameraman jostled forward like muggers cornering a victim. Morwenna held out her palm to show what looked like a dime.

"Iron Age coin," she said. "Dating to around 10 BCE. A gold stater, depicting Tasciovanus."

I shouldered my way to the front and stood alongside Thorn, whose coat bristled with pleasure. I lifted my camera and focused on the coin. Despite the grime, I could make out sharp letters, as though it were newly minted. The archaeologist dropped to her knees, and I kept her in the shot. Her blackened fingernails lifted the edge of a pot that jagged from the earth. "I found the coin by this urn. I can see more inside. If this is a hoard, it'll take days to remove and catalogue."

Lindy tapped her watch. "No rest on the quest!"

Morwenna shook her head. "I'm an archaeologist, not a game show host—"

Lindy emitted a loud bray that I assumed was a laugh and led the cameraman onto the grass, informing the viewers that this was part of the exciting nature of television. I kept my shot on the trench, where the director and Morwenna both puffed out their chests. Then he turned away, walkie-talkie to ear, one finger raised.

"Lindy, river!"

"This must mean another find!" Lindy shrieked into the camera.

The camera was rolling by the time I reached the third site. Access was difficult on the marshy land close to the water. I zoomed in on a freshly cut trench in the riverbank. An object jutted from the mud, about the size and shape of a baseball bat.

"Let's slow this down a bit." Lindy took Ross by the elbow. "Why are we so excited down here by the river?"

"Well, Lindy, my hands are shaking." He turned up his palms, and indeed there was a dramatic tremor. "This is how King Arthur must have felt when he pulled the sword from the stone!"

"Is it that significant?"

"It could be, it could be. My first trench confirmed what we've always believed—this is an Iron Age site. But what was it used for? I think it was a place of ritual, like Stonehenge."

"Tell us why!"

"We had a theory that the natural spring was a holy well. The hoard of coins supports that hypothesis."

"Okay, but what have you found by the river?"

"Let me explain, Lindy. Magnetic readings—"

"What's in the mud, Ross?" Lindy reached down to touch the submerged baseball bat, but he grabbed her wrist.

"Careful!" The snap in his tone stilled the crowd. I was the only person moving, edging forward for a better shot. Claggy ground sucked at my boots. On full zoom, I saw that the find was flatter than a baseball bat. Dull metal. Carved.

Ross whispered, "It's a sword. Known as a La Tene sword. From Switzerland. More than two thousand years old and as perfect as the day it was forged by the Celts."

"What's a sword from Switzerland doing here?" Lindy asked.

"It's been thrown into the river as an offering."

Freezing water splashed my face, and I twisted away to protect my camera. Morwenna ploughed past, her face pink with cold or anger.

"We need to slow down," she said.

"No rest on the quest!" Lindy maneuvered to block Debbie Downer from getting into the shot. I heard Morwenna hiss that she'd walk off the dig, but she'd lost the crowd's attention. All eyes and cameras focused on Ross, stepping down into the river where he sank to midthigh, gasping at the cold. He took hold of the sword. Lindy crouched with a cloth draped over her hands, like a midwife awaiting the final push. The hush was broken only by Morwenna's sighs, which were echoed by the bristling river reeds.

Ross's hands slithered into the mud, and the sword lifted free with an exaggerated kissing sound. He laid the object onto Lindy's cloth. Despite the encrusted mud, the artifact looked impressive; Lindy released a whoosh of air at its weight, its gravity. A burst of applause sent a moorhen crashing into the air.

Lindy turned to the camera and opened her mouth to speak—

"There's more!" Ross's wet curls streamed down his face as he plunged his hands under the water again.

"Another sword?" Lindy off-loaded the first one into the waiting arms of Morwenna, as though it was a female baby born to the king.

"It's not metal," Ross said, hands submerged to the elbows. "I can't see through the murk." Abruptly, he pulled back, flailing, taking a dunk up to the neck. The crowd gasped, but he surged back to his feet.

"Bones," he said, fisting hair from his eyes. "Human bones! Lodged under the wood inside the culvert."

"If it's human remains, then we *have* to stop the dig." Morwenna jostled forward to the water's edge, still cradling the sword. "It's the law. We have to inform the police."

"We're not stopping. There's a police officer here." The director spoke into his walkie-talkie. "Someone get her to the river."

On camera, Ross and Lindy speculated about the age of the bones until Sergeant Ellie Trevelyan arrived. I filmed her stepping into the culvert and the limelight.

"The bones are half-buried in this silty layer wedged between wooden posts." Ross pushed his hand into the murk again. He looked like a vet feeling inside a cow. "Directly below the sword. Maybe the body was sacrificed, a human offering to the water."

"Ridiculous," Morwenna called out. "The river would have changed course in two thousand years."

"Perhaps this was a lake," said Lindy.

"Perhaps this whole thing is a fraud!" said Morwenna, but the onlookers tutted and shushed.

"And I believe we have . . . a tibia!" Ross handed a muddy stick to Lindy. She took it reverentially before dunking it once into the water to wash away the muck.

"It's broken," she said. In her hands, the bone looked more like a weapon, its sharp end tapering to a lethal point.

"This unfortunate individual met a violent end, I'm afraid."

"How old is it?"

"The geochronology suggests it's old. Put simply, it's buried beneath another artifact that we can date quite precisely. But we'll do carbon dating on the bone—"

"It's not old," said Sergeant Trevelyan, dropping to her knees beside the watercourse. "You need to step away from the remains."

"How can you possibly know—" Lindy started to ask, but Ellie reached past her and plucked something from the water.

"This floated to the surface when you disturbed the body." The police officer held up a small ziplock bag containing a black object about the size of her palm. I trained my shot onto it: the black square was topped with a brushed metal shutter. Ellie looked right into the camera: "A floppy disc. What it's doing alongside an Iron Age sword and a skeleton, I have no idea. But using contextual analysis and common bloody sense, I'd date these human remains to the late '90s."

CHAPTER 21

M y breath turned to sand. Hot and dry, too swift to hold, it filled the space where my voice should have been. *This has never happened before.* The voice in my headphones was as clear as daylight. "There seems to be a delay on the line to England. We're hoping to speak to our reporter, who was at the scene of this bizarre discovery yesterday. Human remains found during the filming of a television show. We can see you, Rose. Can you hear us?"

"I can hear you now." I managed the lie. *I can't believe I froze on live TV.*

"You couldn't make it up, could you? They thought these bones were ancient, maybe prehistoric, until a floppy disc was found with the body. The British media are calling it 'Indiana Bones and the Last Upgrade.'" The anchorwoman laughed more heartily than the pun deserved. "You were right there when it happened. Why don't you talk us through it?"

I gave a gritty laugh as the sand threatened to return. *Why so nervous?* My former network, my former coworker. "Yeah, we got more than we bargained for and make no mistake." *Why so folksy?* I pulled myself up straight and planted my fists businesslike on the kitchen table beside my laptop. "They were filming an archaeological dig at a prehistoric site—" I kept talking, recounting the buildup to the discovery of a skeleton with a detail that had clickbaited the world's attention, a computer disc in its pocket. But while I spoke, I spotted over the top of my laptop the front door of the cottage swinging open. A small head bobbed into view.

Aled.

He should be with Gwendoline!

With my earpiece in, I couldn't hear him, but his mouth pursed around the word *Mommy.* "And, um—" *Where was I?* "That's when the police, er, her name is Sergeant Ellie, ah, she spotted a plastic . . . thing in the water."

"Let's take another look at that moment, which was being filmed for British television. I betcha those viewers were not expecting what came next! Take a look at this . . ."

The clip, I knew, was twenty-three seconds long because I'd edited it. My own footage, gone viral again. Twenty-three seconds of a Z-list celebrity falling on his ass in a river and a discovery both macabre and farcical. And now I had twenty-three seconds to stop Aled from photo-bombing my interview while I was cashing in on television gold.

"Hey, baby. Go watch TV," I whispered.

"Mommy?" he stomped into the kitchen.

"Mommy's working. Where's Gwen-ma?"

"She's making a stinky stink. It hurt my throat. I need water."

I rushed around the kitchen table, handing Aled my glass: "Here, baby. Go watch your shows." I gave his shoulder a tiny shove toward the living room.

"This water smells funny. What are you doing, Mommy?"

"I'm talking to a lady, and it's important that you keep quiet, okay?" I checked my laptop: Ellie reached out and plucked the disc from the water. A few seconds to go. "Can you go watch TV in the living room? Please? Just for five more minutes."

"I can't do the button. And my hair smells of the stinky stink." I sniffed him—burnt plastic. *Okay, I'll deal with that later.*

"You can work the button, Aled. You do it all the time. Go on now."

I sat in front of my laptop again, pulling a smile onto my face like a horse's bridle.

"Who are you talking to, Mommy?"

"Dora's waiting for you," I said through clenched teeth, and thankfully he turned toward the living room. On my screen, the camera zoomed in to Ellie brandishing the disc, and it had been reedited so that she repeated *common bloody sense.* Her melancholy accent was more pronounced on the recording.

"That's what I call a cold case!" The presenter laughed as the shot returned to the studio. "So what are the police—"

"Mommy?" Aled appeared at the door, remote in hand. "Who's that lady?"

What did she ask? Something about the police investigation? Under the kitchen table, I slid my leg to the side, blocking Aled from getting into the shot. *Where the hell is Gwendoline?* "Um, yeah, right. The police are—"

"Mommy!" Loud as a wrecking ball.

"Ah, I mean the whole incident may have looked like the Keystone Cops, but it's prompted a live investigation, and the police immediately closed down the dig as soon as human remains were discovered."

"Mommy?"

"And, Rose, from your perspective, what impact has it had on the small town of Hurtwood, being thrust into the public eye?"

"Mommy . . ."

Can they hear him? Blown up large on the screen, I saw myself as a stiff and pale stranger, one arm stretching out of the shot, where my palm closed over Aled's wrist. Time oozed down my spine as though I'd been hit by an egg. Long, sticky seconds passed. I wanted to stop altogether, to step outside time and spool the tape back to the moment when I should have locked the kitchen door. But that's the deal with live broadcasting—no second take. You need power out of the blocks to go full throttle to the finish line. Now I'd lost my footing, and the world tilted as I started to go down. *What was the question? Something about a small town . . .* I forced my mouth to move. "Yeah, so, the small people of Hurtwood have been rocked by—" I had no idea what the people of Hurtwood thought as I hadn't left the holm since the bones were discovered. But my mouth kept going of its own accord, even when Gwendoline flustered through the front door, glanced around for Aled, and bundled him out with one wooden chair, tight in his grasp, screeching along behind them. The louder it got, the wider I grinned, until I must have resembled the skull pulled from the river. As the front door closed, my brain caught up with my mouth, and I heard myself say, "a revelation that has rocked this watery—backwater, ah—" *What the frick? Watery? Backwater?* "This, um, riverside spot in the beautiful heart of rural England."

The presenter thanked me, and I ripped out my earpiece, groaning like a person with diarrhea who got to the bathroom and found there's no paper. My hands shook as adrenaline jolted through my veins. *What a disaster!* I'd been told long ago that my personnel file at the network had a note saying *great live*, but now I heard the producer hitting the delete button on my reputation. A decade to build, three minutes to destroy.

I wanted to bury myself in one of the archaeological trenches on the holm. I pushed the chair back with a scrape and put my face in my hands. I'd only asked Gwendoline to watch Aled for half an hour. And instead he barged in on my interview, smelling like a bonfire. What a stinky stink! Pressure on my eyebrows turned the threatening tears into stars. I heard the front door swing open again.

They're back. I mustn't be rude to Gwendoline. She's an old lady; it's really not her fault.

I looked up.

No one there.

The skin on my back crept closer to my spine. On the pathway outside the front door, a ribbon of smoke swirled to the ground. There wasn't a fire in the cottage. I couldn't get one to stay lit. I sat stock-still as you might if you'd seen a wild animal and didn't want to alert it. The silence tightened. I shifted my gaze to the glass Aled drank from, a sticky handprint whitewashed on the side. Like an image I'd seen days ago: palms pressed against a window. Sliding down, out of sight.

I cleared my throat. "Mistress Payne," I said. "Make yourself at home."

The door behind me rattled in its frame.

Like this day could get any worse.

Slowly, I reached out to shut down my laptop. The screen went blank. Then I walked steadily from the kitchen without looking behind me, picked my keys off the hook beside the front door, and sprinted up the path to see if Aled was safe at the big house.

CHAPTER 22

"Too much of a good thing," Sergeant Ellie Trevelyan heard her father muttering outside in the garden. His arthritic fingers burst from his sleeves like the straw hands of a scarecrow. "Too much of a good thing," he said, digging a toe into the waterlogged lawn. Ellie pulled a carton from the freezer—one of a batch she cooked every Sunday—and slid a tray of lasagna into the microwave. The benefit of caring for someone with dementia was that he didn't complain about the food getting repetitive. He got a week of lasagna. A week of chili con carne. Seven long days of stew. Sunday roast at the pub. "Too much of a good thing," he said to a lake forming on the grass. "The rain, the rain." The microwave pinged.

"One of the wettest years on record, Dad," Ellie called through the open door. He didn't seem to feel the cold anymore; he'd gone out without a coat. Oblivious. A new development to worry about. Last winter, she'd had the locks changed so he couldn't get stuck outside without keys. But if he insisted on going without a coat, he could get hypothermia in an hour. Frostbite. Chilblains. *Oh stop, Ellie,* she thought, *you can't be with him every minute.* Some days, she felt like the nervous new mother she'd never been.

He came in and sat at the table, and she locked the door. Shoveling their meal onto plates—the beef as rich and dank as a slab of turf—she added a handful of cress from the windowsill, which Jim grew on paper towels like a schoolboy.

"Fungus," he said. "Fungus in the root system."

When she was ten, he'd helped her grow a hedge of sunflowers twelve feet tall, and they had their photo in the *Midland Post*.

"Do you remember those sunflowers, Dad? When we got in the paper?"

"Fungus'll blight the apple tree."

Ellie said she'd spread wood chips around the trunk.

"Mildew," he said, but ate his lasagna.

This was one of the worst days. Even then, it wasn't terrible. Jim never got violent or sweary; one of Ellie's colleagues looked after an elderly mother who pinched her caregivers and spat racial slurs at Mr. Samwel, the pharmacist. Often, Ellie and Jim managed lucid conversations. Not based in the here and now—they might discuss the ailments of long-dead friends—but the dialogue had logic, a satisfying pattern of cause and effect. Ellie enjoyed these wandering chats as much as she enjoyed their walks around Hurtwood; you never knew who you might meet.

But that was before the obsession with the "hottie" at the Nail Bar. Jim kept saying the word over and over again, stuck on a loop. Maybe lusting after a teenager signaled a worsening of his condition, the loss of his moral compass. Ellie thought back to his comment about Dylan Kynaston and Giles Hotchen's accident; try as she might, she couldn't get any more sense out of him on that topic. It had been too long. Too long with dementia gnawing his brain.

"Fungus," he said.

"Yes," Ellie agreed. "Fungus in the root system."

But here was Dylan Kynaston on her radar again. Ellie had found a few details about Giles Hotchen online; his bicycle had been in a collision with a truck in July 1999. The *Midland Post* had a terrible online archive, and she couldn't find more. From memory, she knew that Kenny Bale died that summer. And the bones at the holm had to date to roughly the same era judging by the vintage of the floppy disc. Three cases, three links to Hurtwood House. If the techies managed to access the content of the floppy disc, they might get dates. While she cleared the dinner plates, her phone rang. She sent Jim for a bath before answering.

"Sergeant Trevelyan?" The voice on the line sounded harassed.

"That's me."

"DI Harrow."

Detective Inspector Bryan Harrow, known as Broken Arrow. Because, as the oft-repeated joke about him went, he would never go very far and you couldn't fire him.

"I got lumbered with the Indiana Bones case. You were right about the date."

Ellie's heart took a tumble. "Yeah?"

"Coroner reckons it's been in the water at least twenty years. Late '90s. So who went missing from your patch twenty years ago? We need an ID."

"We don't get many missing persons in Hurtwood. Is it male or female?"

"Young male, not fully grown, probably mid-to-late teens—"

Same profile as Kenny Bale, Ellie thought.

"The broken leg was fresh and occurred around the time of death. No soft tissue so we can't say if he drowned or what. No obvious head injury. If it matches anyone, we can request dental records . . ."

"And the floppy disc?"

"It's been twenty years in the water. I'm not hopeful of getting anything off it, but it was inside a plastic bag so we might get lucky. But there was one thing: the boy was missing the tip of a finger."

"From the time of death?"

"No, old injury. Probably happened when he was a kid."

"Farm injury," Ellie said. "So many missing fingers around here, you'd need a football team to count to a hundred."

"That's what I thought. It's a big clue, Trevelyan. Missing kid. Missing finger. On your patch. Any hot tips from the reigning queen of rural policing?"

"Sorry Bro—Bryan." Ellie heard him cough. *He's aware of the nickname.* "No long-lost kids here, not even going way back. But there is one thing . . ." Ellie heard a rush of bathwater down the pipes inside the thin stud walls. "You know what happened at Hurtwood House in 1999?" Ellie recounted the Kenny Bale case. Broken Arrow grunted in conclusion. She didn't mention her father making a link between Dylan Kynaston and Giles Hotchen; the opinion of a dementia patient wouldn't impress the DI.

"So I need a list of the other football players who Stanley Kynaston represented," he said. "If any of them went missing or made an allegation of abuse, we might hit jackpot—ID on the victim and a link to a known suspect. Even better, a dead suspect, so I won't have to fanny about with a conviction. Cold case closed, bury the bones, off to the pub."

Upstairs, her dad thumped around the bathroom like a heavy-footed ghost. Ellie thought of Stanley Kynaston and tried to put aside his reputation, the two decades of slurs that had blown around town, landing on street corners where kids traded lewd jokes, and playgrounds where bored moms gossiped, and pub gardens where smokers told tall tales. All these seeds took root and grew into a shape that resembled reality. A topiary of truth. She wanted to push past that speculation. There was a real man here somewhere. And his living family.

She had a vague memory of Stanley from the time he had been friends with her sister. Cassie's whole class had gone to a party at Hurtwood House—maybe even the one when Cassie did it for the first time in the cottage—but she'd drunk too much, and Stanley brought her home in a tractor he was licensed to drive. Never mind that he would have been over the alcohol limit; country folk considered themselves exempt. Ellie remembered the rumble of his engine outside her window, the carnal smell of diesel and livestock that drifted into her bedroom to mingle with the curiosity and shame of her instincts sputtering to life. Cassie was a crucial eight years Ellie's senior. Hard to believe her sister was in her sixties; their teenage years seemed like a blink ago.

She'd peeped through her curtains to watch Cassie stagger into the arms of Stanley Kynaston. All the girls liked him. Maybe they'd snog. Maybe they'd French kiss. Ellie almost laughed aloud at the memory of how worried she'd been about something as simultaneously alluring and alarming as French kissing, as though it might entail garlic and a level of sophistication that would elude her. But, instead, Stanley held Cassie's elbow in one hand and looped his other arm around her back, supporting her as she tottered up the path toward the door. Even in her innocence, Ellie recognized that her sister was drunk. Once Cassie built up momentum, she dismissed Stanley with a wave. Ellie had watched him, one hand tapping his long thigh until the front door slammed and he drove into the night. Leaving behind that carnal tang of countryside.

But what did it mean, this snapshot? He'd done the decent thing by Cassie. So what? After a twenty-five-year career, Ellie was rarely surprised by contradictions; in her experience, human beings had more messed-up sides than a Rubik's cube.

"Trevelyan?" Broken Arrow had asked her a question.

"Sorry, phone dropped out," she lied.

"I said I need those files on Stanley Kynaston and—what's his name, the boy?"

"Kenny Bale. I had my hand on them earlier this week when I was packing the storeroom; I'll get them sent over."

"Don't bother. I'll work out of Hurtwood tomorrow."

"Don't suppose you need extra hands, do you? I've been out in the cold since . . . you know."

"Since you joined the Kardashians? I could use you, sure. I'm not going to get much support for a cold case. You angling for a promotion to detective when they close Hurtwood?"

"That's not on the cards. Consider this my swan song."

"You're leaving the force?"

"Can't transfer to headquarters. I look after my father, and it's too far."

"Sorry to hear that. Look, I know I took the piss about the Kardashians, but we value coppers who know their patch."

"Thanks, DI Harrow. Appreciate you saying that."

Sergeant Ellie Trevelyan went upstairs to persuade her father that one bath was enough, thinking that maybe she'd resolve the Kenny Bale case after all.

CHAPTER 23

A fter my humiliating live TV performance, I wanted to hide. But the visit from Mistress Payne meant I didn't want to hide in the cottage. Nowhere to go, nowhere to hide. My mind flitted to Dylan's hiding place in the big house, the priest's hole where he'd stashed his treasures. That seemed appealing right now. Except I was a grown woman with a son who needed me to be an adult.

So I decided to take control, starting with making the cottage feel more homey. Gwendoline came down to show me how to build a fire. We needed to warm the flue to prevent smoke from backing up into the room. She lit one end of a knot of paper and held it inside the chimney to pierce the plug of cold air. Simple physics. While she had her arm pushed high inside the fireplace, I took paper from the box of kindling she'd brought with her and twisted the pieces into farfalle pasta shapes. Her scrap paper had jagged edges as though ripped from a book. And it was covered with handwritten calligraphy.

Stockholm syndrome, I read. *The Grim's Holm protects me, and for that I love it and I don't try to escape.*

I twisted the sheet and laid it in the grate. Picked up another piece. *I'm not saying he's on par with the devil. But his name is apt: he's a prick.*

I twisted the words and added them to the pile. His name is apt . . . prick. I stifled a laugh. She must mean Thorn. I picked up another sheet.

He's here. He's back. The isle is full of voices, all whispering his name.

I added that twist to the grate. Gwendoline drew her arm from inside the chimney and dropped the flame onto the kindling. It caught, and the fire strained upward. She dumped the last of her kindling onto the flames and watched the paper burn.

Then she hurried away to the great house. She seemed agitated, bustling and muttering like a person preparing for a trip. Not surprising that she was shaken up after a body had been found near her home. That would rattle anyone. But I worried about the impact on her mind. I'd spent some time reading up on dementia; shocks can trigger anxiety, and disruption worsens the symptoms. And I feared the community's response to a second boy being found dead on the holm.

I put Aled down for a nap and checked the police Twitter feed. Nothing. No news on the identity of the body and nothing about the contents of the floppy disc found with Indiana Bones. Surely that disc would answer a lot of questions if it was readable. It had been protected inside a plastic bag . . . As I trawled news sites, my Facebook page pinged a notification. Plenty of people had seen my car crash of an interview. A woman I'd gone to school with briefly in Japan shared the clip—a part where I was stammering—staking a claim to me now that I was momentarily famous. *Infamous.* I ignored her post—that sloppy-egg feeling of shame dripping down my spine again—and clicked on the Messenger notification.

Victor Carlson would like to send you a message. Ignore. Accept.

I put down the laptop and went to the window.

Vic Carlson.

I opened the window to hear chittering bats. The cold here was different than other places I'd lived. In Chicago, the cold confronted you; it was brutally honest. Here, it was sneaky and insinuating. A sly chill that got under some people's skin more than others, like gossip.

At Vic's cabin, the snow had hidden us from the world. I could barely recall the details of that day at the end of winter when his wife reasserted herself with the brisk potency of spring—she was pregnant and ruthless with new life—and I got kicked to the gutter like the slush that I was. If all was forgiven, why was my first instinct to ignore him? My laptop faded to energy-saving mode. Because I'd never forgiven myself. *My marriage is over,* he'd told me at the start. *But we can't go public until the divorce comes through. She's the daughter of the chairman of the network; it'll affect our careers if this isn't handled right.* And I called myself a cynical journalist? That winter, I hadn't been nearly skeptical enough.

The window blew shut with a soft thump. My son turned in his bed. I slipped the latch into place and sat down with my laptop again.

Is it impolite to ignore someone who saved your life? I scanned his message. Vic had been assigned to London. Promoted. His career at the network had grown as inexorably as a stalactite, the sovereign of cold, dark places. Something glassy glimpsed way up high on the ceiling. When our affair ended, guess who clung on at the network? The stalactite, obviously.

Victor always played with a trump hand: more money, more power, more . . . married.

Did his one gentlemanly act—transferring $10,000 to a bank account in Mogadishu—make up for months of using me for fun? For claiming he'd already left his wife when they were, in fact, trying for a baby? For costing me my job at the network? I hit ignore, just as the front door creaked open. I froze, thinking, *Mistress Payne?* But then I heard "Rosie?" It was Dylan. A long breath streamed out of me.

In the kitchen, he warmed soup while reassuring me—a little too earnestly—that my live interview hadn't been as bad as I thought.

"Although . . . ," he said, pouring the soup into a mug.

"Although?"

"The *small people* of Hurtwood?"

Small people. Keystone Cops. Watery backwater. I had no recollection of saying those words, but I'd been so distracted it was possible. The words wouldn't win me friends in Hurtwood. I took a mouthful and swore as the soup burned my tongue.

"Dammit! You know, Dylan, that interview wouldn't have been such a disaster if Aled hadn't photobombed me. It wasn't an easy situation to handle. And now my reputation is shot, and so is my career."

"Your reputation will outlive this. You'll get another commission and be back on top form. But I'm sorry, if I'd been here, I would have—"

"But you weren't here. And I had to ask Gwendoline to watch Aled. And she got distracted again. I don't know why . . ." I trailed off, putting my thumb into my mouth to rub the sore spot.

"You don't know why what?"

"Why you trust her to look after Aled. Why you can't face facts. She isn't capable. She has dementia; I've been reading about it. Aled said he came home because she made a stink. I think she started a bonfire when she was looking after him, which isn't safe."

"It was probably the manure heap for the ponies. It doesn't burn, it smolders."

"No, he stank of something like burnt plastic. It was toxic. This whole place is . . ." Damn, my tongue hurt.

"Toxic? I think you're overstating it," Dylan said. "Of course I trust Gwendoline with Aled; she's my mum. She's the most trustworthy person I know. But I guess . . ." He dipped a pinkie finger in his soup and lifted away a dried skin. "I need to adjust to her aging."

I questioned his judgment, but it was worse than that: I questioned his loyalty. To Aled. To me. But at least he was listening.

"In other news," I said, "Mistress Payne is haunting us now." I told him about the ghost coming through the kitchen.

"It's the wind."

"It's not the wind!"

"Chimneys—"

"There's no wind, okay? It was still, and then the front door opened, and when I said, *Make yourself at home*, she rattled the back door on her way out."

"Rosie . . ."

"What? Everybody knows the legend. There are ghosts everywhere here. Ghosts and dead bodies." I snatched his saucepan off the Aga to wash it, and the spatula flipped a slash of tomato soup across my white top. "See? This place is out to get me."

Dylan wiped me with a cloth and pulled me to his chest.

"Come to Manchester for a few days. Meet some people—"

"And what about Aled?"

"He'll have to come with us. I got this in the post today." Dylan pulled an envelope from his jacket. It was a lawyer's letter, detailing a request from Gwendoline to give Dylan power of attorney over her affairs. "The solicitor said Mum phoned yesterday and gave instructions to get documents sent out right away. Urgent."

"Because of her dementia?"

"Because of the body. She's scared she's going to prison."

"What? Why would *she* go to prison?"

"She was the only one living here when he died. The only one who's still here, anyway."

"We don't know when he died. Or even if *he* is a he. Indiana Bones could be anyone. And there were plenty of people living here back then: your father, her friend Shawna at Low Farm, and the son who cut off his finger—what was his name?"

"Rhys."

"And even you, Dylan, you were here. All those soccer players coming and going—"

"You know that, and I know that, and the police know that. But she's confused and shocked. Just imagine: there's been a dead body lying at the bottom of the holm for twenty years or more, and she never knew. It's horrible. I'll phone the solicitor now, sort out this power of attorney.

It mightn't be a bad thing considering how forgetful she's getting." He went to make the call, and I went to the living room to stoke the fire. In truth, I needed a moment to think. What Dylan said made sense, but still Gwendoline's reaction jarred: *Why would someone's mind—even a confused mind—turn to prison unless they felt guilty?*

On the hearth, a singed scrap of paper had dropped through the grate, left behind when Gwendoline made the fire earlier. A charred upper corner of her dense calligraphy read *Rose and Aled*, but the blackened paper flaked to crumbs in my fingers like tobacco leaf. Below, the writing was better preserved: *You two arrived too soon, like snowdrops before the last hard frost.* I threw the paper in the fire, wondering what happens to snowdrops who arrive before the last hard frost. Then I realized: they perish. They die.

CHAPTER 24

Robert Elks was a legend, and Sergeant Ellie Trevelyan told him so. It was twilight in the *Midland Post* office, the journalist getting back to his deadline after digging through the archives for a file Ellie needed. The police folder on Giles Hotchen was meager. She laid that to one side. By contrast, Elks's dossier—she liked that word; in her head, she heard it in the voice of Jodie Foster as Clarice Starling—his dossier was stuffed with notes and clippings.

"Why've you gathered all this on Hotchen?" Ellie shouted into the gloom.

Elks pulled off his headphones. "Background."

"For what?"

Elks sighed and stood up, bumping his head on the inflatable crocodile that stalked his desk. "For the obituaries."

"Hotchen is in his thirties," Ellie protested.

"There are rumors he's not been 100 percent since the accident."

Ellie flipped open the file, spilling cuttings across the desk. Elks was as messy as he was thorough.

"Coffee?" he asked.

She shook her head. "Won't sleep. Do you have a file on me, Robert?"

"Yep."

Ellie had been joking. She focused on the paperwork.

Giles Hotchen.

Born 1981, son of Harry Hotchen, a local entrepreneur who turned his family farm into a storage facility. Hotchen Senior diversified into a chain of farmer's market–style shops, and then bought up commercial property in Hurtwood. Finally, he opened a showroom for sports cars.

His only son, Giles Hotchen, was educated at private prep until he won a place at Hurtwood Boys' School.

Ellie found Giles Hotchen amid the monochrome faces of a rugby team photo printed in the *Midland Post* when Hurtwood won a tournament in 1998. How strange to think these youthful faces—frozen in time as impossibly smooth-skinned and, to be honest, smug-eyed young men—would now be showing signs of decay. How many of the team members would now have a widow's peak, a whisky nose, a gut they could rest a beer glass on? How many looked less smug after life had given them more of a kicking than they'd experienced on the rugby field?

But Giles wasn't singled out for praise in the dispatch. Team player, not man of the match. Ellie wondered how he felt about that. Did he live up to the expectations of his rags-to-riches father? She scanned the faces and didn't think she could see Dylan Kynaston. But then, the rugby team might not appeal to the son of a football legend.

Next in the dossier was Giles Hotchen's accident.

July 1999: Giles Hotchen rode his bike at speed down an alleyway from the direction of Whipping Post Lane. Ellie scanned her mental map and found Whipping Post Lane behind the Georgian buildings of Cheapside, close to Hurtwood Boys' School and the police station. It was a narrow street you'd only use to access the rear loading bay of the low-rent shops. *Witnesses said he shot from the alleyway onto the high street, traveling so fast he overshot the pavement and went straight under the wheels of a truck.*

There were several reports detailing extensive injuries. Anniversary pieces with updates on his recovery. A trip to the US for revolutionary therapy to treat the effects of his head injuries—his dad sold a business to pay for that. It must have been a success because, ten years after the accident, Giles Hotchen took over his father's property portfolio. The *Midland Post* ran a profile piece about his bid to "breathe new life into Hurtwood's retail sector" with his purchase of a row of commercial buildings on Cheapside. Ellie found it macabre that Hotchen had bought real estate right where he'd suffered his near-fatal accident.

He'd gone on to be a phenomenally successful developer. But that gave Ellie pause. Why had his Midas touch never gilded Cheapside? That street was a backwater, with its dodgy Nail Bar and the kind of tattoo parlor where you go in for a Chinese symbol saying *peace* and come out with one saying *potato*. It was hard for Ellie to answer these questions because Giles Hotchen was shy of the press. The only other information in the file concerned a legal case that had rumbled on for years after his bicycle accident: *Hotchen Senior sued the manufacturer of his son's bike over faulty brakes. The maker raised a credible counterclaim over possible tampering, and Hotchen backed down before it went to court.* In Elks's own handwriting: *Sources suggest Hotchen Senior fears business rivals may have targeted his son deliberately.*

Ellie closed the file. No mention of Dylan Kynaston. Her dad's comments must have been the result of a jumbled mind. Two boys, two legendary fathers, two tragic accidents. It would be easy to confuse them even while compos mentis, never mind with dementia.

"Elks?"

"Hmm?" The tilt of the journalist's head as he slipped off his headphones made Ellie think of a shire horse with a fly stuck in its ear. She'd outstayed her welcome, but Elks was too polite to say.

"Did you ever hear anything about Dylan Kynaston and Giles Hotchen? I dunno, a falling-out, something serious?"

"They'd have been at Hurtwood Boys' around the same time."

"It isn't a large school. Were they mates?"

"Ellie, I—" Elks reclined in his seat, the lumbar support complaining about the weight.

"You have a deadline, I know, sorry. So Giles Hotchen owns the building where your Nail Bar is located."

"He owns the whole street. I've requested interviews in the past, but he's never cooperated. Don't think he'd incriminate his tenant on my behalf. If anything, he might warn them I'm poking around."

"Shame. I could use a more recent profile of Giles Hotchen." Ellie slid his file back into the cabinet. While she pulled on her gloves, she replayed what her father said. Something to do with a turd left on the headmaster's car. One of them, Dylan or Giles, had provided the turd—*what an undignified story!*—and blamed each other. Later that day, an accident nearly killed one of them. Ellie could feel a connection the way she might feel a cold coming on. A too-warm, scratchy sensation. She called goodbye and headed for the door.

"Ellie?" Elks held up a scrap of paper, and she came back for it. "Back in the day, Dylan went out with a woman called Meredith Fiddler. They were serious. She moved back to Hurtwood recently and started a forest school. If you're after gossip, she might oblige."

"Thanks, Elks, you're a—"

"Legend. I know. Tell my wife, the memo never reached her."

CHAPTER 25

"For the love of God!" said Robert Elks when I walked into the *Midland Post*. He was working in the dark, his face bleached by his screen. "I'm not the local library."

I felt like I'd been nipped by the family pet.

He must have read my face or, given the darkness, my flinch, because he hauled his frame from behind the desk. "Sorry, sorry . . . I'm up against a deadline, and I'm desperately trying to cut down on coffee." He pressed one hand to his throat, as though checking for a pulse. "But deadlines crave coffee, don't you think?"

"I won't disturb you; I came in to look at the archive. I'll make you a decaf . . ."

"Don't be absurd—make me a proper coffee. But I have to get on, so no picking my brain on whatever it is you're looking for." He sat down. "What *are* you looking for?"

"Ideas for documentaries. Maybe true-crime cases." This was true to a degree. It was time to take off my "Rose Kynaston, wife" hat and put on my "Rose Falcone, reporter" hat. I needed to think with the detachment of my former self. Even if I was thinking, mainly, of my husband.

Elks waved his arm at a wall of cabinets. "Make yourself at home. I must file." He sat down, holding his headphones halfway to his ears. The man couldn't resist gossip. "What's happening at the holm? I hear you've been freelancing about Indiana Bones."

Small people of Hurtwood. Watery backwater. Keystone Cops. I wondered what he'd heard. Nothing good. "The police recovered the body. The area is taped off, but we haven't heard any more." The inflatable crocodile above his desk grinned in the gloom. "I hope I didn't mislead you the first time I came in."

Elks wrinkled his forehead.

"By using my maiden name. I didn't think my connection to the Kynastons was relevant"—*that was a lie*—"but since Indiana Bones, I guess it might be an issue."

"I wouldn't be a very good journalist if I didn't know that the young American woman in town had married into the Kynaston clan."

"You knew when I first met you? And you didn't say?"

"Many women use their maiden names, especially in the media. Although you can't report on the Indiana Bones case if—" He stopped abruptly.

"If?"

"Depending on how the case develops. I really must get on."

But he didn't get on. He seemed to be considering his next words. What had he been going to say? *You can't report if . . . the case implicates your family in a murder?* Elks took a deep breath, held it for a second, and plunged on: "You know, as a local reporter, I also function as something of a local historian. All this"—he gestured to the archive—"is backup for what's filed here." He pointed to his head.

"Okay . . ." *Where's he going with this?*

"Most local reporters would have run a piece linking the discovery of old bones with previous unexplained deaths."

"Like Kenny Bale?" Neither of us had time to beat around the bush. "The soccer player who jumped off the Long Drop?"

"The Long Drop? I'd forgotten that's what they call it." He tapped his forehead. "Getting old. It was never established if Kenny Bale intended to kill himself. If he fell. If something else happened."

"Such as?"

"There's always been speculation."

"Show me a journalist who doesn't file away speculation." I tapped my forehead.

Elks smiled in acknowledgement. "I've heard it all over the years. You'll probably hear it too, given time. There's people who'll say it to your face even if you are a Kynaston. This case got under the skin of Hurtwood. There was never any . . . what Americans like to call *closure*. The speculation was left to run wild." Outside, a car with no muffler screeched down the road.

"I can't pretend I'm not curious what people think."

"Everyone has an opinion, but only one person knows for sure, and he died in 1999."

"Stanley?"

"Kenny."

"So what's the leading theory?"

Elks shrugged. "Kenny was abused during football training. Which would point at Stanley."

"But the evidence was thin?"

"Wafer thin. But it was enough for most people. You know, it's a very British mentality to knock down heroes. When the mighty fall, everyone jumps on their back and feels a little taller."

With that, Elks turned the headphones in his hands and clamped them onto his ears. I slipped into the kitchen. While the kettle boiled, I thought about the righteous indignation directed at Stanley. On the one hand, yes, people revel in a public disgrace. It wasn't just a British mentality. On the other hand, righteous indignation could come from a sense of vindication. How many times has one allegation against a person of privilege prompted other victims to raise their hands? Fallen heroes cast a long shadow.

I made a mental note to look for the names of other soccer players who might know if anyone else made a complaint about Stanley. And the neighbors at Low Farm—Shawna and her son, Rhys, who had his finger cut off in the chicken shed—they might know. If I could track them down. I poured boiling water into a French press and delivered it to Elks. I didn't need coffee—my heart was already racing.

As I was settling in at the desk nearest the archive, my chair scrunched a piece of paper, and I reached down to pick up a newspaper clipping. A black-and-white photograph of a sports team holding a trophy. The headline caught my eye: "Hurtwood Boys Win Rugby Cup." Dylan's old school. I checked the date; the clipping was from 1998, when Dylan would have been a student. I scanned the faces but didn't spot him. He wasn't listed below either, but I did recognize a name that had been highlighted in yellow marker: Giles Hotchen. The third side of Dylan and Meredith's love triangle.

I found Dylan's rival in the back row. Giles Hotchen was good-looking, though his hair was slicked back Gordon Gekko–style, giving him a smug air. No doubt he cultivated the image; Dylan said he "flashed the cash" and the girls fell for it. Meredith Fiddler fell for it. Would I have fallen for the attentions of the richest boy in town? Once upon a time, I would have said no. But after Victor Carlson, who was I kidding?

"Elks?" I waved the clipping in the air for him to see. "I found this on the floor by the archive. Do you want me to file it?"

He slid off his headphones. "Ellie must have dropped it. The police sergeant. You can file it under Hotchen, Giles." Elks let his headphones settle around his neck. "You know . . ."

I waited a moment and then said, "You might have to tell me what I know . . ."

"Have you heard of Giles Hotchen?"

I told him Dylan mentioned him once. Old friends. Old enemies. Frenemies.

"If you're looking for your next story, he could be it. I've been trying to do a profile piece on Hotchen for years, but he doesn't give interviews. Guy's reclusive. But he might be willing to speak to the wife of an old friend."

"Even if they were frenemies?"

"Maybe. He might trust you. Or he might be curious to meet the woman who captured the heart of his love rival." Elks's eyes contained a distinct twinkle at all this talk of romantic intrigue. "If you could get him on camera, there would be plenty of local interest. I'd definitely pay you for a profile of Giles Hotchen." Elks went off on a tangent about wanting information on some local building that Hotchen owned, which I could potentially slip into the interview if it was going well . . . and he only stopped when he noticed the time and cursed himself. He passed me Hotchen's email address from his contacts and got back to his deadline. I tapped out a message to Giles Hotchen on my phone, introducing myself and mentioning my recent arrival in Hurtwood, and signing off with my married name for good measure. Nothing ventured, nothing gained. I hit send, then turned to the archive.

Elks kept background files on long-running issues, prominent people, and historical stories. A local journalist has to be creative to fill the pages; anniversaries and updates make easy pickings. It didn't take me long to find a manila folder marked *Bale, Kenny*. I took it to the desk, tilting down the head of a desk lamp so I didn't disturb Elks.

Town in Shock after Death of Young Footballer

The first report implied that the death was an accident, a fall. It included a quote from Stanley Kynaston paying tribute to his mentee.

Coroner Records Verdict of Misadventure in Bale Case

I googled "misadventure" to check its legal meaning: an accidental death that implies no suspicious circumstances. *Misadventure* can be used when suicide is possible but not proven, sparing the feelings of the family. But in the next report, something strange emerged. Kenny Bale's family broke that taboo to argue that their son did, in fact, commit suicide.

Family Claim Boy "Took Own Life" after Abuse

The grieving parents of Kenny Bale have described how he kept a secret diary detailing bullying and sexual abuse by an unknown perpetrator. The journal came to light when Kenny, 12, died after falling from rocks near Hurtwood. Bale was a promising footballer, represented by the talent scout Stanley Kynaston.

Mr. and Mrs. Bale told the Midland Post *of their distress at a coroner's verdict of misadventure. The couple claim that the police have not taken seriously their allegations of abuse. "Kenny's last words in his diary show his anguish," Stuart Bale said, "despite having everything to live for, months of abuse and bullying left him feeling he had no way out."*

Hurtwood Police said everything was being done to support the family and investigate their concerns.

The last person to see Kenny Bale alive was Stanley Kynaston.

My pen hovered over my pad. I scribbled: *Libel?* The laws in the UK, I knew, were stricter than in the US. The *Midland Post* couldn't print wild allegations. But the careful way this report was structured—a claim that someone abused Kenny, followed by a backgrounder on Stanley—linked the two in the reader's mind. A picture emerged, like a magic eye puzzle. Unsaid but seen.

Kynaston told the Midland Post *that the boy set off for home by bicycle at around 4:00 p.m. on the day he went missing. They had spent the afternoon filming and reviewing football drills ahead of a trial for Manchester United's youth team. Kenny's body was found on rocks at the foot of an escarpment known as the Long Drop in the early hours of the following morning, after his parents raised the alarm.*

Stanley Kynaston is a familiar figure in Hurtwood. After a distinguished start to his playing career came to an abrupt end due to injury, he worked as a youth team coach and a talent scout for major clubs. He recently retired due to ill health.

Kenny Bale was a pupil at the prestigious Hurtwood Boys' School. The headmaster, Dr. Adam Alderman, last week defended the school's pastoral care after an anonymous letter to the Midland Post *alleged a culture of self-harm among students who struggle to achieve the grades necessary to be entered for exams.*

I made a note on my pad: *self-harm, exam stress, fellow pupils.* Who could tell me if Bale had been struggling to cope? Journalistic blood pumped through my veins. A sense of direction. There were many reasons why Kenny might have died, reasons that would exonerate my family from blame. In fact, the allegation against Stanley seemed to have originated from Kenny Bale's parents. What if they were trying to deflect attention from themselves? I noted that on my pad too. They claimed the police had ignored them. But I remembered Sergeant Trevelyan's words: "I think we can all agree that, in common parlance, child abuse is evil." She didn't sound like a police officer who was indifferent.

On my pad, I wrote: *Parents, what's their story?* If they had reason to feel guilty, they might have pointed the finger at someone who was dying, someone who wouldn't be around to endure the consequences. Someone like Stanley Kynaston.

Leaving Gwendoline and Dylan to endure it instead.

I cruised through the file, noting dates and the names of people Elks had interviewed over the years, although most of their claims and counterclaims never made it to print. I opened a folded newspaper clipping and found a photograph of Gwendoline that stopped me in my tracks. I wouldn't have recognized her if the picture hadn't been taken in front of Hurtwood House. Her dark hair was in a no-nonsense bob, and she was carrying an extra twenty pounds at least. Her imposing figure was dressed in a wide-legged pantsuit that made the most of her height. She held one end of a giant fundraising check while Dylan—no, I corrected myself: it must be Stanley—held the other end. A caption said the photo had been taken in 1997. It had been reprinted in an article dated after Kenny Bale died.

Scandal Blamed for Demise of Kick Start "Life-Coaching" Service

The director of Hurtwood's Kick Start initiative has been forced to stand down. Gwendoline Kynaston is the widow of the football scout Stanley Kynaston, who was questioned by police following the death of a player in his care.

Kenny Bale fell from a cliff near Hurtwood House, the home of Gwendoline and Stanley Kynaston. Although the coroner recorded a verdict of misadventure, the parents of Kenny Bale allege that he left a diary detailing months of abuse and bullying. Mr. Kynaston denied any wrongdoing, and no charges were brought against him. He died three weeks later following a long-standing illness.

Sources close to Kick Start told the Midland Post *that Gwendoline Kynaston stepped down "to prevent vicious rumors from blighting a service that has helped hundreds of young people." One volunteer said that "Gwendoline is Kick Start," and the service will now have to close.*

The Kick Start scheme, spearheaded by Mrs. Kynaston since 1990, offered youths aged 11–18 vocational training to enhance life skills and employability. A former school nurse and counselor, Mrs. Kynaston . . .

In the gloom, the shape of Elks rose and carried his mug to the kitchen. He was done. I'd have to leave too. I took a last look at the photo of Gwendoline Kynaston. Same name and yet not the same person. Although her hair retained its deep color, it had been left to grow as long and unkempt as the garden around her home. But the changes to her appearance and the dramatic weight loss—that self-neglect was the least of it. The woman who held a giant fundraising check alongside her popular husband had posture and pride. She had purpose. The Gwendoline I knew was a living ghost.

My phone buzzed. Incoming email from Giles Hotchen. I called out to Elks that the recluse had agreed to an interview. He responded with a "Ha!" of triumph. "Told you his curiosity would get the better of him. Often, it's the ones who are most afraid of the media who have the loosest lips once you get them going."

Hotchen said I'd have to visit him the next day as he was flying to his second home in Thailand for the winter. "Sounds like a tough life," grunted Elks. We spent a half hour discussing the line of questioning, and I drove back to the Grim's Holm wondering if Giles Hotchen might put flesh on the bones of a past that refused to be buried.

CHAPTER 26

By the time Ellie got off a Skype call with her sister, the bath was full. She ran the hot tap a little more before getting in. As she sat with her knees steaming, she studied Cassie's postcards from Perth, pinned to a board propped beside the bath. *Wish you were here!* one said. *Don't we all,* Ellie thought. The sea, the sand, the sun. Some comical creature that lives on an island. A quokka. Ellie pitied the quokka. Doomed to live and die in glorious isolation. It should have made the leap to the larger island when it had the chance. Ellie poured Epsom salts into the water. Then she let herself drift, imagining she was in the ocean. Cassie would correct her: The ocean is cold. It doesn't taste like Epsom salts. It's full of predators. *Whatever.* The chance of visiting her sister in Perth was no more than a dream, so it might as well be a lovely dream. Right now, Ellie would take jellyfish over the pinheads. At least jellyfish back up their threats with genuine venom.

Her eyes fixed on the ocean. More shades of blue than colors in the rainbow. But not a soul in the sky, the sea, the sand. *Why don't postcards have people in them? Is it because other people inevitably ruin paradise?* But Ellie ached for that deserted beach—a physical yearning—as another person might long for sex or booze. She imagined walking miles of hot sand and then swimming back across the bay. She hauled herself up to a sitting position, *as graceful as a jellyfish,* and dolloped thickening shampoo on her hair.

Why do I crave time alone and simultaneously feel lonely?

Her phone rang, muffled inside a pile of clothes. She hauled herself away from paradise and returned a missed call from Broken Arrow.

DI Bryan Harrow greeted her at Hurtwood Police Station with a mug of coffee and a pile of pictures. In return, she handed him the Kenny Bale file, which she'd picked up from storage on her way to the incident room.

"Were you turning in for the night?" Harrow asked. "Only you smell—" He stopped, rubbing his eyes. He looked knackered.

"What?"

"Fragrant." Now he looked knackered and also embarrassed. "Coconut or something. Sorry, it's just I feel like I've been awake and wearing this suit for about a month. Anyway, thanks for coming in tonight. I was heading home myself when I got a call from the techies."

Ellie sipped the coffee and winced at the sweetness. But she downed it, finding she was getting more used to it with each mouthful.

"This disc—" he said, but his phone rang. He answered and responded in a series of hums while flicking his wedding ring with his thumbnail. *What would one of those television police psychologists make of his tic?* Ellie thought. *Does it mean his wife is on the line? Is he riven with guilt for telling another woman she's fragrant? Did he only notice the fragrance because he misses his wife?* Ellie had never worked with DI Harrow. His reputation as Broken Arrow preceded him, but he seemed all right. Working late. Dedicated. Exhausted, like the rest of them. His reputation could be driven by envy. Maybe someone enjoyed the nickname so much they forced it to stick? Harrow ended his call and spread the printouts into a neat rectangle.

"Photos," he said, "from the floppy disc you found with Indiana Bones. The images are corrupted, but I'm grateful that forensics got anything at all off the disc." The images were covered by bands of color, like a ham-fisted attempt at modern art. Ellie picked up one picture where the top showed trees and a distant hill.

"That's the Wrekin." She turned it to show Harrow.

"It's in a few of the shots."

"More specifically," Ellie said, "it's the Wrekin seen from north of Hurtwood. Near the Grim's Holm."

"You sure?"

"We can take a drive out there tomorrow, but yes, I'm sure."

Ellie saw that he'd laid the landscape shots together. By jigsawing them, he'd turned several corrupted pictures into one composite photo. Another visible section showed a boy's legs and feet. Football boots and bright-orange socks up to the knees, bulky with shin pads. Another showed the boy again, just his legs and midsection caught in the angular position of a full sprint. Trees in the distance, the peak of the Wrekin. Stripes of corruption obliterated his upper half, but nothing could disguise his energy, his determination, his taut muscles.

Ellie opened the Kenny Bale file and picked out two photos, which she laid on the table for Harrow to see. He tapped the orange socks. "Same football kit."

"Same boy." Ellie pointed to a picture from the *Midland Post* in an article about promising local footballers. Kenny Bale sprinted across a pitch, limbs locked into the same powerful angles.

"You won't like this part," Harrow said. He laid three more printed sheets on the table. "But if you can identify him . . ."

Ellie looked at the pornography. The eagerness she'd felt to help with the investigation drained away and took her words with it. In two shots, the boy was posed full frontal, but Ellie only saw his eyes averted from the camera. How many times had she looked at photos of this face? Bright-eyed in school pictures and joyful on the football pitch. And now this . . . The third picture was graphic—painful even to glance at, let alone imagine what had been in that boy's mind while it was being taken. Ellie turned it facedown on the table.

"Sorry, I—" she said.

"It's okay. No one wants to see that." DI Harrow gathered the pictures, leaving only the graphic one.

"It's him, though," Ellie said. "It's Kenny Bale. Being abused. Like he said."

"We know it's Kenny Bale." Harrow folded the remaining picture so that only half was showing. Ellie glanced down and saw that he'd hidden the part showing the boy. The detective circled another section of the image with his fingertip—the background of the room. "But if you can identify *him* . . ."

Ellie bent closer. In the background stood a long, free-standing mirror. And a figure reflected in the mirror. A man, half-obscured by a camera held to his eye.

"Looks like Stanley Kynaston," said DI Harrow.

"It looks a lot like Stan," said Ellie. "But it's not him."

CHAPTER 27

On the screen, I zoomed in tight on one of Dylan's photographs. A woman's eyes, which held fathoms of experience. I recalled him taking the shot at the displaced persons camp outside Mogadishu. She was a peacekeeper. I'd been hyperaware of Dylan's movements that day, reading his body language like the cover of a book that I—maybe—wanted to read. You can tell a lot about a person by watching them interact with others. Victor Carlson looked over people's shoulders when they spoke; I should have noticed that sooner.

I checked my watch. *Where is he?* Unless Dylan got home soon, I'd be late for my interview with Giles Hotchen.

Dylan was reflected in one of the peacekeeper's eyes. The hard sunlight caught a glint where she'd licked her lips. Nervous, perhaps. I loved the way Dylan had seen beyond her uniform and her age and even her defiant gaze, and brought humanity to the foreground.

I logged in to my cloud. Folders appeared with the many reports I'd filed from Africa. And before that, Chicago and the Upper Midwest. The mouse crept down to a folder titled *Cabin.*

I right-clicked and hovered over delete. It was time. *Do it.* Instead, I double left-clicked, and there was our cabin in the woods. Vic's cabin, but I always thought of it as ours. *Does he, after all this time, think of it as ours? Or does he take someone else there and think of it as theirs?* I used to wait for hours for him to arrive, and I'd gotten artsy with my photos. Now, the images looked as naive as I had been: ripples on the lake, depth of field, raindrops on cobwebs. And then, suddenly, Victor Carlson flat on the bed as though being held down by the strap of sunlight across his torso. If I wanted to blackmail him, this is the shot I could use.

That winter juddered in my mind as though my memory was a video taken while running through the trees. Fleeting sensations of silk skin, snug sheets, rich wine, rare steak, spruce logs, pure stars, bold plans, tail lights. His wife. Their child. My bad.

No one knew about our relationship or the ransom money. Only myself and Vic. And a kidnapper in Mogadishu whom Vic paid off without hesitation. Victor Carlson did a bad thing to me, but he wasn't all bad. After the ransom was paid and I returned to Nairobi, I emailed an offer to reimburse him—in installments—and he shrugged me off as though I'd tried to go Dutch for dinner. He lived in a world where a person could spend $10,000 without his wife noticing. It would only draw more attention to the transaction, he said; he'd passed off the payment as a repair for their boat. A damn boat! That eased my conscience a little. I was working around the clock to survive as a freelancer, while he was entertaining the chairman of the network on his boat. I replied to express my gratitude for the ransom and got on with my life.

I selected the *Cabin* folder and hit delete. Dylan didn't need to know about that winter with Vic. It'd happened before we met. It was ancient history. A buried hoard. Leave that winter to die in the forest.

Downstairs, I heard the front door slam—finally!—and Dylan's footsteps made a smooth patter into the kitchen. I snatched up my camera bag and went downstairs. Dylan eyed gear as he put the kettle onto the Aga.

"You're still going?"

"I have an interview to do." Earlier that morning, I'd told Dylan about the Giles Hotchen profile, and he'd gotten upset. He'd yelled at me. He'd yelled at Aled when he walked in on our argument. The fight was surreal in its intensity—like arguing with a complete stranger—because Dylan had never gone off the deep end before. After he *forbade* me from doing the interview, I refused to discuss the matter, and he stomped off across the Grim's Holm.

Now, an hour later, he tried a different tack. "Let me come with you."

"That's crazy—"

"I won't come inside. Hotchen doesn't have to know I'm there. But I'll be outside in the car in case you need help."

"Dylan, I'm a grown woman, a professional, and he's a local businessman, also a professional." In truth, my stomach felt hollow with dread.

"There are things about Giles Hotchen that nobody knows. Except me and Meredith. You can't be alone with him. Years ago, Meredith alleged—"

"You said yourself that Meredith Fiddler played you off each other. It was a long time ago. Robert Elks doesn't have any concerns." I'd have thought Dylan, more than anyone else, could ignore tired old gossip.

"Hotchen never does interviews," said Dylan. "He's only doing this one because it's you. And he's only meeting you to get at me—"

"Oh my God! You sound paranoid. Paranoid or self-obsessed. If I don't go now, I'll be late. Just stop"—I pushed past him in the narrow hallway—"stop standing in my way."

"I'm coming with—"

"You're staying here with Aled. Two hours, that's all I'm asking. In Africa, I never had to beg to go to work. I never had to beg you to pull your weight. But ever since we got back to this country, you've been acting like a Victorian gentleman. If I'd known you'd turn into Heathcliff, I would never have come." I slammed the door to block out his response.

A half hour later, I pulled up to Giles Hotchen's gate. High and solid. If Dylan had come with me, he wouldn't have had a clue what was going on inside. A marble plaque said "Regency House," which sounded more delicate than the forbidding gateway would suggest. Maybe it was Dylan's words ringing in my ears, but it struck me as something of a fortress.

Elks wouldn't have sent me if it was unsafe. Whatever allegations Meredith made twenty years ago hadn't reached Elks's ears, and it seemed like most rumors reached Elks eventually.

I moved to press the intercom button, but the gate swung open first. Either Hotchen had seen me coming, or Mistress Payne had figured out electronics.

At the end of a winding drive, I parked in front of a pretty house that looked different from anything else I'd seen in Shropshire. Regency House could have easily been the home of a Southern belle, with its fresh, white frontage covered by an intricate veranda. There was one distinctly English element: the wrought iron dripped with rose bushes. On one side of the house, a long stable block had been converted to a garage with four sets of double doors that stood open to reveal a car collection. Despite this testosterone overload, the house was distinctly feminine—not the obvious choice for a bachelor.

I gathered my equipment and walked toward a man waiting under the veranda. Giles Hotchen, recognizable from his rugby photo. Inevitably the muscle had softened, the hair had retreated, and—given his wealth—the wardrobe appeared to consist entirely of Hugo Boss. He also wore frameless glasses, the lenses reflecting the white paintwork so that I couldn't tell where his eyes were looking.

"Mrs. Kynaston." He reached for my hand.

"Mr. Hotchen." We shook.

"Call me Giles." He released my hand.

I wondered if he would ask after Dylan. I wondered if I should mention him to get it out of the way. But Giles held out an arm to direct me inside. I went ahead of him into a gracious hallway.

The house was light and bright. Fresh flower displays. Fragrance in the air, but not floral, something musky. Subtler than patchouli, but similar . . . With Giles close behind me, I continued through to the kitchen. A jug of water with lemon quarters sweated on the island. A candle flickered. Amber and ginger. That explained the scent.

Again, it didn't feel like the home of a single man, not even a single man who likely had a housekeeper. He reminded me of someone, but I couldn't place it. I must have appraised the room a moment too long because Hotchen said, "I rarely have a guest. I made an effort."

"You have a beautiful home. Do you live alone?"

"Yes."

The ultramodern island sat eight. A dining table made from a single slab of grainy wood had twelve chairs. There was a double wine fridge loaded with bottles. It was a kitchen made for entertaining, and yet Giles rarely had a guest. I wondered what he did all day behind his high walls. Another flash of recognition, but the reference flitted before I could grasp it.

As we made small talk, Giles's speech impediment became noticeable. A slur on certain words. But it wasn't severe enough to warrant—as some gossips claimed—his reclusive lifestyle. Nevertheless, he kept his responses short—not abrupt or evasive, but efficient, as though his voice was kept on a tight leash.

I gestured to the window. "Beautiful view."

"It is." But he was looking directly at me. "Imagine waking up to that every morning."

Our small talk dried up, and we stood in silence. He volunteered no questions about me or Dylan or even the forthcoming interview. He regarded me, waiting politely, his glasses opaque again from the light pouring through the French windows. I let the silence stretch, just to see how he would react, and after a few moments he picked up a remote control from the island and pressed a button. In the adjacent room, blinds whirred down to cover the windows. While he poured water into two glasses, I slid my cell from my camera bag into the pocket of my black jeans.

"I understand you don't give many interviews, Giles."

"Not keen."

"I'm glad you agreed to speak to me. As a property developer, you've shaped the town of Hurtwood, and I'm sure people are interested to know what makes you tick." The blinds stopped whirring in the next room. "I'll set up my camera. I don't want to take up too much of your time."

"It's quieter in there." He nodded toward the darkened room. His kitchen appliances were so high-end that there wasn't a hum or a tick. Outside, the trees quaked, but we heard nothing of the wind. *Soundproof glass,* I thought. The house was utterly silent. It couldn't be quieter unless Giles somehow stopped the air from moving.

Then I figured out who he reminded me of. It was so strange—and yet so strong in my mind—that I shook the thought away. The Beast. As in Beauty and the Beast. Waiting in his palace for a princess.

"Here, then, if you prefer the kitchen to my office." He slid onto a stool at the island.

"A homely space helps the viewer feel as though they're seeing the real you." I unpacked my camera. In truth, I wanted to pick up my bag and get out of there. I calmed myself by straightening my cables. Hotchen had done nothing out of line. I was spooked, that was all— Dylan's fault for creating a scene before I came here. Yes, Hotchen had an unnerving habit of leaving a beat every time he spoke. The delay was probably an aftereffect of his injury. I should be empathetic. But I couldn't shift the sense that he kept considering what course of action to take next.

Finally, my gear was ready and I laid my notepad on the island. Hotchen took it and spun it around to read the questions.

"Oh no, I'm sorry." I caught the notepad and drew it back. "I never show my questions in advance. But rest assured, I'll stick to the topics mentioned in the email. No surprises."

"I'll sound better if I'm prepared."

"People just want to hear about you, so you're already perfectly prepared. It'll make the interview more natural, more spontaneous, if we have a conversation."

"Spontaneous?" He slurred the word.

I got the camera rolling. He answered everything I asked him, personally and professionally. I even managed to squeeze in Elks's question about the buildings on Cheapside, and Hotchen said he'd never been able to develop them because of complaints about the lack of parking. We touched on his accident and his plans for development in Hurtwood. We covered a lot of ground, but his curt answers made for a short interview, and I soon packed away my camera. He mentioned Indiana Bones, and I asked about Kenny Bale, but Hotchen only shrugged. "He was younger, a couple of years below me at school. I didn't know him personally."

I stood, ready to leave. "Well—"

"I refurbished the swimming pool. I've been dying to show it off." He extended an arm in his courtly way—"Lead on, Macduff," he said— and we passed through a library to a modern extension. The glass-roofed atrium was heated to tropical humidity. Sweat prickled on my skin the moment the door closed behind us, cutting off the cool air. The surface of the pool flickered with sparks like a shattered lightning bolt. At the far end, water dribbled down a child's slide.

"So." Hotchen turned to me. "Is there anything else?"

"No, I have everything I need." I exited the pool room and made for the front door, sensing Giles an arm's length behind me all the way. "It's a beautiful pool," I gabbled. "My son would love it." As soon as the words left my mouth, I wanted to scoop them up as though hiding a child in my skirts. Relieved to reach the frigid outside air, I turned to say goodbye.

"How is Dylan?" Hotchen asked. At last.

"Glad to be home."

Hotchen sniffed. Waited. Considered his next move. "You could bring your son for a swim." His eyes sought mine, although his glasses were still misted slightly from the humidity of the pool room. I felt sad for him then. The Beast.

He walked me to my car, opened the door, and held it, so that I brushed his arm as I got behind the wheel. He slammed the door, and I opened the window a little to thank him.

"How is Gwendoline?" he asked.

"Well."

"Really?"

"As well as can be expected."

He nodded at that, more satisfied by the answer. "I heard she has dementia. Shame, she can't be that old."

"She's in her sixties," I confirmed.

Hotchen smiled, and I realized it was the first time he'd done so. "Meredith's back too. I saw her with Dylan. We can put the band back together!"

My insides tensed. I realized then why I recognized Hotchen. Nothing to do with this Beast nonsense—I'd seen him in real life. Hotchen was the driver of the Range Rover on Hurtwood high street. The one who nearly ran me down. Who snarled at the sight of Dylan and Meredith. That hatred must have been wrestled under control in the same way as his slurred speech.

"I met Meredith last week," I said. Weak as I was, I couldn't resist digging. "She seems lovely."

Hotchen laid a forearm on the roof of my car to lean closer to my window. "She's a backstabber. You'd do well to avoid her. You know her marriage failed?"

"I heard she was divorced." I started my engine.

"Strange how they both gravitated back to Hurtwood. Like nails drawn to a magnet. First she came home. Next thing, Dylan's back."

"They're lucky to have family roots."

Hotchen smiled, echoes of the snarl on his face. "Don't worry, you've got no competition from Meredith. She's not in the same league."

"I wasn't worried." I returned the smile, showing my teeth.

"No, it's Shawna you need to worry about." Hotchen pushed himself upright and slapped the roof, a period at the end of a sentence. "Shawna Dourish. The one who got away."

CHAPTER 28

Giles Hotchen's high gate slid to a close behind me. I let the car idle, gathering myself. *Shawna Dourish. The one who got away.* I had to stop that guy's voice from getting inside my head. Despite his cultivated manner, I'd seen his real face on Hurtwood's high street—full of hatred. A tap on the driver's window made me duck for cover.

"Sorry!" Dylan and Aled were peering at me from the road, holding plastic pots filled with blackberries. Aled smiled with black teeth. My insides unclenched at the sight of them. I hit the button to unlock the doors, and they climbed into the car.

"Didn't mean to startle you," Dylan said. "Gwen-ma dropped us off to go foraging for fruit."

I put the car into gear and drove toward home. My throat choked to think of my boys standing guard for me.

"Thanks for coming," I said.

"You okay?" Dylan asked in a low voice.

"Fine. I got the interview and got out." A car hurtled past with mere inches between our vehicles. I flinched at the near miss.

Back at the cottage, Aled ran up to his room. Dylan put the kettle on. I placed my camera on the kitchen table. I wasn't looking forward to editing. I suspected the interview wasn't as revealing as it needed to be, plus I didn't want to spend any more time than I had to in Hotchen's company.

"What's his house like?" Dylan asked while splashing boiling water into the teapot.

"Lovely."

Dylan put down the teapot, frowning. "Lovely or lonely, did you say?"

"Both."

He nodded, unsurprised, and made the tea.

"Hotchen mentioned Shawna Dourish," I said. Dylan dunked a cookie into his mug. "Is that Gwendoline's friend? Whose son lost his finger?"

Dylan nodded, his mouth full. He licked his lips and swallowed. "Rhys hurt his finger when he was young. I'll never forget the screaming."

"What was Shawna like?"

"A survivor, but she never made it easy for herself. In fact, this chicken business tells you everything you need to know about Shawna—she was completely idealistic, no common sense. Spent more time in our kitchen than doing any work. Looking back, I suppose she was only in her twenties, but it frightened me to see an adult so out of their depth. My mum didn't show her much sympathy, of course."

"Sympathy for what?"

"Her drama. There was always something requiring hot, sweet tea. A fox got in the barn. The flock got cholera. Rhys got hurt."

"How did that happen?"

"So . . . her slaughterhouse was at the back of the barn. She must have rented it, or my parents let her use it for free, I don't know. I wasn't allowed in, but Rhys used to play in the hay while she cut the heads off chickens. Have to say, I wouldn't let Aled watch that. Anyhow, on the day Rhys got hurt, I was in my room. It was hot, I had my window open, and I heard an almighty scream. Sounded like an animal dying. And Shawna came running across the yard. She was the one screaming, not Rhys. He was bundled against her chest. I just remember her dress all rucked up so I could see her legs. And my mum started shouting, and the door slammed, and then it all went quiet."

"Horrible."

"It was. So I went downstairs, of course. My mum was calling an ambulance. Shawna sat on the floor by the Aga. Her skirt pooled around her. Apron covered in blood."

"Where was Rhys?"

"With my mum. He wasn't even crying. Shawna was making the noise; I thought she was the one who got hurt. And on the table was a tea towel with a bit of meat on it."

"His finger?"

"Mum shouted at Shawna to pick it up. She didn't want me to see it, I suppose, but she was stuck on the phone. Shawna was spaced, didn't move. Mum swore at her—I'd never heard that before—and *screamed* at me to get out. Honestly, that scared me more than the finger. So I ran off and hid upstairs."

"In the priest's hole?"

Dylan nodded.

Suddenly, my jealousy of Shawna seemed crass. Single mom. Tough life. Zero coping skills. Her prettiness didn't seem to have done her much good. "I'm not surprised she moved away after that."

"Oh, they lived here for years after that. There were many more dramas. They're written in tea stains on my mother's pine table—if you could read the ring marks, you'd find a tragicomedy worthy of Shakespeare."

He didn't say any more. I tried to resist, but couldn't help myself. "Did you see a lot of her growing up?"

"It was hard to miss Shawna Dourish." Dylan went to wash his mug. "But she got away in the end—sold Low Farm to Tony Thorn, went to live by the coast. Never saw her after that. Mum keeps in touch."

"Did you—" I stopped myself. I was letting Hotchen's voice get in my head.

"Did I what?"

Might as well get it out in the open. "Hotchen implied that you and Shawna—"

"Me and Shawna what?"

"He wasn't specific."

"Slander is often short on details. What exactly did he say?" He sounded weary.

I was trying to recall the exact words when I heard footsteps. Heavy footsteps outside the front door. Dylan and I looked at each other. We didn't get visitors. More footsteps and a knock.

Dylan went to answer it, and Aled came racing down the stairs. He clamped himself around his father's leg, driven by an instinct that was far more attuned than ours. Dylan opened the door to a man with a badge. Behind him, Sergeant Ellie Trevelyan. We made eye contact over the men's shoulders.

"Dylan Kynaston?" the man asked. "I'm DI Bryan Harrow, and this is Sergeant Trevelyan, who you met during the archaeological dig. We have questions relating to the human remains that were found."

"Come in, I—"

"If you could accompany us, it would be better to go through these questions at the station."

Dylan turned to me, his hands on Aled. "Rosie . . ."

"I got him." I slotted my hands under Aled's frozen shoulders and pulled him off his father's leg. "Is my husband under arrest?"

"He's helping with our inquiries."

Dylan plucked his coat from the hook and tussled his arms into the sleeves. The police officer was already halfway to his vehicle, keys in hand, eager. I tried to make eye contact with Ellie, but she kept her gaze directed toward Low Farm and gave me only a fleeting glance as she stepped in line behind my husband. I tried to analyze her look. I remembered her expression from the film we'd made, the set of her mouth while she picked up the remains of the teenagers' petty drugs. No surprise, no anger, no irritation. Instead, pity and fatigue. Sergeant Trevelyan felt sorry for me. And that's when I realized they suspected Dylan of doing something very bad indeed.

CHAPTER 29

A led wouldn't settle, so we looked at photos on my laptop. He liked seeing pictures from Africa. When Dylan's assignment shots popped up, Aled wanted more. He took control of the mouse and flicked through. He wanted to see the displaced persons camp, and I told him no, it's not for kids. He brushed my hand from the mouse, and I thought, *It's reality, not a horror movie.* If the people living in the camps can't switch it off, should we? Aled put out a hand toward the screen as though to touch a child's face . . . And laughed. The child held a broken beaker that spurted water from its sides. Aled laughed, and I held him while he laughed.

I clicked off the laptop and carried him to his room. *He's too young to understand; he's not really laughing. It's not messed up like it would be if an adult laughed.* The full moon outside turned everything to shadow. Even Aled. Laughing at refugees. What was wrong with him? What was wrong with me? Maybe it wasn't the moonlight that made me lose perspective. Maybe going to those places had messed me up so much I thought it was okay for a child to look at those pictures.

"Sleep now," I said. "It's late."

"Mommy's angry."

"I'm not angry, I—let's go to sleep." I got into his bed and coiled my leg around him like a boa. Long after I thought he was asleep, he laughed and rolled out of my grip. Meredith claimed he'd scared the other children at the forest school. I recalled my fear that he had a darkness in him, a taste for the macabre, a bad gene inherited from Stanley. Did it work like that? Did badness run in the family?

What did Meredith know? Even if she did share roots with my husband—even if there was some kind of magnetic attraction, as Hotchen suggested—I knew Dylan better. *And I know my son.* If someone asked me, "How can you ever really know another person?" I'd say it's not a matter of knowing. It's faith. You feel it, like a ghost in the room. I unwrapped myself from Aled and crept to my laptop.

In Dylan's photograph, the peacekeeper's eyes fixed on me. She felt it too; she'd trusted him. But what did she think now, years after he'd gone? Might she think that he took what he wanted and walked away, leaving her with nothing? Events look different in hindsight.

I checked my phone, but there was no message from Dylan, even though he'd been gone for hours. I checked the police Twitter feed. A press conference was scheduled for the next day. Maybe they had found something on the floppy disc? Surely it couldn't have anything to do with Dylan? I logged into the *Midland Post* intranet: Robert Elks was due to attend. I decided to join him at the news conference in the morning, assuming Dylan was back from the police station by then.

The hours stretched as thin as a spider's thread twisting in a beam of moonlight. Waking in the black of night, I heard a fox bark and went to the window. Dylan stood outside by the fence where we'd stroked the pony on our first day. I knew it was him from the shape of his back, even though he was no more than another layer of darkness, a hill against more hills.

I pulled on my boots and went to bring him inside. Instead he took my hand, and we walked to the summit of the holm, past the craggy hulk of the great house. He told me what happened at the police station. A photo they showed him. They'd managed to retrieve some images from the floppy disc found with Indiana Bones. One picture showed Dylan himself, his reflection caught in a mirror. The heat of the officers' eyes. An instant sweat that made him aware of his stink.

"It's me in the photo—I'm definitely reflected in that mirror—but I was never in that room. I don't even recognize the room. I feel like I'm going mad." He led me toward the Long Drop. "You know me, right?" His grip tightened. "I wouldn't hurt a child. The most important thing right now is that you believe me. You won't take Aled and leave?"

"Photos can be faked. I know you, Dylan—it must be fake." I'd be lying if I pretended a voice in my head hadn't asked, *But do you know what he was like twenty years ago?* I'd been busy worrying about Meredith, and yet Hotchen said Shawna Dourish was "the one who got away." *What does that say about my insight into my husband's past?* We stepped out from the cover of the trees and crept forward into blackness. Different depths of darkness like the sea. "Why are we here?" I asked. "Aled's alone in the cottage . . ."

"I've been thinking that home is a time rather than a place. And a happy home is like a great pub; the winning formula is a kind of alchemy." I smiled at that. But he lost me as he went on. Leather on willow. Jumpers for goalposts. He seemed to sense that he was rambling and using terms that were unfamiliar to me and stopped. "I needed to come out here," he said, "because I thought I might feel him."

"Your dad?"

"Kenny Bale. Is that stupid?"

It wasn't stupid. This is where the boy died. Something drove Kenny Bale here, and our lives depended on finding out what. Dylan wrapped his arms around me from behind. With my hands trapped beneath his, my hair blew over my face. In the distance, clouds cocooned an electrical storm.

Dylan whispered against my ear: "The wind shows how close we are to the edge."

"Where have I heard that?"

"Joan Didion," Dylan said. "You gave me her book on our first anniversary."

The wind found its way into the small spaces between us, and I shivered.

"Living here makes me feel small," I said. "The wind is too strong; it could fling me over the Long Drop. Maybe that's what happened to Kenny Bale—maybe it was an accident."

"I'd like to believe that. It's better than the alternative." Dylan's voice suggested that he didn't, however, believe it. The wind plucked my clothes, but my feet remained on the ground. "I don't feel small here," said Dylan. "I feel significant. A link in a chain. The Grim's Holm endures; nothing changes."

"But it does change, it's just that we don't see it. We're too small to get the perspective."

Dylan hummed. "But we're not just one life span. Think how long that house has stood. Other houses before it. Hundreds of generations, thousands of years."

"There was a landslide last winter. There will be another and another until the house falls into the river, and another and another until the holm is gone."

"Inevitably."

In the trees, a bird gave a pook-pook of alarm. The first call of the day.

"I'm sorry I got you into this," he said.

"You're my hero, you know that."

There was a long silence. "Do I?"

I turned in his arms. A hint of dawn let me see his eyes.

"I didn't save your life in Mogadishu," he said.

I tried to protest, but his look silenced me.

"You've told the story so many times, it's become our mythology." He held up his hands when I tried to speak. "I'm happy to go along with your truth if that's what you prefer."

"Surely the truth is the truth."

"The truth depends on who's telling the story. We can lie to whoever you like, but I can't lie to myself; I don't see the point anymore."

The pook-pook alarm again. A blackbird emerged to watch us from a rock. "What are you talking about, Dylan?"

"After I went back to work in Nairobi, my boss told me they never paid a ransom. But someone paid a ransom, so it must have been one of your contacts. You didn't offer an explanation, and frankly I was happy to put Mogadishu behind us—"

"Why bring it up now?"

"Because you make me out to be some kind of hero, and it's a lie. I'm not a child who needs to be told he's a good boy."

I turned away, eyes streaming tears in the wind. "I left you in that cell to take a beating that nearly killed you. You deserve to feel like a hero."

"I would have got that beating whether you left me or not. If you'd stayed, I would have got a beating *and* I would have heard you getting a beating."

"The man who paid my ransom—"

"I'm not asking for an explanation. I just want to stop the pretense."

"The man who paid my ransom—I'm not proud of it . . ." The blackbird hopped around for a better view. "I did something in the past that I'm truly ashamed of. I didn't want that to be the first thing you knew about me. I wanted you to see the new me, the person who evolved from the woman who made mistakes. The better person."

"I married the best person." Dylan kissed my messy hair. "I also did something in the past that I'm truly ashamed of. It's nothing to do with Kenny Bale or the bones in the river, I swear to you, but I've never told anyone, and I don't intend to now. It's buried—not literally!—but I don't want it dug up."

I wondered if he meant Shawna Dourish. Maybe Hotchen was right, and she was *the one who got away*. I thought about that while dawn turned the clouds the color of Aled's skin.

"Rose?"

"So we're even?"

"We're even."

We went back to the cottage, and Dylan slept, but I was too uptight to rest. I shouldn't have deleted my photos of Vic's cabin. I wanted to see his face. To study it and try to recall if I ever saw deceit in his eyes. His manipulation came down like snow that winter, settling so softly I didn't notice until I was all snowed in. One of his lies was that we had to keep our relationship secret for the sake of his wife. I'd applauded myself on how mature we were being, considerate. I didn't tell a soul. And that meant there was no one to tell me I was a fool.

Would anyone tell me I was a fool to believe Dylan? Would the police?

Wise up, I told myself. *You need more information.*

I washed and dressed, then raced to the *Midland Post* to find Robert Elks. When I pressed the reluctant door open, light pouring in around my feet, I heard his voice from the gloom.

"Wasn't expecting you today, Rose."

"I thought I'd accompany you to the press conference."

He moved his bulk between the desks with careful haste, as though the floor was covered with thumbtacks or sleeping children. "I don't think—"

"I'm loaded and ready to go." I held my camera bag aloft. "What do you think of a film about the police investigation?"

"Rose—"

"Starring Sergeant Ellie Trevelyan, the reigning queen of rural crime!"

He grasped the end of his tie as though it were a rip cord. *He's going to say no.* I could see it as clearly as if he'd raised his arm to slap me down. And suddenly I was as tearful as I would have been if he had actually hit me. I chewed the inside of my cheeks while Elks explained the most basic tenets of journalism. "You can't report on a story that involves your own family."

"I need to go to that press conference, Robert. The police questioned Dylan last night."

His snort made his bulky shoulders swell. *There you go then.*

"I'll go by myself." I snatched up my camera bag. "I'm freelance."

"They won't let you in without accreditation. Even if you use your maiden name, as soon as you open your mouth, everyone will know who you are. You're not exactly inconspicuous among the *small people* of Hurtwood . . ."

The fight went out of me. He'd watched my live interview. "I didn't mean to say that."

"Go home to your *watery backwater*, and I'll call you after the press conference. I'll update you before the news goes on the wires. It's the best I can do."

"I'll come to the police station and wait outside."

Elks said in a flat voice, "Free country."

We walked the short distance along the high street and down an alley that cut through to the police station. Elks left me on the sidewalk without a backward glance. A journalist's curses clattered through the morning mist, along with the sound of heels on cobbles. I tried to slip into the station along with the crowd, but an officer asked for identification, and when my name wasn't on his list, he told me to step outside to let a BBC journalist come through and then shut the door in my face. I was left with the rubberneckers, mostly teenagers working hard to look disinterested. They settled along a low wall like pigeons, and I perched in the last remaining space.

"Are all these reporters here for Indiana Bones?" said a kid with a wolf tattooed on his knuckles.

"Suppose." The girl wore ballerinas without socks, and her cold feet looked like pâté.

"Hurtwood was on the telly last night. You could see the chip shop."

"Yeah?"

"Mum says it's the football coach who killed him. You know."

"I don't."

"Yeah you do, at Hurtwood House." He grabbed the wolf and cracked his knuckles by ringing its neck. "The Grim's Holm."

"Dad delivers hay there. This one time, Lady Muck wouldn't let him come inside the house to have a wee."

"Rude."

"And after, his mates said he got off lucky because it's haunted." She flicked her shoe on and off her gray heel. "This is boring. I thought there'd be like . . . a media scrum."

They heaved themselves off the wall, and I saw that the rest of the teenagers had vanished. I got my phone and went to Twitter. #Hurtwood was trending.

Press conference: police appeal for help to identify human remains found during TV show #IndianaBones #BBCNews #TheQuest #Hurtwood

The door to the station swung open, and a reporter clacked away over the cobbles with a phone pressed to her ear. I jumped off the wall and swung my camera bag over my shoulder. When Robert Elks emerged, he spotted me and jerked his head toward the *Midland Post* office. I fell into step beside him.

"No arrests. No cause of death. No word on whether it was accidental or foul play. Official statement on the floppy disc is that they're 'examining the contents.' They appealed for help in identifying the bones, so that's the news line. Teenage boy, dead around twenty years, five feet ten, slight build, leg broken during the incident that killed him, missing the tip of one finger."

My bootheel slid on the wet stones. Elks caught my elbow.

"Missing finger?"

"Tip of a finger." He unfolded a piece of paper from his pocket. Handed me a photocopy of an X-ray showing the bones of a hand raised in a high five.

"The pinkie," I said, pocketing the picture. "I'll see you later. Thanks for the update, Robert."

"Rose . . ." Elks stopped beside the crossing, ignoring a car that had stopped to let him go. The driver threw up her hands and drove on. "Do you know something about this case? Something you're not telling me?"

"My husband was questioned by the police last night, and I should be there for him."

"The dutiful wife," said Elks with an up-flick of his chin. "There's a surprising amount of that on the Grim's Holm."

Robert Elks didn't believe me. As I hurried to my car, I figured I'd tell him—and Ellie Trevelyan—as soon as I proved my suspicion about the identity of the boy with a missing pinkie finger. But first, I'd tell my husband.

CHAPTER 30

*C*all Elks. Sergeant Ellie Trevelyan picked up a note someone had left on her desk. Maybe the journalist knew the name of this kid with the missing pinkie finger? The appeal in the media had ignited the switchboard, all the officers in the incident room massaging their temples as they dealt with cranks and busybodies. Callers keen to identify a killer when Harrow hadn't even said there was a killer.

Elks answered on the second ring.

"D'you know who this boy is?" Ellie greeted him.

"'Fraid not. Can you tell me what's on the floppy disc?"

"'Fraid not. I need to ID this child." Ellie's sigh rattled the speaker.

"I didn't call about Indiana Bones," Elks said. "The girl from the Nail Bar—"

"I don't have time for that today."

"This might help you too. Remember Giles Hotchen owns the building where the Nail Bar is located?"

Ellie told him to go on.

"He owns the whole row of shops. Lets them out for peppercorn rent. They back onto Whipping Post Lane. There's also a gate from Hurtwood Boys' School on Whipping Post Lane—"

"That's the direction Hotchen came from when he had his accident."

"It was assumed he was cycling home from school. But his accident was in the early evening, so that doesn't make sense. I did some digging, and those buildings were unused at the time, condemned. At one point, we ran a story about it with the headline 'The Shame of Hurtwood.'"

"What's that got to do with the accident?"

"No idea. But Giles Hotchen bought the shops from his father. He owns them personally, not through his company."

"Hmm."

"And listen to this: Hotchen was seen arguing with Dylan Kynaston in Whipping Post Lane on the day of his accident."

"How do you know that?"

"Because you left your file here."

Ellie's heart skipped. "That's a confidential police file."

"Yeah, I know. I showed you mine, you showed me yours, if that isn't too ghastly an image."

"And?"

"Well, that's it. You were asking about a link between Dylan and Hotchen. And there's one, buried in the statements. A witness saw them arguing. Unfortunately, that witness is dead. But Meredith Fiddler, the girlfriend I mentioned, told police that she and Dylan drove to her family's cottage in Wales right after school that day. Hotchen's accident occurred at rush hour, so Meredith effectively gave Dylan an alibi. That's what I've got for you. In return, can you help me out with something for this Nail Bar story?"

"Elks, you've got nothing for me. A suspect with an alibi!"

"A wobbly alibi. I only mentioned it because you were asking. You should come and collect your file."

"Don't tell anyone I left it, will you?" Ellie noticed DI Harrow add a name to the whiteboard in the incident room. *Progress?* She should get back. "What's going on with the Nail Bar, then? Between you and my father, I spend more time thinking about that place than I do my cases."

"I sent my wife undercover."

Ellie laughed. "Of course you did."

"She got her nails done by the girl. Hardly any English. *Please, thank you, what color you like*—that's about it. The radio was turned up so loud Mrs. Elks could hardly hear the few words the girl did say."

"And?"

"And she slipped her my business card. I'd written *Are you okay?* in Vietnamese. Got it off Google Translate. This morning, the girl turned up in my office."

"And?"

"She's twenty. About the size of my little finger."

"What else did she say?"

"We couldn't communicate. She was as jumpy as a deer. Only stayed a couple of minutes. But I took her visit as an answer to my question: *No, I'm not okay.*"

Ellie agreed. "I'll line up a translator if you can get her to the station."

"I'll see what I can do, but that's not why I called. Is Giles Hotchen clean?"

"As far as I know. Keeps to himself because he has speech problems from the accident. You know what people are like—they take the piss."

"I've heard some of the nicknames they call him. Politically correct, they are not."

"Why do you ask?"

"Something's wrong at this Nail Bar. If their paperwork looks kosher, then I wonder if someone's helping them falsify it."

"Why would Hotchen help a dodgy nail bar? That would be small fry for him."

"It doesn't make sense, I know. But it also doesn't make sense that he lets those shops sit there—a whole row, right in the center of town—without making any money off them. He did an interview with Rose Falcone—Rose Kynaston—and told her he'd never been able to develop them because of a lack of parking, but my contact at the council says they've never received an application for planning permission for those buildings so that was a lie."

"Rose got an interview with Hotchen?" Ellie nodded. "I'd like to see it sometime. But not today." She couldn't get sucked into one of Elks's conspiracies, not with Indiana Bones rattling her cage. "Let me know how you get on," she said. "And remind me of the date of Hotchen's accident . . ."

"It was"—rustling—"Friday, 23 July 1999. Emergency call received at 6:10 p.m."

Ellie hung up and, without really knowing why, wrote the date and time of Giles Hotchen's accident on her notepad.

CHAPTER 31

The early dusk sapped my energy. Driving up the Grim's Holm on a path worn by the soles of two thousand years, I had a fleeting fear that the washed-out sun might fade for good. A primal fear. The end of days. The land was spent, and I would be left alone, like that film Aled watched, about the robot who stays on Earth to clean up the mess. Scavenging and dogged.

I am dogged too. As though in response to that thought, the spaniels swirled with the motion of eels under the stone arch and into the trees. I drove on and stopped beside the great house. Through the kitchen window, the tall figure of Gwendoline faced the corner cupboard, throwing a comment over her shoulder like lucky salt. I figured someone must be there to catch it. I cut the engine and got out.

I had to ask Gwendoline about Shawna Dourish. I hoped she remembered her friend today. It was hard to imagine how she could forget someone whose son lost the tip of his finger in a chicken shed.

Was it possible that Shawna's son, Rhys, had gone missing long ago—and that Gwendoline had lost that knowledge to dementia? Was it possible they weren't friends at all, that Shawna only returned to the Grim's Holm because she couldn't let her child go, as some bereaved parents do, circling, like restless ghosts, back to places haunted by the missing? Or was Shawna actively looking for Rhys? Hoping he was alive after all this time. If so, she would surely have come forward after the public appeal. She couldn't have missed the coverage, wherever she was living.

The spaniels sped ahead of me into the kitchen, splashing a trail of hairy footprints that made Gwendoline flap her tea towel at them. "It's time for the ponies," she complained, as though the dogs' crime was tardiness rather than filthiness. Deep inside the house, a clock tolled. She shrugged on a coat. No one would call me a horsewoman, but even I knew that it would be easier to tend to the ponies in the light. Gwendoline's rules of timekeeping didn't always make sense.

"Gwendoline, can I just ask you—"

"Ponies."

I trailed after her into the dusk. The sky had the rich blue-black luminosity of crow feathers. The tireless wind turned mild around this time, flagging at the close of day. Gwendoline bustled to the stables, skirting the flint barn, me hurrying to keep pace with her long strides.

"Gwendoline," I tried again, "was it your friend Shawna whose son lost the tip of a finger?"

"Rhys Dourish."

Good, she remembered. "They lived at Low Farm?"

"These days, of course, it belongs to Tony Thorn." Gwendoline sucked her teeth. "And now look."

"Did Rhys go missing?"

"All the time. Feral child, that one."

"I mean did he go missing . . . seriously? Did she ever have to call the police?"

"Shawna call the police? I don't think so. That would require a degree of responsibility. Even the police would best describe her as a flibbertigibbet."

"The thing is, Gwendoline, the skeleton found in the river near Low Farm had a missing finger. Tip of a finger. And Rhys Dourish had a missing finger . . ."

She stopped dead, like someone who has walked into a room and forgotten why they came. Then she strode on toward the stables. "Farming injuries are very common." She flicked on the lights, and the stable block became an ark in the gloom with room for two ponies, two spaniels, two people. A refuge from the flood. The veil of my breath whipped away; the wind had rested and now returned at full force. We set out across the pasture to open the gate for the ponies. Deep hoof-prints in wet mud had frozen into a sea of breaking waves, making the going rough.

"Gwendoline? Where does Shawna live now? I think the police need to talk to her."

"Look at the buzzards." Gwendoline pointed to Low Farm, as bright as a circus tent below us, where two birds dipped in and out of the light like trapeze artists picking up momentum. "She comes and goes."

"Is she visiting soon?"

"She's a law unto herself."

"Sounds like you're mad at her?"

"I am a bit, yes. She takes things that aren't hers. Like your scarf, which I found lying in her car. She preaches her *make do and mend* philosophy, doesn't let anything go to waste, but I'm not sure what to believe." At the gate, the ponies clanged the metal with their knees, a discordant one-two rattle. Across the valley, we must have sounded like a death knell. Gwendoline slipped a halter over Morgana's flattened ears and tugged the lead rope to make the old mare keep up.

She takes things. My scarf. I remembered what I'd read on the web-site about dementia: confusion often leads to paranoia.

"If I wanted to speak to Shawna Dourish, how could I contact her? If the police wanted to ask her about her son—"

"Water under the bridge."

"Surely she'd want to know if Indiana Bones is her son?"

The ponies clattered into their stalls.

"Don't you think Shawna Dourish would want to know?" I pressed.

Gwendoline stamped her foot onto the kick-bolt, and it slotted home with a snap. "Between you and me"—she glanced around—"Aled's not here, is he?" I reminded her that he'd gone with Dylan, and she fixed me to the spot with a look. "Shawna Dourish is a terrible mother! I'm not speaking out of turn because I say as much to her face. Now, these ponies need their feet washed and dried or they'll get mud fever. They don't like cold water, but sometimes you have to do what's best even if it's uncomfortable."

For a moment, I watched Morgana snatch mouthfuls of hay and suck them down like drags on a cigarette. The pony's cussedness was quite appealing. I took my cell out of my pocket and checked for a number I'd copied from Gwendoline's phone. I didn't want to go behind her back, but . . . *sometimes you have to do what's best even if it's uncomfortable.*

I walked a short distance into the trees and found a sheltered spot. I dialed Shawna's number. A voice answered after three rings. "Hello!" Male, somehow familiar. "Can I help you?" The tone: imperious, impatient. *Tony Thorn.* Shawna was still listed in Gwendoline's phone under her old home, Low Farm. The number must have stayed with the property.

"Oh, I'm sorry, I misdialed." I made to hang up.

"Rose?"

Damn. "Yeah, hi, Tony."

"What can I do for you on this blustery evening?"

I looked down the holm, and I could see him inside the atrium of his home. I felt like I was spying, although he was the one who'd chosen to live in a glass house.

"Sorry to bother you. I was trying to track down Shawna Dourish."

"Can't help you there, I'm afraid. I used to give her post to Gwendoline to pass on, as she left no forwarding address. But her mail dried up years ago."

"Any idea where she moved to?"

"I only know she left the place in a mess. The house was empty, but the outbuildings were full of rubbish—the boy's toys and computer equipment."

"Is any of their rubbish still in the outbuildings?"

"Of course not, it all went in a skip."

I thought of Gwendoline saying that Shawna had *left them to clean up her mess*. This must be what she meant.

"You mentioned the son, Rhys . . . This is going to sound weird, but did he go missing? Is that why she moved away?"

Pause. "No, no, I saw him at the notary on the day we signed the contract. Grungy sort. But surely Gwendoline should be able to help you? They've been friends for years."

"This is the number she has listed for Shawna. I guess I could contact the notary. Do you recall when you signed the contract? Roughly?"

"Can't recall the exact day, but it was late July 1999. We rushed the sale through because I was due to fly to Paris to watch the Tour de France. First year Lance Armstrong won. Very exciting at the time, though he wasn't all that he seemed, was he?"

"Sometimes I feel like no one is all that they seem."

"Speaking of which, have you managed to get Gwendoline to a doctor? I went to her GP once, but the blasted woman wouldn't show me her notes. Family only."

Thorn requested Gwendoline's medical records? *There's a thin line between concern and control.* "I'm sure Gwendoline was grateful for the help—"

He laughed harshly. "Come now, she resents me. But I went ahead and ordered some equipment for her, so maybe I did some good. I don't hear her yelling in the barn like I used to."

"Yelling in the barn?"

"Shouting at her husband. *Help me!* She must have kept him on a tight leash . . ."

I rolled my eyes at the ball-breaker cliché. "What equipment did you get for her?"

"A special clock that tells the day as well as the time, dated boxes for pills—that kind of thing. A journal that encourages people to write down memories and information, like a cross between a diary and an aide-mémoire. It has an elephant on the cover, which I thought was amusing."

"Does she let you go inside the house?"

"Beyond the kitchen? Never! I do wonder if she's a hoarder and the place is full to the gunwales with vacuum-packed toenail clippings or something like that. Don't you go inside?"

"The roof is dangerous."

Pause. "I don't think so. I had my surveyor take a look over it—only from the outside—and he said it's in good condition for its years."

I thanked him and hung up, wondering if Gwendoline knew that Thorn had had her home looked over by his surveyor and that he'd requested her medical records. Maybe she was right; Thorn wanted Hurtwood House for himself by any means. Maybe he made her dementia out to be worse than it was in an attempt to get her put into a residential facility?

I backtracked to the stables and invited Gwendoline to join us for supper. She checked her watch as though she might have a hot date, then agreed. Back at the cottage, I took Aled for a bath while Dylan cooked. Sitting with my arms folded on the edge of the tub, I asked him: "Do you remember Gwen-ma's friend?"

He hammered a toy fish against the tap. "Gwen-ma has a friend."

"Do you remember her? Shawna?"

"I sawed her."

"Do you remember what happened to her son, Rhys?"

"Chicken bit his finger off."

I smiled. "That's right, he lost the tip of his finger in the chicken factory. Did she tell you that story?"

"Gwen-ma's friend."

"Shawna, yes. Did she tell you the story?"

"I sawed her in the barn. Mustn't go in the barn."

"No, it's dangerous. Was Shawna in the barn with Gwen-ma?"

"She was in the barn with Gwen-ma and Stanney."

A dark sparkle ran through my muscles. "Stanley? Stanley was there?"

"Yep. In the photo."

"Aled, this is important. Did you see Shawna in the barn or in a photo?"

"In the photo of the barn." He gave an exaggerated nod that soaked his forelock.

I pushed the hair back so the shampoo didn't get in his eyes. "Aled, have you ever seen Shawna in real life?"

"Yes! In a real-life photo." He threw the fish, and it bounced off my eyebrow.

"Ouchy," I said, "that hurt." Aled laughed. Okay, I'd been pushing him, and he'd found a way to make me stop. But I didn't like that laugh. I picked up the fish and kept it, going to the window where I looked toward the great house. Thorn said Gwendoline had a book where she could write important stuff. Might Shawna's address be written in there? Could it contain the photo Aled was talking about? I persuaded him out of the bath and settled him in front of the television. I slipped my phone inside my bra before going into the kitchen. Dylan and his mother were discussing a story in the newspaper.

"I need to go get my phone," I said. "I must have left it in the stables."

"It's dark. Shall I go?" Dylan asked.

"I know where it is." I took a flashlight from the drawer. "I'll be quicker."

I trotted out of the back door into the field, before making a sharp turn toward the great house.

CHAPTER 32

As she drove the patrol car out of town, landmarks that other drivers might not even notice reminded Sergeant Ellie Trevelyan of various largely avoidable calamities caused by pinheads. At an oak tree where a boy once totaled his car an hour after taking his driving test, she turned onto the road that led to the forest school.

Meredith Fiddler. Ellie told herself to focus as she worked up through the gears on the old Roman road. Meredith wasn't active on social media. Her Facebook account remained in her married name. She hadn't replied to birthday messages from a month ago. It looked like she'd been a regular humble bragger once—#SoBlessed—but she'd gone dark. It didn't matter. Ellie needed only a rough sketch of the present. It was the past she wanted to spotlight.

She parked and got out into the pitch black of the trees. The wind thrashed around in the canopy like a huge infuriated hand searching its handbag. Every winter it surprised Ellie how dark it got in what was still, indisputably, a key part of the working day. It was inconvenient. She picked her way to a well-lit shelter.

A woman watched her arrive, sleeves rolled up, hands dripping. Ellie had seen her before, but couldn't place it. *Let it percolate,* she thought.

"Meredith Fiddler?"

The woman took the time to find a towel and dry the skin between every finger before coming over. She wore her hair in an intricate braid that suggested she didn't object to looking at her own face in the mirror. Ellie was more of a scrape-it-back-and-hope person. In fairness, if she looked like Meredith, she'd probably have a mirror in the hallway. Instead, she had a hatstand.

Apart from the exasperated wind, the camp was quiet.

"Too blowy for kids today; a tree could come down," Meredith said. "I'm doing some housekeeping instead."

She chatted easily, showing no curiosity about the reason for a police officer's visit. She gave every impression of being open and at ease, explaining that she'd moved home to Hurtwood after her marriage ended. "He had an affair. I didn't care. Which is probably why he had the affair." Frequently enough to count as a tic, Meredith's fingers touched the braid that encircled her head—front, side, back, front—as though it might come undone.

"Does the date 23 July 1999 mean anything to you?" Ellie asked. "It was a Friday."

Meredith's hand rose. Front, side, back, front. As though she was crossing herself. "That's a long time ago."

"It would have been your last day of school."

Front, side, back, front. "July 1999. Could have been."

"It was. Did anything unusual happen that day?"

Meredith pushed both hands into her pockets. "Yes, actually. Although I didn't know about it until afterward. There was a guy in our year named Giles Hotchen; he's still around."

"I know of him."

"He had an accident that day. Last day of school, I mean; I don't recall the exact date, but if it was the last day of school, then it happened on that date."

"You were friends?"

Front, side, back, front. "Not at that time."

"You had been friends?"

"It's a long story. Do you want tea?"

Ellie followed her under the shelter. Meredith placed a camping kettle on the open fire. Behind her, a woodworking area was strewn with branches whittled to vicious spikes.

"So, Giles Hotchen," Meredith said. "I was going out with a bloke named Dylan Kynaston. You might know the family . . ."

And then Ellie knew where she'd seen Meredith Fiddler before: in Hurtwood, the leggy woman Dylan Kynaston had been chatting up when he should have been watching his son. "I know the Kynaston family," Ellie said. "From Hurtwood House."

"Right. We were on and off for ages. We were kind of"—she shook her head at the ground, abashed—"kind of the golden couple, I suppose. Dylan made life seem effortless. Nice-looking. Straight As. His dad was cool, his mum was cool, even his house was cool—bohemian, a bit tumbledown. They weren't loaded; that wasn't why people liked him. Dylan had to work all summer to buy a car." Meredith snatched up the whistling kettle and poured water into the teapot. "And it was so crummy, a Fiat 500, tiny little thing; and some of the other boys—I'll get to Giles Hotchen in a minute—tried to take the piss, like this was their opportunity to diminish him, but Dylan gave zero fucks, and the girls fancied him even more because he looked cute in his daft car." She handed Ellie a mug. "And it was crushing for the likes of Giles Hotchen, you know? His father bought him wheels—serious wheels, something German—but he wasn't cool. He wasn't bad looking, got good grades, played on the rugby team, drove a Mercedes. Still not cool. That's gotta hurt."

Ellie blew steam off the surface of her tea.

"Giles never went short of girls, though. There was always someone willing to let him buy the drinks, you know what I mean?"

Ellie did.

"And I did too sometimes. Not proud of it. Sometimes Dylan would blow hot and cold. When he went cold, I'd rub his nose in it by going out with Giles. Looking back, I . . ." To Ellie's surprise, and apparently her own, Meredith choked up.

"Slowly does it," said Ellie.

Meredith shook the tears away with a sharp twist of her head. "Why are young women so insecure? Even when they have so much going for them. Looking back, I had so much going for me, but I . . ." She shook her head again, hard enough to make her teeth rattle. "When Dylan said he needed to work, I thought he'd gone off me. Now, of course, I realize that his effortless cool took more effort than we thought. He worked for his grades. He worked to buy his daft car. He worked to help his dad. When he said he needed to work, he genuinely needed to work."

Ellie offered a consolation: "Youth is wasted on the young."

"A good bloke is wasted on the young."

"How did Dylan react to your relationship with Giles Hotchen?"

"Typically . . . cool. Which was infuriating. I wanted him to fight for me, but he seemed to think I had the right to make up my own mind."

"Surely that's true?"

"Of course it's true, but it's not what you want to hear, is it?"

Ellie smiled into her tea.

Meredith pressed one palm against her own forehead. "And it took me a long time to work out that Giles Hotchen used me as a stick to whip Dylan. That was not my insecurity, that was a real thing. He was obsessed with Dylan. It was as though Giles was trying to work out what he was lacking by studying Dylan, deconstructing him. So Giles courted Dylan, in the same way he did the girls—by paying for stuff. Weed and booze, mainly. His dad owned some buildings near their school, and they'd break in to smoke. So, yeah, even Dylan fell for the flattery."

Buildings near the school? The ones on Cheapside? "Did you ever join them?"

Meredith wrinkled her nose. "Grotty little flat with a stained mattress on the floor. One of those electric heaters you put coins in. The boys hung out there, listening to the soundtrack of *Trainspotting*, two privileged boys playing at being losers. Cocksure it would never happen to them for real. But the place frightened me. It's your basic middle-class nightmare, isn't it? Failing and ending up somewhere like that."

"These are the buildings that back onto Whipping Post Lane?"

"I don't know what the road's called; I haven't been there since."

"Was Dylan there on the day of Giles Hotchen's accident?"

"Are you investigating the accident? After all this time?"

"I'm interested in that day."

"Right." Front, side, back, front. "Dylan and I drove to Wales straight after school. He picked me up, and we went to Abersoch, where my parents had a place. We spent the weekend there."

"That's what you said in a police statement in 1999."

"Yes, I did. That's what happened."

"Tell me about the headmaster's car." Ellie watched Meredith's hand fall to her side.

"That had nothing to do with Dylan."

"Giles Hotchen claimed that Dylan defecated on the headmaster's car on the last day of school." Ellie struggled to recall a detail her father had mentioned. It flickered in her mind, like the sun behind the treetops. "Is that when he earned the nickname Nasty Boy?"

"Nasty Boy? I don't remember." Front, side, back, front. "Dylan wasn't the kind of person who . . ." Meredith pulled her face into a grimace of disgust. "That wasn't him."

"Was Giles Hotchen the kind of person who . . . ?"

"What kind of person poops on a car?"

Ellie shrugged. It was a reasonable question, but one she wanted Meredith to answer.

High in the trees, a wood pigeon hooted. "I think Giles Hotchen would have done anything to disgrace Dylan, yes."

"And how did Dylan react to being disgraced?"

"He was furious." Hand to hair. "But he was with me. In Wales."

"Was he?"

"Yes. Yes, he was." Front, side, back, front.

CHAPTER 33

The kitchen of the great house was submerged in silence. Even the spaniels lay sprawled in their bed as though tranquilized. I stood with one hand on the stripped pine table, the wood grounding me to a living thing. The door to the rest of the house was ajar, the first time I'd seen it left open.

If you're going to do this, do it now.

When I opened the door, it gave a soft creak, like the exhalation of a person steadying herself. I thought of the house as female, its defining parts hidden inside. The passageway was painted the blue-gray of veins seen through the skin. It branched off to both sides and up the wooden stairs. I followed flagstones to a scullery, where a wooden drying rack was strewn with underwear.

Back along the passageway, I found a formal living room. A fireplace made of veined marble like slabs of fatty meat. Two couches in wilted florals. No decorations, no photos, no life. I crossed the room on the diagonal, emerging in the entrance hall. There was a wide front door through which the wind whispered, a mahogany staircase with a frayed runner. It was freezing, a deep cold that comes from the earth, as though this part of the house was built on permafrost. The sort of house that would be cold even in summer.

There was hardly any furniture. Tony Thorn was wrong; the house wasn't stuffed full of clutter, it was pared to the bone. It didn't even have a smell. It wasn't a house, but the skin of a house. I thought of the shed skin of a snake, frightening only in relation to what it once was, not what it is. Fear tinged with relief.

Then I thought of Mistress Payne or, at least, the fact that I hadn't thought of her until now. Her presence was absent. I backtracked to the servants' staircase beside the kitchen. Each stair crunched under my feet. *What am I looking for?* A clue to help me find Shawna, but also, I realized, a clue to help me find Gwendoline. And a small voice inside me added: *And Dylan, and Aled. Yourself.*

On the landing, too many doors. I found myself inside a crazy game, a riddle, a dream even. The landing light had been left on, but the far reaches faded to black. I shone my flashlight into corners. There was nothing there, except snowdrifts of dog hair. I grabbed the nearest handle and pulled, but inside was a hidden staircase, narrow and mean and dark, leading maids to the attic. *What am I looking for?* A notebook, an address book, the journal Thorn had mentioned. It was so quiet. Not even a ticking clock. Where was the grandfather clock that chimed the hours, which you could hear in the kitchen? Everything had shifted so that the kitchen that once felt threatening now seemed like a safe harbor. The house vibrated with the choked echo of a bell that's been silenced between fingers.

Focus, Rose.

The master bedroom had to face the front of the house. I orientated myself and grabbed another door handle. It opened to a vast room with long sash windows. In the darkness, the panes were black as bomb craters. I let my beam scurry around like a rat. So, Tony Thorn was right after all. Full of junk—books and paperwork, bulging bags, clothing, and boxes. A four-poster bed made an island on one side. Gwendoline's slippers beside the bed. Glasses folded on the nightstand.

Unlike the rest of the house, this room smelled of dried lavender. Picking my way with care, I reached the bedside table. Glass of water filled to the brim. A biography of some English king with a masculine cover. I traced one finger over the title and left a dark trail in the dust. A car key on a fob shaped like a car. A house key on a fob shaped like a house. And a hardback book spread wide with an alarm clock propped in the fold. A journal. I lifted the cover to see the front, and there was the photo of an elephant. Thorn's aide-mémoire, the one he foisted on her.

I tucked the flashlight under my chin. Printed in capitals on the top of the first page: *You are Gwendoline Marina Kynaston.* Underneath in red pen: *You are a silly old woman with dementia.* Dementia was underlined twice. Next: *Do as you are told, or you will starve and your animals will starve*—and underlined—*or you will all die of dehydration.*

Next, a military timetable.

06:00—You are awake. Reset alarm NOW.

06:01—Drink the glass of water. Refill glass of water NOW.

06:02—Put on your slippers and the clothes laid on the floor and make the bed.

06:04—At the next alarm, go to the kitchen, to the corner cupboard, and follow further instructions.

06:05—Alarm is ringing downstairs, go NOW.

I picked up the travel alarm clock and saw that it was set for 6:00 a.m. A second identical alarm clock on the nightstand was set for 10:00 p.m. In the journal, I read:

22:00—You are tired. It is time to go to bed. Reset alarm NOW.

22:01—Do not drink the water or you will WET THE BED. The water is for the morning.

22:02—Lay clean clothes for the morning on the floor HERE.

22:04—Brush your teeth and wash yourself. Leave your dirty clothes in the basket in the bathroom. Pee NOW or you will WET THE BED.

I flipped through the pages. *Dylan has to see this. He should agree to that power of attorney because this is crazy.* Using my phone, I photographed Gwendoline's timetable. I turned to a page headed *Information*: bank account numbers, doctor's address, insurance details. I copied those too. The next page was titled *Friends and Family* and contained only Dylan's and my numbers, our last address studiously struck through and replaced with our current details. Nothing about Shawna. The next page—*Reminiscences*—was blank and so were the next several pages. According to her journal, Gwendoline had nothing worth remembering.

I left the journal where I found it, put the alarm clocks back in place, and closed the bedroom door behind me. In the kitchen, the spaniels slithered around my legs while I checked the corner cupboard. Gwendoline had pasted handwritten notes to the inside of the door and hidden a row of identical alarm clocks, which were set to sound at various hours.

The first note picked up at 06:06—*Feed dogs.* 06:07—*Eat toast and tea NOW. Don't wait or you will starve.* (This was underlined.) 08:00—*Drink tea and eat an egg. Go for a pee or you will WET SELF.* 09:00—*Ponies. Put on coat or you will FREEZE. Go to stables for instructions.* I ran my finger down her list, every moment of the day itemized. A new piece of paper had been tacked up, noticeably less finger-grubby than the rest. *If Aled is here, make him a drink and cake. You mustn't let him go HUNGRY. Ask if he needs to pee. You mustn't let him WET SELF.*

My eyes stung with tears. *Poor Gwendoline.* I rubbed my hands over my face, exhausted by the thought of her routine, impressed by her ingenuity, and touched by how she had incorporated Aled into her scheme. No wonder she seemed strict; this was how she held it together. All alone. Tony Thorn was right, annoying though that was to admit. Gwendoline was sick, really sick.

I set off toward the cottage. The wind picked up and the trees howled. Gwendoline couldn't help me find Shawna; I'd have to do it myself. I wanted to offer Sergeant Trevelyan something concrete, but the best I could do was tell her my suspicions and let her track the woman down. I got my phone and dialed her number as the wind nudged me along, a faithful mule carrying me home.

CHAPTER 34

Early start for Sergeant Ellie Trevelyan. The sun was stuck behind storm clouds, slow-moving behemoths like the farm traffic on the road out of Hurtwood. Ellie rode up front in DI Bryan Harrow's car, directing him to the Grim's Holm. Her nerves fizzled, as did the wet road under their tires. Broken Arrow drove fast and jagged. It was, as her father would have said when he still had access to his memory bank of similes, *like being dragged along on a shovel.*

Possibly, he was trying to impress her. Harrow, that is, not her father; Jim Trevelyan had long since treated Ellie no differently than any of his more occasional caregivers. One day the previous week, he left her a tip on a plate.

"The turn is coming up," she said. Harrow nodded, lips slightly pursed. At the junction, he tossed the car into the lane, and they hurtled along between hedges higher than a house. Harrow had badgered two junior detectives into accompanying them. After the call from Rose Kynaston the previous night, which Ellie had duly relayed to Harrow, he'd spoken to his commanding officer and bumped the investigation up the priority list. The whiff of farce that lingered about the Indiana Bones case had intensified to a more piquant stench of crime. Local boy. Local victim. Local embarrassment, if it turned out a dead kid hadn't been missed, let alone investigated. Better get it solved before the fallout had time to settle.

"What do we know about Dylan Kynaston's movements in July 1999?" one of the young detectives in the rear asked, hands on the back of Harrow's seat like a child inquiring how much farther. To Ellie, the young woman seemed like a girl wearing her mother's suit. *She looks sharp, though,* Ellie thought, *with her androgynous edge. I should have dressed like that back in the day.* Foolishly, Ellie had always believed that appearances didn't matter, that she'd get ahead by doing the job better than anyone else. Instead, she'd done the job so well they made her keep doing it. The force took her for granted. Her father, *bless him*, took her for granted. Even her sister took it for granted that Ellie would stay in Hurtwood to look after Jim while Cassie swam in the ocean. Maybe Ellie should pop Jim on a plane with a Paddington Bear tag printed with the words *Your Turn.* Her sister had always been sanctimonious about sharing.

"He's a journalist, isn't he?" Harrow said with a side-eye at Ellie. "Dylan Kynaston?"

"Right, yeah. I called my contact at the local rag last night," Ellie explained. "He says Dylan was an intern on the *Midland Post* in his last year at high school. This was 1999. Very bright kid, he says; Dylan had a place at Cambridge. But, weird this, he didn't take up the place. His father died earlier in the year of heart problems—"

"This is Stanley Kynaston," Harrow said for the benefit of the kids in the back seat. "A football coach who was questioned and released after the death of one of his players. The boy alleged child abuse. He never named Stanley or any other abuser, although in his diary he used the initial *S*—which was never made public, by the way. As there was no further evidence, no further action was taken."

"The allegation stuck, though," Ellie picked up. "Even after Stanley passed away. His wife, Gwendoline, who we'll meet soon, went to pieces. Publicly at first—defending Stanley to the hilt—but when the tide of public opinion turned against her, she shut herself away. Went from socialite to recluse pretty much overnight. God only knows why she didn't leave Hurtwood. Robert Elks was one of the few people to attend Stanley's funeral—most boycotted it. I tried to go myself, but Gwendoline took against the police and wouldn't let me in. Then Dylan skipped Cambridge and took a menial job at a newspaper in London."

"But why skip Cambridge?" the young DC said. "You don't turn down a place at Cambridge."

"I asked Elks the same question. It surprised everyone. He reckons Dylan Kynaston wanted the anonymity of the big city. Only took him a few years to get posted overseas. Seems all he ever wanted was to get away from Hurtwood." Ellie stopped talking as the last line came out sounding more wistful than professional.

"Get away from a rumor?" the young DC scoffed.

"Or from his crazy mother," suggested the other kid.

"Or," said DI Bryan Harrow, "from a crime."

The car plummeted down a sharp dip into a huge puddle, hydroplaning a few yards until Harrow got control. He slammed on the wipers to clear the windshield.

"There's that view of the Wrekin," Ellie said. "The one from the picture." The lone hill sat like a clenched hand on the horizon.

"Distinctive," said Harrow.

"It's a different shape from every side."

The distant hill was echoed in the foreground by a smaller mound of earth, although this one was too uniform, too structured to be natural. The Grim's Holm.

"What the flip is this place?" said the girl wearing her mother's suit. Ellie explained that the holm was an Iron Age hill fort, a vast raised mound upon which sat Hurtwood House and its estate. Low Farm perched on its lower flank. Conveniently, Thorn's house came into view, and the kids cooed over the television producer's home. Technically, the site where Indiana Bones was found lay on land belonging to Low

Farm, but remains in a watercourse could have—most likely would have—moved. Harrow nosed his car through a set of iron gates and powered up the driveway, sending puddles of gray water leaping over the precipice. He rolled down the windows as they crunched to a halt on the gravel beside a mansion.

"What's that?" asked one of the kids, pointing to a crumbling structure across the yard.

"Dovecote," said Harrow.

"For actual doves?"

Harrow ignored her. "I don't like these storm clouds. Best get a look at the outbuildings as soon as possible." He rubbed the bridge of his nose, and Ellie wondered if he had a headache. She'd downed two painkillers with her morning tea, but the air was so dense under the iron sky that the pressure pain wouldn't go away until it rained. Harrow got out and two spaniels appeared, white apparitions that squirmed around his legs like fish fertilizing his shoes.

"Used to be a beautiful house," Ellie said. "Shame really."

"Certainly got potential." Harrow brushed dog hair off his shins, creating a white cloud that eddied and blew back to coat the upper half of his trousers. He tutted. "Would make a great hotel. You could develop those barns. Wedding venue. Little goldmine."

"Thinking of retirement, boss?" said the young detective.

Harrow was just informing her that he was *only bloody fifty* when Gwendoline Kynaston appeared from inside the flint barn. Ellie was shocked at the change in the woman's bearing; back in the day, Mrs. Kynaston had been fond of wearing Marlene Dietrich–style trousers, the kind that would make a short woman look like a child standing on another child's shoulders inside a trench coat. But now her shabby slacks were stuffed into the tops of her boots. Harrow walked to meet her, identification held aloft in his left hand, right hand held out to shake. His words carried on the breeze.

"Mrs. Gwendoline Kynaston? I'm Detective Inspector Bryan Harrow. We're investigating the human remains found in the river near Low Farm."

Ellie knew they had a warrant, but there was no need to go in all guns blazing. Harrow's voice sounded authoritative but reassuring. Mild. So Ellie was most surprised when Gwendoline ignored his offered hand, put one palm to her chest, and collapsed at his feet.

CHAPTER 35

The wind-harassed trees pointed toward the big house. I dressed Aled and myself while Dylan went out in response to a banging noise. He came rushing back for his coat.

"Police." He knocked over a chair in his haste. "And an ambulance."

Clouds sped over the holm like shallow waves. Everything turned upside down. Aled refused to let me carry him, so it took frustrating minutes to get to the summit. Then he ran to the ambulance, where Gwendoline sat wrapped in a blanket. A paramedic tried to take her blood pressure, but she shrugged him off. Dylan came out of the big house, followed by Sergeant Ellie Trevelyan.

"The warrant covers your property too, Mr. Kynaston."

"Fine." He threw out his arms as though submitting to an airport search. "I've got nothing to hide. As I told you at the station." He looked at me. "These officers are going to search the cottage."

"What are you looking for?" I directed the question to Ellie.

"I'm not at liberty to divulge—"

"Bollocks!" said Dylan. "You're trying to pin Indiana Bones on me, just like you pinned Kenny Bale on my father. Much easier than finding the real perpetrator."

"Perpetrator of what?" Ellie said. "Has a crime been committed, Mr. Kynaston?"

He scoffed. "Well, something was committed. Commit suicide. Commit murder. Bodies don't turn up in the river without something happening first."

I watched as Dylan and Ellie trudged down the path toward the cottage. Her back gave off a deadpan expression that annoyed me; *I know you,* I thought, *and you're shutting me out!* Aled came over and lifted his arms. I picked him up, and he buried his face in my shoulder. He shouldn't have to witness this. *Police picking over his home like rats at a landfill.* Gwendoline folded the blanket for the paramedic, who was advising her about the aftereffects of a panic attack.

"Nothing of the sort," Gwendoline said. "Low blood sugar. I forgot to eat this morning. My routine has gone to pot."

I knew I should take her inside, make sugary tea. But instead I shifted Aled onto my back and carried him to the cottage. I'd never felt animosity toward the police before, but my aggression was instinctive; it came from a sense of vulnerability that made me want to kick out in a preemptive strike. I put Aled right in the car. Through the upstairs window, I saw Dylan with his arms hugging his own chest. When I started the engine, he looked at me and gave a single nod. I nodded back, even though I wasn't sure what we were agreeing to. *Get Aled out of here.* Agreed. *But where to?* Not agreed.

I rolled down the hill, taking the route past Low Farm. At the bottom of the slope, I stopped between the iron gates. Inside the zippered section of my purse, I found Aled's and my passports. I'd been meaning to put them in a safe place, my bedside drawer perhaps, or together with Dylan's documents in his nightstand. And yet I hadn't. And here they were. Aled and I could go to my mom's in Chicago.

I didn't have more than a couple of hundred bucks; setting up our home had wiped us out. Payments for my recent freelance work wouldn't come close to buying two plane tickets. But Vic was in London. Victor Carlson, who'd rescued me from a stinking cell in Mogadishu. It was a sure bet he'd pay for flights if I asked him nicely. My hands kneaded the steering wheel. I would refund Vic this time for sure, but how could I ever repay Dylan for abandoning him? I left him once in Mogadishu. If I left him now and took Aled too, there might be no coming back. What sort of wife left her husband at a time like this? *One who's leaving him for good, that's who.*

I drove through the flooded dip, keeping the car on the road. There was one other person who might help, even though it would crush my female pride to ask her. A few miles later, I parked up at the forest school. Aled ran toward the shelter, and I spotted Meredith.

"We're closed. This wind is going to put me out of business." She carried a box of food toward her car. "The police came here yesterday. Asking about Dylan."

This stopped me in my tracks. "What about him?"

"Tell him they're asking about Giles Hotchen. He'll understand."

I recalled her standing on this very spot, telling Dylan that he owed her one. My female pride didn't stretch to letting this woman think that she and my husband kept secrets behind my back. "I know you've helped Dylan in the past—"

Her face turned gray. "What has he said?"

What's she so worried about? "The police are at Hurtwood House now. Dylan asked me to say Nasty Boy needs a favor."

When I returned to the holm—leaving Aled with Meredith—there were more officers. The ground was littered with snapped branches, as though a tidal wave had passed through. I stepped out of the car and the wind, a devilish, irritating bully, spun my hair into a knot. I pulled up my hood, and a gust snatched it down again.

The focus had shifted to the barn. The leper house. Gwendoline and Dylan stood in the yard, their arms limp. A knot of police was moving around inside the double doors where I'd once seen Shawna's green Land Rover. When Dylan saw me, he hurried over and ushered me into the kitchen.

"What are they looking for?" I asked.

"They called for police dogs." The wind had pounded his face to the color of dough.

"What? Why?"

"They found something. The atmosphere in there is tight as a rubber band." His head tipped back, staring up at the ceiling. His arms crept around himself. I thought of his hiding place, the one in the space between the walls, where he'd gone as a kid. Why would a child hide in his own home? I went up behind him and layered my arms over his.

"Dylan . . ." I hesitated. "I'm sorry, but I have to ask you something. Did your father abuse you? You and Kenny Bale?"

"Jesus, Rose!" He pushed me away, and I bumped into the table, its edge digging a line into my butt like a cane. "My father wasn't like that. When will people accept it . . ."

"Some kids repress memories—"

"Maybe, but I remember everything. I haven't blocked it out or rewritten it. He was just . . . my dad. A regular dad. He picked me up when I fell down. He told me I could achieve whatever I wanted. He spent hours teaching me to bend a football into the back of the net. And yes, he got distracted by work. Sometimes he was short-tempered. And he didn't do a great job of hiding his disappointment when I couldn't bend the ball in the slightest. But I remember when he tried to get interested in history because that's what I liked. It took him months to read a single book . . ." Dylan ran out of steam for a moment, one hand raised in the air like he could grasp the light bulb of an idea. His version of a father, one with normal human foibles, sounded preferable to my own, who made us think he was perfect right up to the moment he left us. Dylan carried on: "He wasn't a saint. But he wasn't a pedophile. He wasn't a killer." Dylan gulped in a breath. "Nor am I."

I took his hands again. "Okay, then let's—"

"I'm so sorry." His face crumpled, and for the second time in my life I saw my husband cry. I held him the way I'd wanted to the first time, in a cellar in Mogadishu, while I was being led away by a man with a gun and a leer.

"What are you sorry for, Dylan?" I held him tight.

"I've done it again, haven't I? Dragged you into danger."

"I came of my own accord. To Somalia. And to Hurtwood." I took hold of his shoulders and pushed him back so I could see his face. "Gwendoline needs help, Dylan. When this is over we could sell this place and use the money to get her into care. And we can go somewhere nobody knows us."

"We can go anywhere," Dylan said.

"So let's make a plan. We're good at plans."

"They took my phone," Dylan murmured into my clavicle, leaning in again, "and my laptop. They think I'm a pervert." His arms tightened around my waist. "What if they keep me away from Aled?"

"Do you remember when we climbed Mount Kilimanjaro? We got to the summit by taking baby steps." He hummed. "And do you remember"—my voice dropped lower; this memory was a place we revisited on tiptoe—"Mogadishu? In the cell, we celebrated each time we heard the muezzin because we'd survived long enough to hear another call to prayer."

He grunted. "It was my fault you were in that cell."

I kissed his brow. "You did save me, whatever you may think. You got me through it."

We heard boots. The side door opened. DI Harrow came in, followed by Ellie Trevelyan. Her face wind-bleached.

"What's happening?" I asked.

"The dogs picked up a scent in the barn," Ellie said. "One is a cadaver dog, and one is trained to search for historical human remains. They led us to a hatch for the cellar—the medieval undercroft—which had been buried beneath the hay."

"That barn's been full of hay for years," Dylan said.

"Evidently. In the cellar, we found human remains." Harrow let this drop. The skin on my back made its familiar creep into the lea of my spine. All eyes were on Dylan. Two high spots of red appeared in his blanched cheeks.

"Which dog?" said Dylan.

"What?" Harrow.

"Which dog found the body?"

"The one searching for historical remains."

"How long?" said Dylan.

"The coroner will tell us that. I have a hunch she's going to say it's about twenty years."

"So it's connected to Indiana Bones?"

Harrow shot a look at Ellie, who in turn glanced at me. I placed a hand on Dylan's arm. "Stop being a journalist," I said. My lips attempted a smile, but my muscles were too tight. "Let DI Harrow ask the questions."

Dylan zipped up his coat. Harrow shifted his weight so that he balanced squarely on both legs. "Dylan Kynaston." His hands formed fists. "I am arresting you on suspicion of involvement in the deaths of Rhys Dourish and an unidentified woman. You do not have to say anything, but it may harm your defense . . ."

I didn't hear any more as I stumbled outside into a spiteful wind.

CHAPTER 36

"Throw me a bone, Robert!" It was an unfortunate choice of words, which Elks ignored as he walked away. His long strides alternated black and white over the crossing. I chased him into the cobbled street where the media gathered. There was no way I'd be waiting outside the press conference this time.

Elks flashed his accreditation and went into the police station. A BBC reporter strode past the officer at the door, pointing a finger over her shoulder at a cameraman hauling a tripod. From inside my camera bag, I found a lanyard and slung it around my neck, loading my hands with equipment. When the next journalist came clacking over the cobbles, I dropped into her slipstream and pointed at her back as I breezed inside. Yes, I was the only female "cameraman," and no, the officer didn't dare question me.

A sharp right turn into a conference room and I slid into a gap, camera covering my face. My breath came in short gasps. The crowd of thirsty reporters sucked oxygen out of the stiflingly hot space. A table at the front was covered with a royal-blue cloth. A solitary glass of water rippled as DI Harrow slid into a seat behind the microphone. *This is the man who's been questioning Dylan. Who thinks my husband is capable of . . . what?* It wasn't possible. Just like Dylan knew his father wasn't capable of evil, I knew Dylan was innocent. If he had a dark shadow, I would have felt its chill slide over me, a cloud across the sun. I would have tasted bitterness on his tongue. *Wouldn't I?*

I studied Harrow for any clue to his mood, to what had happened in the couple of hours since they'd taken Dylan. But his face was a stopped clock. Sergeant Trevelyan stood on the dais, hands behind her back like a nightclub bouncer. Looking right at me. I lowered the camera an inch. She tilted her head to one side. *What are you doing?* I gave a small shrug. *Can you blame me?* Ellie opened her mouth as if to say something to the officer next to her, the one who had manned the door, but then the room reverberated with the thump-thump of an index finger on a microphone, and a squeal of feedback made everyone wince.

"Sorry about that," said Harrow. "Thank you for coming."

Removing me now would make a scene. Ellie widened her eyes once. *Don't do anything stupid.*

"Ladies and gentlemen, I have an update and an appeal for information. We can confirm that the human remains found in a river near Hurtwood belonged to a local teenager named Rhys Dourish. Rhys spelled with a *y*. His identity has been confirmed by dental records. It is still not clear when and how the young man died, but his death is being treated as suspicious." A couple of raised hands prompted Harrow to frown. "Not yet." The hands went down. "During a search in the vicinity of the original discovery, officers uncovered a second set of human remains." Hands thrust into the air and stayed there. "A thirty-eight-year-old man has been arrested and remains in police custody."

Don't name him, please don't name him.

A reporter's voice called out: "What can you tell us about the suspect you've arrested?"

"Man. Thirty-eight. In custody."

Another journalist: "Was he known to the victims?"

Please don't name him.

"I won't be releasing any further information regarding the arrest."

My stomach gave a contraction of relief.

A third reporter wearing a hipster flat cap got to his feet: "Are we looking at a serial killer?" Titters in the crowd.

DI Harrow pulled back from the microphone as though it had squealed again. "I believe the definition of a serial killer is someone who murders three or more people over a period of time. We have two sets of human remains; the cause of death is not established and neither is the timeline. So, no, no serial killer. Next?"

The hipster stayed on his feet. "But there *are* three deaths. There was a football player who died during the same period. Fell from rocks near Hurtwood House." He flicked through his notepad. When he spoke again, I mouthed the name with him. "Kenny Bale." The reporter shifted to a wide-legged stance. "Kenny Bale died in July 1999. Your previous statement said the bones had been in the water for up to twenty years, so that takes us back to"—he flipped the notepad shut—"1999."

No tittering now.

"Kenny Bale committed suicide," said Harrow.

"According to the coroner, it was 'misadventure.' He might've fallen. Or he might've been pushed. Which leaves the possibility—"

"You won't get to use your 'Shropshire Slayer' headline today."

The BBC reporter stood, and the hipster conceded the floor. "Are there connections between the *three* people who died at the holm?"

Harrow's hesitation was enough to get pens scribbling. He was cornered. He edged his chair an inch closer to the microphone before he spoke again. "Our priority is to establish the identity of the second set of human remains, and, to that end, I have an appeal for information. We'd like to hear from members of the public who have information on the whereabouts of a Ms. Shawna Dourish. She is the mother of Rhys Dourish, whose body was found in the river. We have been unable to trace Ms. Dourish since she moved away in July 1999. We would like to establish any sightings of her in the local area—or, indeed, anywhere in the country—after that date."

I saw her, I thought, *only last week.* At least—my stomach constricted—I saw her car. And she mended my scarf. And she told Aled a scary story. *Did she really do any of those things?*

A reporter: "So you think the second set of human remains belongs to Shawna Dourish? A mother and son found dead on the holm?"

"Until DNA results establish a link between the two sets of bones, we can't be sure. There are no dental records for Shawna Dourish, but maybe she was scared of the dentist. Or she couldn't afford dental work. Or nature gave her perfect teeth." Harrow stared into the glass of water, as though divining the best answer. Then he looked up and nodded. "But yes, there is evidence to suggest it's Shawna Dourish."

The body can't be Shawna. She's Gwendoline's friend. She comes to visit when she feels like it because she's a flibbertigibbet . . . The facts took a moment to penetrate; I resisted, like skin shrinking from the point of a needle. The truth stung. Gwendoline's friendship with Shawna was all in her mind. An echo of the past. Who mended my scarf, I didn't know, but I'd read on the dementia website that advanced patients may hallucinate . . . maybe Gwendoline had sewn the scarf herself. I delved into the wool around my neck, feeling the rough stitches that overlapped like bad teeth. But, no, it couldn't be true: I'd seen Shawna's car with my own eyes. A few reporters left the room. The remaining journalists swayed side to side to see around the obstruction, making me feel like I was in a boat in the throes of the sea.

Robert Elks stood. "What evidence points to Shawna Dourish?"

"Remains of clothing and a set of keys were found with the body."

Elks: "House keys?" Robert was trying to keep his information close to his chest. I knew how he felt; local reporter pushed aside when the nationals parachute in with all their resources, their clout, their big dicks. But he was the only journalist in the room who knew that Shawna Dourish had lived at Low Farm, which was now owned by the famous TV producer Tony Thorn.

As Harrow brought the press conference to a close, I wondered if Thorn had been questioned. I scanned the reporters as they chattered, mouths wide with words or wonder. It made me think of birds gathered in a circle in the paddock. *A parliament of rooks.* The flock had turned on one of its own in judgment. They'd pecked away at Stanley. They'd pecked away at Gwendoline. Now Dylan. Would they turn on Aled in the future? When would it end? When I turned back to the royal-blue table, only the half-empty glass remained. Harrow had gone. Sergeant Trevelyan stood in the doorway. *I should tell her about Shawna's car, the green Land Rover.* I raised one hand. *Or maybe I'd make it worse for Dylan somehow, inadvertently give evidence against him?* Ellie weaved between chairs in my direction. *Or maybe the information would clear his name?* Or maybe . . .

Or . . .

Or . . .

Uncertainly cawed in my mind like a circle of rooks. My only certainty was that Dylan, my Dylan, wouldn't hurt a soul, not even to defend himself. I'd seen him make that choice in the flesh; given the chance to hurt an innocent person in order to save himself, he'd laid down his weapon. And it nearly killed him. Could that same man have hurt someone in the past?

"Rose Kynaston," said Ellie Trevelyan. "Bold decision, coming here." Another officer shouted Ellie's name from across the room, and they communicated with hand signals. My phone buzzed. I'd missed three calls. I glanced at the text that had just arrived.

Meredith: *Police have taken me in for questioning. Dropped Aled at Hurtwood House with Gwendoline. The road is flooding, but she said they'll be safe. Sorry.*

"Did you have something to say, Rose?" said Sergeant Trevelyan.

Gwendoline can't look after Aled: she doesn't know a real person from a hallucination.

Sergeant Trevelyan frowned at my camera. "You aren't reporting on this?" If I told her about the car, she'd make me stay to give a statement. I had to get to Aled.

"Does Dylan have a lawyer?" I said.

"He's been offered the duty solicitor."

"Okay then." I picked up my bag.

"You blagged your way into a press conference to ask that?"

"I've been worried."

"Is there something you need to tell me?"

Around me, cameramen dismantling their tripods made the cracking sounds of gunfire in the desert. "Only that . . . Dylan saved my life. We got kidnapped in Mogadishu, Somalia, when we were working there. There was a guard, just a kid. The kidnapper treated him worse than us, screaming at him, slapping him upside the head. He was terrified—"

"What has this got to do with—"

"On the first night, Dylan worked a brick out of the wall. Pried it loose with his fingers until they bled. It was just the kid and us, the others had gone to prayer, so we made a plan. I'd call for water, and when the kid opened the door, Dylan would smash him with the brick. I called and the kid came. He was too trusting, stepped right into the room, turned his back to Dylan. It was perfect. Dylan raised the brick right over the kid's head. I wanted him to do it. To hit him. Even though the boy was innocent, just as much of a victim as we were, in fact, because he would never get out of that place. But still, I wanted Dylan to hurt him. I would have done anything to get out. Anything at all."

Sergeant Trevelyan nodded.

"But Dylan dropped the brick on the bed. He couldn't do it. Said it wasn't the kid's fault. Do you see?"

Ellie nodded again.

"Dylan didn't hurt Rhys Dourish. Or Shawna Dourish. He couldn't."

Ellie opened her mouth to speak, but I cut her off: her eyes told me all I needed to know. They reminded me of the conflicted gaze of the kid in Somalia. How could a boy deny the word of God? How could Sergeant Ellie Trevelyan question the law? Both of them afraid they might let a guilty man walk free. I headed to my car. I needed to reach Hurtwood House before floodwater stranded Aled with his sick grandmother. And I needed to show Ellie that these deaths had nothing to do with my husband.

CHAPTER 37

"So why didn't you go up to Cambridge, Dylan?" DI Harrow glanced at Ellie's hands, which were resting on the police file. On cue, she opened the folder and flicked through photographs of Kenny Bale. She laid them one by one in a fan shape on the table, feeling like the world's most sour-faced croupier.

Dylan's voice remained steady. If the photos distracted him, he didn't show it. He was earnest. Helpful. Emotional at times, but appropriately so. Even his lawyer glanced often at his profile, subconsciously flashing her eyebrows at his handsome face. Dylan looked a lot like his father, who Ellie had responded to in the same primal way a generation ago. *We're just apes,* she thought, *highly trained apes. In evolutionary terms, no more sophisticated than the people who built the holm. Eat, breed, kill if necessary. Repeat for three thousand years until the process becomes so streamlined we hardly notice it anymore.*

Focus, Trevelyan.

Why hadn't Dylan gone to Cambridge? He was explaining that when his father got blamed for Kenny Bale and died soon after, he wanted to get away from Hurtwood.

"Cambridge is a long way from Hurtwood," Harrow said.

"But people I knew were going. School friends. Well, not friends, more like acquaintances."

"Such as?" Ellie prompted. As Dylan counted off names, her lips pursed. At the school she'd attended—also in Hurtwood, but at the less prestigious end of town—precisely zero pupils had gone to Cambridge. Ever. The Canon High School. The kids from Dylan's school—who were now politicians and lawyers and newspaper editors, the architects of society—used to call it the Cannon Fodder School.

"Giles Hotchen got a place," said Dylan.

That name again, Ellie thought.

"And my girlfriend at the time, Meredith Fiddler. She went to Hurtwood Girls' Grammar."

"But you wanted to get away from your peer group?"

"Yes, I—" Dylan glanced away. The psychology of someone looking to the creative side of the brain for a convincing lie. According to the textbooks. "I'd tried to split up with Meredith once, but . . ." Dylan gave a single huff of laughter. "She reminded me of Anne Boleyn. Does that make sense? Same ruthless ambition. I told her that once, and she thought it was a compliment." Dylan tipped his head back again. *Remembering? Fabricating?* "I tried to finish with her before the Kenny Bale thing happened, but she spread horrible lies about me. After a while, we drifted back together. That's the trouble with a small town, you can't get away from one another; it's like everyone's floating around in a bathtub."

"Circling the drain?" said Ellie, and felt Harrow's side-eye like a flick on the ear.

"With all the logic of a teenager, I figured that if we went to the same university," Dylan went on, "I'd have to keep going out with her, or she'd tell everyone about my father and Kenny Bale. I'd be saddled with it—or her—forever. So, I didn't go." He ended on a shrug.

Harrow leaned forward with his elbows on the desk. "You gave up Cambridge for that?"

Dylan held out both hands. "My father was accused of being a pedophile who drove a child to suicide. Is that how you'd like to be introduced at a party?"

Ellie cut in with a question. "If the media treated your family badly, why did you become a journalist?"

"To do it better," Dylan said without hesitation.

"And do you?"

"I'm principled, yes."

"There are a few of us left." Harrow glanced to the door and gave a nod. A young constable carried in a tray of toffee-colored tea. Harrow picked up a packet of sugar and gave it a rough shake. "Tell me about Shawna Dourish."

Dylan took a plastic cup but didn't drink. "She was our neighbor."

"She sold Low Farm to Tony Thorn and moved away in July 1999?"

"Sounds about right."

"Did Shawna Dourish influence your decision to split up with Meredith?"

Dylan sighed. "Did Meredith tell you that? It's the same lie she spread when we split up the first time."

"Tell us the truth, then."

"Meredith told everyone I fancied Shawna Dourish. A Mrs. Robinson thing. Looking back, Shawna was younger than I am now, a 'yummy mummy,' I suppose we'd call her today. She used to wear floral dresses over her wellies, kind of demure but busty, like something out of the 1950s. Meredith used to call her Wilma Flintstone."

"Was she aware of it—her allure? Did she flaunt it?"

"I didn't think so, but she probably caught me staring at her cleavage. I'm sure she was aware of more than I realized. Looking back, all the women were more aware than I realized." Dylan's shoulders folded into his chest like wings, the first time he'd looked uncomfortable. "Meredith started calling me Nasty Boy. From Ky-NAST-on, you know.

It was a punishment, I guess, after I dumped her. Or maybe she just couldn't accept that I would walk away from the smartest and prettiest girl in town, so she had to invent an explanation."

"Her explanation was that you were in a sexual relationship with your neighbor, your mother's friend, Shawna Dourish?"

Dylan shifted back in his chair, unfolding his shoulders. "Yes, I think it's fair to say that, regarding Shawna Dourish, Meredith's jealousy may have got the better of her."

CHAPTER 38

My car radio hummed with reports of flooding. Surreally, it wasn't even raining, but the wettest winter on record had saturated the land, and water draining down from higher ground had overwhelmed the river. Its banks burst like a bag of corn with a sharp knife run down its side.

Floodwater had inundated the pastureland surrounding the Grim's Holm, and I had to abandon the car at the ghostly dip, which was as deep as a pond. I continued on foot. Wind whipping across the surface raised white-crested waves, and the holm lived up to its name, looming like a mythical island. I thought of a mirage I'd reported on in my cub days, when the Chicago skyline appeared to hang over Lake Michigan, visible but impossible. A fata morgana, trick of the light, which had the power to lure sailors to their death. I blinked the memory away, but the holm remained. *Aled is safe,* I told myself. The flood would need to reach biblical proportions to threaten them up on the hill.

I splashed through ankle-deep water that pooled between the iron gates and climbed up the incline to dry land. I wanted to run, but the slope was steep. *Aled is safe at Hurtwood House.* I forced my cold muscles on. *Unless Gwendoline forgets and leaves him alone in the house, and he gets scared and runs outside and ends up at the Long Drop and—stop!*

I passed under the stone arch and jogged the final stretch. The side door was open, and I found myself in an empty kitchen. Aled's backpack was on the pine table. But no Aled. No Gwendoline. My wet jeans felt cold and tight, as did my heart. I opened the door to the interior, calling for them. The house absorbed my voice. An acrid tang dried my throat. Creeping along the passageway, I reached the stairs, eyeing my own damp footprints, which made it look as though I'd been followed.

Upstairs, the landing was a mess. Clothes were strewn along the corridor as if someone had undressed in a passion. And the tang was stronger, metallic on my tongue. I noticed a box with a broken bottom and realized its contents had dropped out as someone was carrying it. I bent down to pick up a flowery scarf, a long sock for wellington boots, a dress in floral fabric. The cotton smelled fungal, subterranean. I followed the trail to the attic door. Bags and boxes circled it like offerings at a shrine. Piles of books: I fingered faded copies of poetry and folklore. One linen-lined cover revealed a bookplate signed *Shawna*.

This is all Shawna's stuff.

I flipped open the lids of boxes, revealing a load of junk—floppy discs and shoeboxes containing curled-edge photos. Photos. And floppy discs.

There must have been hundreds of pictures. I got down amid the mess. Glossy ones were stuck together, others pockmarked by time. There were school portraits of a boy in uniform—Rhys, I assumed. His hands were folded in his lap, so I couldn't check for a missing finger, but it had to be him. I flicked past vacations and Christmases. Shots taken around the holm. Low Farm as it had been before Tony Thorn built the glass *monstrosity*—I had to disagree with Dylan on that point; the old house had been a hovel. But there was nothing that might shed light on the pictures Dylan said the police had found of him and Kenny Bale. Or even—my stomach clenched—him and Shawna Dourish.

If only I could access the floppy discs, but without an old-fashioned disc drive that would be impossible. I shifted them aside to give to the police. Underneath, lying on the bottom of the box, were several sheets of card. Printed photos. Blown-up copies, presumably, as no one printed snaps that large.

The first image showed a woman on a bed. I squinted. Long hair in a plait. *Meredith.* Only much younger, a teenager. And she was naked. *Why does Shawna have photos of Meredith?* I checked the lid of the cardboard box and saw *Rhys's Stuff* written in marker. Okay, that made slightly more sense. But *how* would Rhys have gotten photos of Meredith? Another picture showed her in a different position, also naked. Had he secretly photographed her? No, these pictures were posed. They weren't explicit—people share much more revealing stuff on Snapchat—but they were certainly private. I wondered who Meredith had trusted to photograph her like this.

The next image was taken from another angle, the other side of the room. There was a freestanding mirror in the shot. I lifted the image closer to my face. Someone was reflected in the mirror.

Dylan.

I had no idea how my husband's "artistic" pictures of his ex-girlfriend had come to be in Rhys's possession, and I didn't much care. I remembered Dylan's description of the photos the police showed him of Kenny Bale: *I'm definitely reflected in that mirror.* And here he was again, reflected in a mirror. How these images of Dylan and Meredith fit together with the images of Dylan and Kenny, I didn't have time to work out, but I got my phone and made copies. Then I called Sergeant Ellie Trevelyan. When she didn't answer right away, I WhatsApped the photos to her number. Instead of the disgust you might expect at finding your husband in nude pictures with another woman, I felt the heady delight of possibly clearing him of a murder charge.

CHAPTER 39

When Sergeant Ellie Trevelyan and DI Bryan Harrow reentered the interview room, she had a new batch of images in her folder.

"You've been gone a long time," Dylan said.

Harrow restarted the recorder, gave the necessary details in a low voice, then: "We received new information."

The silence was filled only by the whirring of the machine. Dylan gave in first: "Why are you so focused on Shawna Dourish?"

Ellie said quietly, "Do you have any idea whose remains we found in the barn?"

Another pause. Dylan this time, his face falling into a deep frown. "Your line of questioning is making me wonder if it was Shawna Dourish."

"How does that make you feel?"

"Sad. If it's true. And confused, because she's my mum's friend. My mother says Shawna still comes to visit."

"Recently?"

"Yes."

"You've seen her?"

"No, but my mother said—"

"Your mother may have dementia?"

Longer pause. Dylan rotated his plastic cup counterclockwise on the table, turning back time. "She's imagining it . . ."

"Looks that way."

"Bloody hell." Dylan scrubbed the frown off his face with the palm of one hand.

"Earlier, you said your girlfriend was jealous of Shawna Dourish. Why?"

"I had a crush on her. Schoolboy crush. She was the first woman I noticed, sexually, you know what I mean? That made it quite powerful, I suppose—the excitement, the confusion, the guilt—and even years later I went a little giddy around her. And Meredith noticed. There was nothing to be jealous of, not really—Shawna was my mum's friend. It never occurred to me that my crush might turn into something real. That we'd hook up. I didn't even know the phrase *hook up*."

Harrow nodded. "Did she encourage you?"

Dylan showed his palms. "She treated me like a boy. I was a year older than her son."

"Did she turn you down? Resist your advances?"

"I never made advances. In my mind, it was as much of a fantasy as hooking up with Debbie Harry from the Blondie poster on my bedroom wall."

Harrow turned the pages of the new file the techies had given him. "Why did Shawna Dourish sell Low Farm?" he asked. "She lived there all her life. Why leave?"

"Rural poverty isn't much fun. My dad patched up her roof because she couldn't afford to pay anyone. Meredith said Shawna made dresses out of curtains, and I thought she was being a bitch, but, you know, it might have been true. Then all of a sudden, Shawna sold the farm, and we didn't even know it was on the market. My mum said it had something to do with Rhys too. I didn't spend much time with him after we went to different schools. He went to the Canon; hated it."

The Cannon Fodder School. Ellie asked: "Was he bullied?"

"From what I heard, he was the bully. He had a knack for making himself unlikeable. He stank. He wore the same *Grand Theft Auto*

T-shirt all the time. The girls called him Sniffer. Because of the smell, but also because he sniffed around them like a dog, walking too close, pressing against them by the lockers, staring at their legs. If they complained, he'd get aggressively sexist. He'd call them things like *cock tease*, and if the boys told him to back off, he'd say they were pussy whipped. That kind of stuff. A nuisance. Shawna moved away to give him a fresh start. Or so we thought."

Harrow sat very still in his seat. "Did your father kill Rhys and Shawna?"

"No!"

"Did you kill them?"

"Absolutely not. Why would I—"

"Who else might want to kill them?"

"I don't know. Rhys was unpleasant, but not enough to kill him. And Shawna—definitely not, she was well-liked."

"And yet not a soul reported her missing."

"I don't remember her having any family. People thought she moved; they lost contact. This was before Facebook and the other one— what was it called?—Friends Reunited. It was easier then for people to just . . . leave. As I discovered myself."

"Shawna was an attractive single woman. She could be considered a threat?"

"To whom?"

"Your mother?"

"Dad spent most of that year in treatment for his heart. I don't think infidelity was on either of their minds."

"Rhys lived at Low Farm, right across the holm from Hurtwood House. You knew each other. He would have known secrets."

"What secrets?"

Ellie laid photos on the table. A child on a bed. An older boy reflected in a freestanding mirror. Harrow slid one picture across the table to Dylan, who deflected it with the back of a hand.

"I told you I don't know anything about that. I was never in that room with Kenny Bale. I never touched him, or photographed him, or knew anything about this." Dylan's body pitched forward as his gaze flitted between Harrow's face and the discarded image that had come to rest faceup.

"We know it's not you in the picture, Dylan," Harrow said.

"What?"

"Our technicians say the person in the mirror *is* you, but the whole photo is a composite image. Someone superimposed part of one image onto another. We have in our possession a photograph that shows you reflected in a mirror, which may have been used for the purpose. Did you ever take nude photos of another person?"

"Meredith! But those pictures disappeared, how the hell did you find them?"

"We have our sources."

"They disappeared not long after I took them. Meredith was livid, accused me of keeping them to show other people, which was untrue. I thought maybe my mum had found them and burned them, and I was too scared to ask so I just left it. Meredith and I split up over that for a while."

"Well, now you know. The composite image that we found on the floppy disc is ham-fisted by modern standards, but quite skilled for someone using Photoshop back in 1999."

"Someone made it look like I'm abusing Kenny Bale?"

Harrow said nothing. Dylan threw himself back in his seat as though a thought had struck him between the eyes.

"Then it couldn't have been my father who abused him because he never would have framed me. That's right, isn't it? You know who abused Kenny Bale, and it wasn't my father."

"The thing is, Dylan, I'm not investigating the death of Kenny Bale. I'm investigating the death of Rhys Dourish, aka Indiana Bones. And your photo was on the disc we found with his remains."

Dylan barely moved, but his chest deflated as the breath went out of him.

"So let's say you're right," Harrow went on. "Let's say someone else hurt Kenny, drove him to suicide, and then tried to frame you for it." Harrow leaned forward on his elbows. "Let's say this image was used to blackmail you, Dylan. What does that suggest?" A beat. "It suggests to me that you would have done anything necessary to destroy this picture. You would have gone to any lengths to protect yourself. Even murder."

CHAPTER 40

No reply from Ellie, but WhatsApp showed that the images had been received. I hoped the boy innocently photographing Meredith Fiddler—well, if not "innocently" then at least "legally"—would match the boy photographing Kenny Bale. *I knew those pictures had to be fake. I said so as soon as Dylan told me about them.* Now I had to trust Ellie to interpret them in the same way because I needed to concentrate on finding my son. I left Shawna's belongings on the landing and went into Gwendoline's bedroom. The acrid smell wasn't as strong here. The huge space was as clean as a fresh hotel room.

I shivered in a way that makes superstitious people claim that someone has walked on your grave. But I forced myself over to the bedside table. It had been cleared. No alarm clocks, no journal. Only the keys remained, one with a car fob and one with a house fob. The house key was an old iron thing, heavy in the hand. I picked up the car key too, thinking of the green Land Rover in the barn, and pocketed them both.

Where were Gwendoline and Aled? Why had she cleared her room and moved everything to the attic? If I could find her schedule in the journal, I'd know where she should be on the holm. She could be doing one of her many chores. Maybe she'd put the journal with Shawna's stuff? I went to the attic door, which opened without a sound.

My throat closed in response to a smell. *A stinky stink.* Burning. The stairs led to a narrow landing, and the smell drew me into a bare room that reminded me of our cell. On the far side, a small brazier stood in the fireplace, a metal garbage can with holes, like a homeless person might use to stay warm. Hot to the touch, a mulch that looked like tar pooled in the bottom. Beside it, more of Shawna's belongings. More flowery dresses, books with her name in them, envelopes addressed to Low Farm. *Gwendoline must have brought the stuff up to the attic to burn it.*

A hardcover notepad with an elephant on the front had been laid to one side.

Hunkering down, I gathered up Gwendoline's journal.

It was messed up, its pages crumpled, some torn out. Holding it upside down in my hands, I opened the back cover to straighten the paper. My fingers smoothed a sheet of handwriting. *What?* The last page of the journal had been written in; in fact, it was covered in text. As was the second-to-last page, and the one before it, and the one before that. The writing went on and on, sometimes a scrawl that covered a whole page and sometimes a verse inscribed onto the middle of a sheet, stranded like a holm in the river.

The journal was two books in one. At the front, with the elephant on the cover, bullet-point notes detailed Gwendoline's strict daily routine. But at the back, with a plain black cover, an inner world: quotes from books, stanzas of poetry, a stream-of-consciousness script that was so intense at times the words eroded the paper. Even the handwriting changed from a neat print at the front to a fluent cursive at the back. As though two minds pushed the same pen. I closed the journal and turned it between my palms. I felt as if I had Gwendoline's chin in my hand, turning her face from side to side to see asymmetrical profiles.

But this was a mystery that would have to wait. *I must find Aled.* Adrenaline sharpened my mind. They would be somewhere on the holm; Meredith had brought my son here, and the flooding prevented them from going elsewhere. I took the journal with me as I ran down through the house. *Where now?* Feeling like Mistress Payne in her eternal restlessness, I knew this is how I would spend the rest of my life if I let anything happen to my son. I slipped the journal into my bag and ran out into the wind.

At the flint barn, I broke the blue-and-white police tape and called for Gwendoline and Aled. Nothing. Worry nibbled my insides, not a biting panic—not yet—but a persistent gnawing. I hauled the door open. Stillness told me no one was there. Swags of cobweb hung like forlorn bunting. More police tape around the trapdoor, incongruously colorful in the drab light. A jumble of vehicles in the far corner. I went into the gloom, past the carcass of a tractor. And there was the green Land Rover. My heart gave a jolt, even though the sight of the vehicle came as no surprise. It was a jolt of acceptance; if Shawna died twenty years ago, then she hadn't been coming and going. Her car must have been here all along. And Gwendoline must have kept it running. *Why?* Maybe she used it to get around the holm—I'd seen it by the door of the barn. I recalled her saying the car was Shawna's *pride and joy.* Did she believe she was looking after it for Shawna? In which case, why store it in a dingy corner of a tumbledown barn? It felt more like it had been hidden.

I opened the driver's side door and smelled the same fungal air as the floral dress I'd found in the house. *Well, I can use it to get around the holm—I'll find Aled quicker that way.* I dug the key from my pocket and slipped behind the wheel. The engine started without complaint. I shifted into reverse and eased past the tractor to the barn doors. Only after I drove it outside did I consider that Shawna's car might be evidence. *Stupid!* I stopped on the gravel by the big house, left the key in the ignition, and ran toward the Long Drop, anxiety nipping at my heels.

Darting between trees, I climbed through the new fence to glance over the cliff. My stomach swirled as violently as the water that eddied below, a brown mass like the heads of people in a crowd. My relief at finding no sign of Aled was replaced by a new rush of anguish. I ran on toward the stables, my hot breath bouncing off the cold air. I found the ponies inside, their ears flickering with tension. It wasn't dark yet, which meant Gwendoline had put them away earlier than usual. *Why has she broken her routine?* This rang an alarm bell inside my head. I'd been relying on the idea that Gwendoline and Aled were somewhere on the holm, busy with her usual chores. But they could be anywhere. I staggered across the field until I saw Low Farm, the lights of its glass room glowing orange as twilight fell. Tony Thorn's home. The last place I'd have expected to find Gwendoline and yet the only place left to search.

CHAPTER 41

Sergeant Ellie Trevelyan felt the energy in the interview room ebb. Despite a deluge of questions, Kynaston left behind him answers as smooth as river stones. He'd been a foreign correspondent, made a living interviewing war criminals and unscrupulous African politicians and, indeed, their British counterparts. He gave little ground.

A rap on the door made Harrow announce a break and switch off the recording equipment. The grind of their chairs on concrete stung Ellie's ears. Outside in the corridor, the DI released a huge sigh. "He's a brick wall. My head hurts."

"The girlfriend is here," said his young colleague. "Meredith Fiddler."

"All right, let's give Kynaston time to juggle his thoughts. Hopefully, he'll drop a ball when we come back to him. Where is she?"

"Suite two. There's something else." The detective held out a photo. "Maybe Dylan Kynaston knew about the sword?"

"What bloody *sword*?"

Ellie squinted at the picture. "That's the La Tene sword, the one they found in the river during the televised dig. Came from Switzerland—two thousand years old, they said. Is it fake?"

"No, it's the real deal." The girl grinned. "But it came from prehistory via the internet. Amazing what you can buy on eBay."

Harrow studied the picture for a long moment, then slotted the sheet into the file. "All right, I can't work out where that fits in right now."

Ellie frowned. "The senior archaeologist on the dig—Morwenna something—she was calling it a hoax while they were filming. We should talk to her. And Tony Thorn is the show's producer, and he bought Low Farm from Shawna Dourish . . . there's another link."

"Bring him in." Harrow sent his detective to do the legwork. "Trevelyan, sit in on this interview with Meredith Fiddler. You know her history." They marched down the corridor.

"What did you think about Dylan?" he asked.

"Talked a lot about Meredith." Ellie shook her head at that. "I barely remember the name of my childhood sweetheart . . ."

Harrow nodded his head to one side. "I married mine."

"There's still something between them."

"Leftover feelings? Resentment? A secret?"

Ellie thought back to seeing the pair on Hurtwood's high street, Dylan's hand on Meredith's bicep. Flirting, so she thought, but what if it was something else? Not caressing her arm, but gripping it. A warning? And she thought of her father's words: *Dylan Kynaston. Nasty Boy they called him. Afterward.* Dylan had tried to run away from his reputation, but Meredith carried it like a recurring cold sore on her lovely lips. Dylan wouldn't like that . . .

"I don't know how, but it's got something to do with Giles Hotchen." Ellie told Harrow the brief details of what her father had said about the accident. "The problem is, my dad literally doesn't know what day of the week it is."

"My mum had Alzheimer's," said Harrow as they arrived outside suite two. "Bloody cruel." He slapped the file against his thigh. "She forgot all our names, but never forgot how to cook a roast dinner. Some things are ingrained."

"My dad was a copper for thirty years. Everything he does is ingrained."

"Then maybe we should listen to him." Harrow opened the door. In stark contrast to the airless room where Dylan would sweat it out until they returned, suite two was bright and comfortable. Meredith perched on the edge of a sofa, one hand on her bag as though she didn't expect to stay long. After performing the legalities, Harrow warmed Meredith up with chitchat—Ellie noticed she was big on eye contact—then Harrow looked out the window for a moment. Meredith studied his face, but Harrow instead turned to Ellie.

"Were you already in the force in July 1999, Sergeant Trevelyan?"

"I've been a police officer in Hurtwood for almost twenty-five years, so . . ." Ellie widened her eyes at her own longevity.

Harrow now turned to Meredith. "Sergeant Trevelyan tells me that three unusual things happened in Hurtwood in July 1999, all within the space of forty-eight hours. On 21 July, a boy named Kenny Bale died after falling from rocks near Hurtwood House."

"The Long Drop," Ellie said. "That's the name of the place where he died."

"Event number one: Kenny Bale died at the Long Drop on 21 July. Two days later, on 23 July, event number two: Shawna and Rhys Dourish went to the notary in Hurtwood to complete the sale of Low Farm to Tony Thorn. We have no sightings of them after that meeting. Event number three occurred an hour later, just after 6:00 p.m.: Giles Hotchen rode his bike under a truck on the high street. Your boyfriend at the time, Dylan Kynaston, had links to all of these people: Kenny Bale, who trained with Dylan's father; Shawna and Rhys Dourish, who lived on the holm; Giles Hotchen, who went to school with Dylan."

Meredith nodded, earnestly. Her hand reached up to her trademark plaits.

"Let's work backward. Can you tell us what happened between Dylan and Giles on that day?"

"I already helped the police with their inquiries. And I told Sergeant Trevelyan when we spoke about it the other day. Dylan and I drove to Wales right after school."

Harrow selected a stapled sheaf of papers from the file. "I'd like to go over it again. Just to recap your statement from 1999."

"Is that the original?" Meredith's eyes flitted between the paperwork and Harrow. "You'd think they'd be computerized."

"Can you recap your movements on 23 July 1999?"

"Dylan picked me up after school—"

"What time?"

"As soon as we got out, so we'd have left Hurtwood by four, latest."

"Where did he pick you up?"

"He used to park in a side road."

"Which road did he park on that day?"

"Whipping Post Lane."

"Go on."

"We drove to Abersoch, where my parents had a place."

Ellie read out the exact address of the holiday cottage. "That's a drive of approximately three hours, less if the road is clear."

"His car was slow."

"Really? Because in your original statement"—Harrow flipped a page—"you said, *We took the route via Shrewsbury and across Snowdonia; we didn't hit any traffic and arrived in plenty of time for supper.* What time do you have supper, Meredith?"

"Normal time."

"Normal time. Most people think of suppertime as, say, between six and eight. Unless you live in Madrid. Would you agree?"

"Yes."

"We know you were there in Abersoch." Harrow pulled out another statement, which he flipped open to a highlighted section and laid on the table for Meredith to read. Ellie watched the woman's fingers scramble through her hair. "This statement from a neighbor confirms it.

She watched the two of you on the patio eating fish and chips. *Beautiful couple*, she said, *they lit candles and everything*." Meredith's fingers fell still. "Why did you light candles before eight o'clock on a July night?"

"Maybe it was a little later, by the time we got the fish and chips."

Harrow slapped the neighbor's statement. Meredith startled, her fingers dragging loose a long twist of hair. "We both know it doesn't get dark until late in the summer. If you want, I can google the precise time of sunset on 23 July 1999 to confirm that you weren't eating fish and chips by candlelight until much later than you swore to the police. Look, I need to know what happened that night. Why you covered for Dylan. It's clear the two of you left Hurtwood later than you said, and that has implications on an investigation into a suspicious death. It's serious, Meredith. If you want me to come after you for perjury, then I will, if that's what it takes to find out where Dylan Kynaston was that night."

Meredith laid both hands flat on the table. She consulted the ceiling for inspiration and, after a beat, tapped all ten fingers. "Dylan asked me to give him an alibi. Earlier that day, Giles Hotchen told the headmaster of Hurtwood Boys' School that Dylan had put"—her nose wrinkled in disgust—"feces on his car. Giles told everyone Dylan did it. Nobody really believed it, but that wasn't the point. When Giles's accident happened a couple of hours later, Dylan thought he'd get the blame, that people would think he'd done something to get back at Giles. So we pretended we left for Wales before Giles got hurt. That's what happened. I don't know anything about Kenny Bale, though, or the Dourishes."

"Tell me about Giles's accident."

Meredith tried to push the errant curl back into the plait with one finger. "I don't know where to start."

"Take your time."

"I was at the flat with him. The one on Cheapside. I met him after school, and we stayed for an hour or so, smoked a bit, but then he wouldn't let me go out the front door onto the street, so I went out the back way—you used to be able to climb through a window onto the fire escape and down to Whipping Post Lane. As I was climbing down, Dylan was coming up. He was steaming because he'd just been dragged in to see the headmaster. He was on his way to confront Giles, when he noticed I'd been crying."

Harrow spoke gently now. "Can you back up a little? Why wouldn't Giles let you out the front door?"

Meredith drew in a ragged breath. "People think the head injury changed Giles Hotchen, and I'm sure it did in some ways. But he was always . . ." The taut fingers of her hands pressed together to form a cage. "He had a side that he didn't let people see, but I think they sensed it, and that's why he wasn't popular."

"What kind of side?"

"It's hard to explain. He came up with nicknames for everyone— Nasty Boy for Dylan, Brains for this idiot who smashed his car into a tree. He tried calling himself Hottie, but it didn't catch on because, frankly, he wasn't. When the other boys bantered, he could only quote from television scripts and memorized jokes. None of it was spontaneous." She straightened up. "That was the thing about Giles; it was like he was acting a part. He only wanted me because Dylan loved me, and envy was the closest Giles got to an emotion. Looking back, I genuinely think he was a psychopath."

Ellie wanted to go back to the mention of *Hottie*, but didn't dare stop Meredith's flow.

"A lot of insecure people hide behind a facade," Harrow said.

"He wasn't insecure. Quite the opposite. He thought everyone was stupid. Too stupid to recognize his innate superiority. I read a book about serial killers, and that's a sign of a psychopath. Not that I'm suggesting he was a serial killer, just that the bike accident didn't change him; he was always a control freak."

"Is that why he wouldn't let you go out of the front door?" Ellie asked. "Because he was controlling?"

"We had an argument, and I was upset, and he didn't want anyone to see me and report back to his father."

"Can you tell us about the argument?"

Meredith traced her plaits. "He tried to get off with me, like he always did, and I let him kiss me for a bit, but this time he wouldn't stop. Normally, when I started to, you know, shrink away—signal that I didn't want to go any further—he'd get the message. But his mood had changed. I don't know what it was; maybe he'd smoked more than usual, or maybe it was the end of term and he knew he wouldn't get another chance. But I could tell the moment he started pawing my buttons that something was different. He wasn't going to stop, so I just . . ." Meredith looked down. Her thumbs battled each other in her lap.

"Can you go on?" Ellie said.

"I just let him."

"He raped you?" Ellie asked.

"No, I let him get it over with quickly because I didn't want it to turn nasty. It doesn't make me a loser or a victim; I know loads of women who've taken the easy way out."

Ellie pressed her lips together. Harrow said, "It doesn't sound consensual."

"That's what Dylan said when he found me on the fire escape. Well, he didn't use the word *consensual*—we didn't know that word or even the concept back then—but he said it sounded like Giles had forced himself on me. He got all chivalrous about it." Meredith rapped her knuckles once on the table. "Anyway, that's what happened. And I just wanted to get out of there and go home and enjoy the summer and go up to Cambridge, where bloody Giles Hotchen would be going too, but I didn't want to think about that on a fine summer's evening on the last day of school. I just wanted to get away from that disgusting little flat. And then Dylan was right there on Whipping Post Lane, climbing up when I needed to climb down, and I ended up telling him, and he was so angry he was spitting, so I told him not to go inside or he'd end up killing Giles, and it wasn't worth the hassle of prison." Meredith gave a dry laugh. "So we both climbed down, and I said, *Let's get out of Hurtwood*, and we got in his car and drove to my parents' place in Wales. And that was it. End of story."

"Why didn't you go to the police?" Harrow said.

"That's why." Meredith pointed a fingernail at Harrow. "That's why. Because I knew it would be my fault somehow. I knew I shouldn't have gone to his skanky flat. I knew I shouldn't have played him off against Dylan. I knew I shouldn't have accepted his drinks or smoked his weed. I knew I should go to the police, or he'd end up doing it to someone else. I knew all of that, but I thought bad things like that didn't happen to strong women, so either I wasn't a strong woman or it wasn't all that bad. I was wrong, but that was what I thought at the time. In my defense, I was only fucking eighteen. Clever enough for Cambridge, but naive as that question you just asked me."

"I didn't mean to imply it was your fault, and I'm sorry I phrased the question badly," Harrow said. Meredith responded with a curt nod. "Did Dylan suggest going to the police?"

"He wanted to get away from Hurtwood."

Harrow tilted his head. "But, Meredith, this is what bothers me: First, Giles Hotchen told everyone that Dylan crapped on the headmaster's car. Then Giles forced himself on Dylan's girlfriend—you. Two reasons for Dylan to want revenge. Why didn't he go to the police and get Hotchen strung up like he deserved? Is there another reason Dylan didn't call the police?"

Meredith hesitated a moment too long.

"I think one of you was involved in Giles Hotchen's accident."

Meredith stared out the window, eye contact lost. Her nod was barely perceptible.

"For the tape, the witness is nodding. Can you elaborate, Meredith?"

"I don't know exactly what he did—"

"Dylan?"

"Yes. After I told him what Giles did, Dylan was raging. He wanted to go inside the flat, but I stopped him, almost pushed him down the

fire escape. While I was climbing down myself, I heard all this clatter-
ing. Dylan had got hold of Giles's bike—which we knew cost more
than Dylan's car because Giles was always gloating about it—and he
was ramming the front tire against a wall, and then he pushed it over
and hauled it back up by the cables. And Giles came out to find Dylan
trashing his bike and, of course, they ended up fighting."

"In Whipping Post Lane?"

"Yes. Pushing and shoving each other. They were terrible fighters;
no one even managed to land a punch. It would have been comical
except"—she gasped another ragged breath—"except Giles got Dylan
up against the fire escape with his hands on Dylan's throat, so I grabbed
the bike and rammed it into the back of his legs. Giles buckled and
released Dylan, who fell on the ground, choking. And Giles didn't even
hesitate to see if he was breathing—he grabbed his bike and rode off
down Whipping Post Lane. He cycled straight onto the high street and
straight under that truck. It was all over in half a minute."

"And you think one of you damaged the bike?"

"The brakes, I guess. But we had no intention . . ." Her hands fell
still in her lap.

"And then what did you do?"

"We went to Wales."

"You kept this secret between the two of you?"

Meredith shrugged one shoulder. "One other person knows. Dylan
was upset. He felt responsible even though he hadn't meant to hurt
Giles. So he called home to find out if anyone knew Giles's condition.
We never dreamed he'd be so badly hurt . . ." She waved one hand to
encapsulate a life changed by serious head injuries.

"So who else knew what happened?"

"His mother. Gwendoline. She was the one who told us to pretend
we'd left right after school. She knew all along that we caused Giles's
accident, and never said anything."

CHAPTER 42

I leaned my full body weight on Tony Thorn's bell. It rang with the exasperated air of a fussy old man. His front door was peppered with black iron studs like something from Tudor times. Maybe it was from Tudor times. I pressed the bell again. The old-fashioned lock was huge, big enough to take my pinkie finger. I thought of the iron key I'd found on Gwendoline's bedside table. Did she keep a spare to Low Farm? I pulled it from my pocket, and it turned in the lock with a clunk. I stepped inside Thorn's home.

"Hello?"

My voice echoed off the hard surfaces of a shelf filled with television awards, arranged right inside the door. Thorn didn't want anyone to remain unaware of his success. I followed a light to the glass atrium and found myself inside his dining room, where a table gleamed with places set for ten diners. Instead of a view over the road, where Thorn must have seen our headlights on the night we first arrived at the holm, I saw only water and the Wrekin rising like a shark's fin in the flood.

"Thorn?" I went through to the kitchen amid a scene of disarray like the one in the great house; clothes and shoes were strewn over the flagstones. I went to the foot of a stairwell, but going upstairs felt like an intrusion too far. I'd hoped Thorn might have seen Aled and Gwendoline. At a stretch, they might be here. But the house seemed abandoned, the mess giving it a jilted air. As though Thorn had left in a hurry.

Has he taken them somewhere? How would anyone get off the holm through the flood?

I went back to the atrium. It was strange to hear nothing of the outside world, not the circling water, the thrashing trees, the crying buzzards. Thorn had conspired to capture the real world, mute it, and put it under his control. I recalled seeing this room from the road and thinking it had to be a place of hospitality, but now I felt a dread so strong it was like I had woken up in a fairy-tale house made of candy. Outside, the light was fading fast.

I had to find them.

I pulled out Gwendoline's journal. To find Aled, I needed to find Gwendoline, and I had her daily schedule right here. I flicked open the front of the book. It was almost time to put the ponies away, but she'd done that already. Her timetable was shot. I turned to the back of the book instead, flipping past stark, isolated phrases—*I may forget, but I feel*—and torn-out scraps that she'd pasted in. *Last night I dreamed I went to Manderley again. Land as had been cursed. The devil wants for a new servant.* Snatches of stories like the voices of strangers on the street, distracting but meaningless. I flipped past them all until something caught my eye:

To my precious Dylan

The letter was dated just a few days ago.

> *You're back, my precious boy, and now the holm is flooding again. It's been almost twenty years since the last one, which makes it twenty years since you left. We are an island once more. Strange, what comes to the surface in a flood.*

For years, I tried to forget that flood, and now, here I am, hoping I can remember. They say old people live in the past, but they've got it wrong, I live in a perpetual present. The events of that night flap around my mind like a bird trapped in a greenhouse. Maybe I'm the one who's trapped. But I never want you to get stuck here, so I'm writing this to set you free.

Now that you're a father, you understand what we'll do for our children. Raising a child is like caring for Hurtwood House. You never own it, you merely shepherd it toward the next generation. I was your mother, your confidant. I hope I have been a good shepherd.

I'm straying off topic—like a sheep! I have to focus before I forget. Why do I write this letter, Dylan? Now that you're here, why not tell you? That's the nub of it—I'm a coward, hiding up here on my hill, gutless. "Cowards die many times," Shakespeare said, which is true because every time I remember what I did on the night of the flood I die of shame.

But you're no coward, Dylan; that's why I've never been able to look you in the face and tell you what you need to know. You owned up to your mistake. You phoned me that night—after Giles got hurt—and you were brave enough to admit what you did. And how did I respond? I sent you off to Wales, into hiding. Poor boy, you were always hiding.

But I can't hide anymore. I have to tell you about the night of the flood. Because if a place has flooded once, it will flood again, and it will keep on flooding. That night haunts me. I thought I could keep it hidden, but I'm weak now, and my grip is starting to slip. The police are here. They know. So you need to know too. Here it is, Dylan.

It's fresh and bloody in my mind, I've been picking it like a scab, so I'll write quickly before I forget.

On the night of the flood, you go to Wales with Meredith. I don't tell your father about Giles Hotchen. Stanley's grieving for Kenny Bale, and that's enough for him. It's late in the day, but he can't rest; he's like one of those windup toys that keeps marching even when it's hard up against a wall. He's down in the cellar in the barn, and I'm grooming the foal, Morgana. Sweet-natured thing, I'm not sure the name suits her. Then Shawna arrives, haring into the barn in her Land Rover, so fast that Morgana tugs on her rope in fear. Stanley comes up from the cellar, head and shoulders popping through the hatch in the floor, hammer in hand.

Rhys is with Shawna even though we asked her to keep him away. Stanley looks at me and shakes his head. He can't believe she would bring Rhys to our home after everything we told her about Kenny Bale.

Yes, I should have started with Kenny. You don't know about that. A week before the flood, Kenny told us what Rhys had been doing. Sniffer—did you know that's what the kids at the Canon school called Rhys? Horrible name, but it suited him. Rhys—Sniffer—took Kenny into our barn to show him pictures. Disgusting pictures; we found them stashed in the hay later. Stanley wanted to go to the police. Those pictures aren't legal, he said, some of them show kids.

It was me who said we should tell Shawna. I'll talk to her, I said, one mother to another. She'll do the right thing. But I was a coward even then. We don't like talking about child abuse, do we? Hardly dare say it aloud. Pornography. Pedophilia. The words feel dirty, as though we're dirty just thinking them. I should have been brave enough to march her down to the police station in Hurtwood and say those words aloud. But I wasn't. I didn't. And neither did she.

On the day of the flood, she gets out of the Land Rover in her best dress, the one she made from the Liberty print curtains. I've sold up, she announces. City fella— more money than sense. We cleared the house this morning. You can keep the key and give it to the new fella.

I ask where she's going.

Her eyes dart to Rhys, and I know then that she's running away. I remember feeling angry, and I see from the way Stanley is tapping the hammer against his thigh that he's angry too, but I also feel sorry for her. She looks jaded; she's losing her bloom, I think. Pretty as she is, time won't be kind to her. But I was wrong there too—she proves to be perennial, coming back year after year from under the earth. Another coward, dying many deaths.

If only we'd marched Rhys to the police station when Stanley wanted. We would've saved Kenny. We might've saved Stanley too, because the guilt stopped his heart. And, I suppose, we'd have saved Shawna and Rhys. But I made Stanley wait. So I only have myself to blame.

That's why I'm writing this letter, Dylan. Forgive me for hiding the truth for so long, but I'm not such a coward that I'd let anyone blame you for Kenny. You're a good boy with a good heart. The police will see that, my love, as do I.

The letter was signed. The following pages were blank. I laid the journal on Thorn's dining table, rattling his china.

Rhys. *Sniffer.* Shawna's son abused Kenny Bale.

Gwendoline's letter wouldn't count for much in a court of law. And it didn't tell us how both boys—Kenny and Rhys—ended up dead. But Dylan needed to see it. I glanced over it one more time, growing colder with each line. *I was your mother, your confidant.* The letter had the air of a suicide note. If so, where was Gwendoline now? *And where is Aled?* I stuffed the journal into my bag and called Dylan's number, but he didn't pick up. I called Sergeant Trevelyan again, glancing up the hill to the great house. A strange light hung over the roof. An aura. The glow of heat.

I disconnected the call.

Then I was running toward the summit of the Grim's Holm, where the burning roof of Hurtwood House shot distress flares into the night sky.

CHAPTER 43

Sergeant Ellie Trevelyan kept her phone pressed to her ear while her father, on the other end, continued his monologue. Her phone beeped for an incoming call: Rose Kynaston, who would have to wait because Ellie needed to ask Jim a question right away. His waterlogged garden was making him agitated. His trembling fingers tapped against the handset as though his unconscious mind was sending a coded message to help it escape.

"Dad?"

"Too much of a good thing," he said.

"Dad."

"Too much."

"Dad! I need to ask you about Hottie."

His breath hard down the line. Dash, dot, dot, dash went his fingers against the handset.

"Who is Hottie, Dad?"

"Been keeping my eye on 'em. All in my logbook."

"What's in your logbook, Dad?"

"Times and dates. Visits."

"Whose visits?"

"Hottie. It's in my logbook, sweet, his times and dates. Someone needs to keep an eye on the young girl. Too much of a good thing—that's it, Giles Hotchen."

Ellie let Jim ramble while she typed Giles's name into the vehicle database. He owned a stable of cars, including a Range Rover with a personalized license plate: *HOTT 11EE*. Ellie swore under her breath and told her dad she had to get back to work. He put the phone down immediately.

"Trevelyan?" Harrow called as he strode past the incident room. "I'm going back in with Kynaston."

"I'll catch you up. One minute." Ellie called the duty inspector to request CCTV from outside the Nail Bar and any cameras that showed its rear entrance on Whipping Post Lane. Then she texted Robert Elks and told him to visit her father and consult Jim's logbook for sightings of a Range Rover, license plate *HOTT 11EE*, then come to the station and lean on the duty inspector for the CCTV footage. Then she texted Rose to say she'd return her call as soon as she could. Then she muted her phone.

Too much of a good thing, Ellie thought as she trotted down to the interview room to join Harrow. Giles Hotchen had been able to get away with too much for too long.

Back in the dismal room with Dylan Kynaston, Sergeant Ellie Trevelyan laid a photo on the table. Dylan silently studied the green patina of an ancient sword.

Harrow said: "So you arrive back in England, walk into a job with Tony Thorn, and then this valuable artifact is found on the Grim's Holm, right where you live."

Dylan's lawyer interrupted. "To clarify, this is a photograph of the actual sword they found in the river during the archaeological dig? And it was found near the remains of Rhys Dourish?"

"It had been buried in mud on the riverbank above the submerged remains."

"But why?" said Dylan.

"You tell me. Why were you digging there in the first place?"

"The location of the dig was decided before I joined, months ago. The team scoped out the sites to make sure there was archaeology ready to be *discovered*." Dylan made quote marks in the air. "Obviously, television is stage managed—everyone knows that. At the river, there were magnetic readings, evidence of timber piles that could be prehistoric, probably a jetty. But no one was expecting human remains. Or a sword."

"The sword was Iron Age. Made in Switzerland." Harrow folded his arms across his chest.

"Fascinating." Dylan didn't sound sarcastic; he was studying the photo with interest. "I went all over the holm with a metal detector when I was a boy, but never ventured down to the river. I thought that explained why I'd never found it."

"It wasn't there. This sword was purchased from a collector last year and the trail leads to none other than—" Harrow held out his palms.

"Tony Thorn," Dylan said in a flat voice.

"Your groundbreaking archaeological dig—if you'll excuse my pun—was a hoax."

"Thorn buried the sword to make it look like *The Quest* made a big discovery?" Dylan covered his face with both hands.

"My colleague spoke to Morwenna, the senior archaeologist, and she reckons the hoard of coins was also fake. They originate from different eras hundreds of years apart. It's not a hoard, it's a collection. A collection that Thorn purchased and planted."

Dylan groaned through his hands, a curiously sheeplike bleat. "She was right."

"Morwenna?"

"No, my mother. For all that she's losing her marbles, she was right that Thorn was up to something."

"Did you know about the hoax?"

"This ridiculous scam? No, I did not. Thorn offered me a job, and I realized straightaway that he only brought me on board to win my mother round. But there was no way she was ever going to let him dig inside the barn—" Dylan stopped abruptly.

"Why would your mother oppose an excavation of her barn?"

"She thinks Thorn wants to force her to sell Hurtwood House. If the barn got listed as a historic building, she'd have to pay for its upkeep, which she couldn't afford. It's not the first time he's bought a house at a rock-bottom price from an impoverished woman."

"That's a convincing explanation. Or maybe she didn't want anyone to find the body of Shawna Dourish?"

"No, no, no." Dylan thought about it for a few seconds. "If my mother knew her friend was dead, why would she keep talking as though she were alive?"

"If everyone thinks she's alive, no one's looking for her body," said Harrow.

Ellie's head reeled with thoughts of Gwendoline Kynaston. She'd heard the gossip. She'd heard people say her dementia was a sham. Ellie had little affection for the woman, but maybe they were right? *A woman with dementia could never face trial.* And what about Stanley? Ellie had felt sure he wasn't capable of murder, but what if they had been in it together, Gwendoline and Stanley Kynaston, like Fred and Rose West or the Moors murderers? What if—?

"Where were you on the evening of 23 July 1999?" Harrow asked.

"1999? That's so long ago—"

"It's the day Giles Hotchen had an accident. If that jogs your memory."

If Dylan was rattled, he didn't show it. "It does, yes. Our last day of school. I went to Wales with my girlfriend, M—"

"Meredith's in the interview suite down the corridor. She told us about the false alibi."

The only reaction on Dylan's face was a slight flare of the nostrils. "Look, I never meant to hurt—"

"We don't care about Hotchen. That was the last day Rhys and Shawna Dourish were seen. We think they died that evening. And we know you were in Hurtwood, not in Wales. So tell us what happened to Rhys and Shawna."

"I don't know, I swear. I was in town the whole day. At school, then Giles's flat, then we drove to Wales."

"You phoned your mother."

"Did I?"

"Meredith says you did. You told your mother that you caused Giles's accident."

Dylan's mouth hung open for a moment. Then he closed it. "She never forgave me."

"Your mother?"

Dylan nodded. "What I did must have disgusted her because she changed that day." Dylan snapped his fingers. "Shut down, just like that. She did her duty as a mother—she never turned me in—but a spark went out when she lost her perfect son."

"Maybe something else happened that day. How did she sound when you phoned?"

"I can hardly remember."

"I don't believe you." Harrow folded his arms. "Must have been the worst phone call of your life, having to tell your mother you nearly killed someone."

Dylan stared into the middle distance, his eyes flickering as though studying someone's face. "She was angry the moment she picked up the phone because I'd promised to help my dad build a fence, and then, of course, I hadn't come home after school. He was trying to do it by himself, and she said he was going to work himself to death. This was right after Kenny Bale died, and I think that was exactly what he was trying to do."

"Work himself to death?" Ellie said.

"He blamed himself for Kenny's accident—we still thought it was an accident then—he kept saying, *I should have done more.* I think he meant he should have built a fence across the Long Drop; he'd been meaning to do it for years. So when I phoned, Mum was annoyed I hadn't come home to help. I could hardly get a word in edgeways, and when I managed to explain what happened to Giles she went very quiet. I remember her saying: *Don't tell your father, the shame will kill him.*"

Ellie's phone buzzed with a text from Rose Kynaston: *Help me.* Ellie turned the phone to show Harrow, and he nodded. Outside in the corridor, she called Rose. The voice on the line was strained, breathless. She recognized the accent, but not the tone of anguish: "You have to help me!"

"Where are you?" Ellie heard a rushing sound that could be water. Or wind.

"I'm at the holm. I need help."

"Where's Gwendoline?"

The rushing sound turned into a roar, and Ellie realized it wasn't water or wind—it was flames.

"Gwendoline's in the great house. It's on fire. She's inside, and she's got Aled with her."

CHAPTER 44

The fire seemed to have sentience, a purpose. Flames chittered through a skein of dead ivy like a swarm of critters, circling the house, looking for a way in. I held Gwendoline's coat and Aled's soccer scarf, which I'd found lying just inside the kitchen door. They hadn't been there when I searched the house before. Gwendoline and Aled must have come back after I set off around the holm. I threw her coat into the kitchen, where it could go to hell amid the swirling smoke. *Stupid woman; where is my son?* I stood on the threshold and screamed their names. Nothing. The fire raged overhead.

I looked around as though help might be idling in the trees. They bent sideways in the wind, clinging to a world that was spinning too fast. The same wind fanned the flames. Sergeant Trevelyan had said she would alert the firefighters, but how long would they take? Tinkling glass was followed by the husky woof of flame feeding on air. Too long; help would take too long to arrive.

There was nothing to do but go in. I ran around the outside of the house. There was no ivy on the cold north side, so it wasn't burning as fiercely. Despite a growing panic, I felt myself coldly note that the vehicles were parked up out of harm's way—no risk of explosions.

If I can stay calm, I can do this.
I have to do this.

I ran to the Land Rover and draped Aled's scarf over the side mirror for safekeeping. He'd want it back without a stinky stink. I removed my own scarf and soaked the wool in a puddle, then squeezed it out and tied it around my face. In the trunk of the Land Rover, I scrabbled through the tire-changing kit until I found a metal tool. Running to the front door, I jammed it between the wood and the stone lintel, and put my weight behind it. The door burst open. A rush of smoke pushed me back onto the gravel with the force of a hand in my chest. My eyes streamed. I blinked away tears, and as my sight swam, I recalled my earlier vision: hands pressed white on glass, sliding down the panes. I scanned the upstairs windows. There. I was sure I saw hands on glass, but the image dissolved into tears. I scrubbed my eyes. A shadow moved in the corner farthest from the fire. *They might be trapped up there.* I grabbed a handful of gravel and threw it at the glass. *If she's trapped, why doesn't she open the window?*

I thought of Dylan's hiding place between the walls. How many lives had been saved by that priest's hole? I heard his voice in my head. *Go on, run.* I put my hands over my ears. The heat from the flames, as scorching as the sun in Mogadishu, where Dylan had once said that: *Go on, run.* I heard his voice clearly, and this time it urged me to go inside and find our son. Pulling the scarf over my nose and mouth, I went in.

Smoke amassed high over my head in the heights of the Georgian ceiling. Up the staircase, the air was thicker on the galleried landing, and I threw open a door only to find a room I'd never seen before, with bare floorboards and a ceiling that sagged like a full diaper. I retreated and fell through another door into a wishbone-shaped passage—a servant's sneak-through—that delivered me to the familiar corridor at the back of the house.

In the haze, I saw a glimmer through the door to the attic; the fire overhead. Contained, for now. I shouted for Gwendoline and Aled, but my throat clutched. I didn't want to gulp in smoke. I hit the floor and focused on drawing shallow breaths.

With my breathing under control, I crawled to Gwendoline's bedroom and pushed myself inside. It was less smoky here, and I closed the door, going over to wrestle with the sash window, which resisted then shot up. I drank down oxygen. Tendrils of smoke leeched through cracks in the ornate plaster around the center light. How long before the ceiling collapsed?

I tried to focus; I didn't have much time. From outside, I'd seen a movement in the far corner of the house. Must be the last door on this hall. I crouched along the passageway and fell into a small room. One sash window, which I couldn't budge. Must be painted over. In the gloom, I made out the shape of an old-fashioned sewing machine. But no Gwendoline, no Aled. I started to cough, panic and smoke invading my body. I held the wet scarf tight over my mouth and forced my lungs to stop spasming. Then I pulled off my boot and pushed my hand into the toe, punching out one pane of glass, then another. Smoke streamed out like a spirit released. I gulped cold air into my burning lungs. Then I heard a thump behind me.

Spinning around, I noticed another door tucked into the corner. I went to it, but the handle wouldn't turn. It was locked. With both fists, I hammered on the wood.

"Leave us alone!" The voice from inside was high-pitched, afraid.

"Gwendoline! It's Rose. Is Aled with you? Is he in there?"

Her voice was suddenly low and slow: "Why don't you move on, like you want to?"

Did Dylan tell her we're thinking of moving to the city?

"The house is on fire, Gwendoline, but we can still get out."

"If you take him away, you know what'll happen."

I hammered on the door again. "He'll die if he stays in here. You both will—"

"I'm warning you, you'll be the one who gets hurt."

"Not if we go now—"

"You always say you'd do anything for your son, that you'd sooner die than let him get into trouble, but when it comes down to it, you're not strong enough!"

I stepped back half a pace. *When have I ever said that?*

She released a growl, a sound of pure frustration. "You're such a . . . flibbertigibbet!"

I dropped to my haunches. The old door had a gap at the bottom, through which I saw her dark shape moving over a tiled bathroom floor. *Flibbertigibbet?* Gwendoline's favorite description of Shawna Dourish.

She thinks she's talking to Shawna.

I can work with that.

"Gwendoline, is my son with you?"

There was a long pause, darkness shifting at the base of the door.

"Are you there, Gwendoline?"

"Where do you think I am?"

"Is the boy with you?"

A sulky tone: "Why would he be with me?"

My heart expanded in my chest. *Okay, if she thinks she's talking to Shawna, then she thinks my son is Rhys.* "I'm desperate to find him, Gwendoline. We both know what Rhys did to Kenny. You understand why I have to find him."

"You have no right to take the boy away. He'll only do it again to some other poor child."

"I'm trying to find him so I can take him to the police, Gwendoline."

"About time! We told you about him, but you wouldn't listen. Flouncing around in your dresses. Everything rosy and rose-tinted, while Rhys was—" She made a sound of disgust. "It's abuse, Shawna. Not teasing or ragging or leg-pulling or whatever you want to call it. It isn't boys-will-be-boys or you-show-me-yours-I'll-show-you-mine. You said you'd deal with it, and I trusted you. I thought you'd go to the police, but what have you done?"

Even though I wasn't really Shawna, I felt shame: "I tried to run away."

"I know we stand up for our own—God knows, I lie for Dylan, but he's got a good heart and he'll learn from his mistakes. But people like Rhys—pedophiles—they don't get better. It's a sickness, and you need to be strong for him. But you aren't strong."

"I can be strong now."

"I don't know about strong, but you're ruthless, I'll give you that. More ruthless than anyone realizes, with your flowery dresses. But it won't get you anywhere in the end."

In the end. How had it ended with Shawna dead in the cellar? "I can't recall what happened in the end . . . You know what it's like, when your memory doesn't work like it should."

"Then will you go away?"

"I'll leave you in peace."

"Because you're making me crazy by taking everything I love. Like Stanley! The shame of people thinking he'd touch a young boy . . . And Dylan can't live here anymore. And I can never leave. I can never go anywhere else, just in case—" Gwendoline fell silent.

"Why can't you leave? Why didn't Stanley tell the police that Rhys abused Kenny Bale?"

"You know, Shawna!" Gwendoline's hand slammed the door, making me jump to my feet. "Stanley had to take the blame because otherwise someone would have found your body. And then they'd know that I killed you."

My head throbbed. My heart too.

Suddenly I didn't care how Shawna had died and whether or not Gwendoline was a killer; I wanted my boy whatever it took. I was the same as Gwendoline, same as Shawna: I'd turn a blind eye to anything so long as I could keep my son safe. "I don't care what you did, Gwendoline. I want to find Aled. Where is your grandson? Where is he?" I was still yelling at a locked wooden door when a crumpling noise above me sounded like a vast piece of paper scrunched in a fist. The bathroom door blew open in a shower of sparks, and everything turned to flame.

CHAPTER 45

Sergeant Ellie Trevelyan froze, mesmerized by fiery threads waving from holes in the roof like the arms of sinners' souls. She heard no sirens now, only flames licking the house, as hungry as slavering dogs. Maybe the fire engines had taken a roundabout route to avoid the flooding. *They've gone all around the Wrekin,* she thought. Or maybe they'd been diverted to another incident; on a night like this, there would be car crashes, fallen trees, residents trapped by rising floodwater. Who got priority?

Ellie faced the same decision. There was no sign of Rose. Or Gwendoline—Harrow would want to talk to her. But the boy had to be Ellie's priority. Inside her pocket, her phone buzzed: Harrow. She heard a long hiss as his vehicle rushed along a wet road.

"You won't reach the holm now," she said. "The road is flooded. I barely made it myself. I can't find anyone, and the house is going up like a wicker man."

"Stay outside, sergeant. What about—"

"There's no sign of Rose or Aled. They must be inside."

"Firefighters are on their way; there's been an accident on the main road. Just stay outside." Harrow's voice was insistent. "We're yet to locate Tony Thorn."

Ellie frowned. "D'you think he might be involved? Is he dangerous?"

"Maybe. Or—"

"Or Gwendoline might have hurt him." Ellie pictured Tony Thorn in his peacock coat; a soft-handed man if ever she'd seen one. Even so . . . an old lady couldn't overwhelm a grown man, could she? But the crack of a shotgun wouldn't raise eyebrows when farmers culled rabbits and crows all the time. The idea of Gwendoline committing a reckless act of anger or revenge didn't sit right. She'd kept Dylan's secret for twenty years. She'd kept quiet about Rhys and Shawna too; whatever had happened to them, she must have known. She lived like a recluse, never leaving Hurtwood House, hovering over the holm like a raven at the tower. No, it didn't make sense to draw attention to herself by hurting Thorn, not even if she hated him for digging up her buried past and bringing it all to light. Ellie looked up at the burning house . . .

. . . and thought of a cat who knows its time is coming to an end. Slinking away to starve itself. Maybe Gwendoline had found a quicker way to hasten her demise: fire.

"Gwendoline's inside, I'm sure of it. And Rose may have gone in to find her."

"Don't go in, Ellie."

"She called me for help. What else can I do?"

"Don't go in the house—"

She hung up. Inside the main entrance, the air was so thick she couldn't make out the top of the stairs. She wouldn't last a minute if she went that way. She soaked her scarf in a puddle and wrapped it over her mouth and nose before setting off toward the side door.

The kitchen was as cloudy as a crystal ball. Ellie hesitated. Then a splintering crash sent the door on the far side of the room slamming back against the wall. Sparks rained down the stairs in the passageway beyond. And a voice: a woman's cry. The blast cleared a path through the smoke, and Ellie followed it through the kitchen and up the stairs.

More screaming—"Aled," she heard, "Aled"—led Ellie along a debris-strewn hallway and into a small room at the far end of the corridor. The ceiling gaped like a gunshot wound. Ragged edges of paper and plaster hung down, the color of burnt skin. Amid the wreckage, a woman's cries. Ellie wrenched aside a door that hung painfully from one hinge. Rose was there, clambering to her feet, so stunned she barely reacted to Ellie's sudden appearance. Instead, she froze, listening to the groans of the house as though it was a language only she understood.

Ellie took the woman's arm, but Rose barely noticed. "Aled," she whispered. And before Ellie could stop her, Rose rushed into an adjoining bathroom that had suffered the worst of the ceiling collapse. Ellie registered a bath full of embers and the wall beyond riven into a huge V where a beam had smashed down. Ellie tried to keep up as they crossed an entirely empty room, where Rose shoulder-barged through another interconnecting door. *Damn house is a rabbit warren.*

It was less smoky in the next bedroom; the ceiling was intact and the window was open. Rose stood in the middle of the room, screaming her son's name, her voice a high whine of pain. Ellie closed the door behind her and laid her wet scarf along its bottom edge. Through the gloom, she made out a four-poster bed and a tall chest of drawers. Then a movement on the bed made Ellie yelp. She grabbed Rose, and both women clung together as a recumbent figure stirred to a sitting position. It started coughing. Only then did Ellie recognize the figure as Gwendoline, as gray and stiff as a tomb effigy.

"Where is he?" Rose rushed toward the old woman.

"Hiding, most likely. Dylan often hides."

"Aled!" This one word emerged from Rose like a growl. "I'm talking about Aled. Where is he hiding?"

"If I knew that, it wouldn't be a good hiding place, would it!"

Ellie caught Rose's arms from behind as she launched a strike at the old woman, who didn't flinch—a stone martyr. Rose's arms jerked in Ellie's grasp with the taut movements of a deer, one snap away from panic. Ellie tugged her around to make eye contact. "Go and look for your son. I'll deal with Gwendoline."

After a moment's hesitation, Rose pulled off her bag and thrust it into Ellie's hands. "In here is a journal." She nodded toward Gwendoline. "She wrote everything down before she forgot. The deaths had nothing to do with Dylan. Gwendoline killed Shawna; she told me herself. What happened to Rhys, I've no idea, but he was the one who abused Kenny Bale."

"Sniffer!" Gwendoline swung her legs over the side of the bed, the movement making her cough. "They call your son Sniffer, Shawna. Once again, we've got to clean up your mess."

Rose widened her eyes at Ellie, inviting her to understand. "That's right, Gwendoline. I didn't go to the police even though I knew Rhys was abusing Kenny. I tried to run away, and you stopped us."

Sniffer, thought Ellie. The police never made public the words written in Kenny Bale's diary. The claim that he was abused by S. They'd thought *S* meant Stanley. But it didn't explain how Rhys—*Sniffer*—and his mother died.

Gwendoline came closer. One side of the old woman's face was blackened by a burn. She grabbed Rose by the arm. "Tell the officer what happened, Shawna. This horrible business can be over."

Ellie saw a chance to get Gwendoline out of the house. "It's not over, I'm afraid. I'll have to take your journal to the station. We're going to charge Dylan with the deaths of Rhys and Shawna, unless you can explain . . ."

Rose joined in: "Gwendoline, Dylan will go to prison unless you tell her."

The old woman released Rose and grabbed Ellie instead. Her papery fingers had surprising strength. "I'll tell you while it's fresh in my mind." But the old woman started to cough, bent over as she scanned the room with the close attention of a hotel guest checking out for the final time. "I hope you find your son. He must be in here somewhere."

Gwendoline dragged Ellie by the wrist across the huge room, opened the door to the hallway—smoke flooded the bedroom—and went down the stairs. Ellie pressed her free hand over her mouth and nose until she felt gravel under her boots and the relief of cold night air in her lungs. Through streaming eyes, she made out the Land Rover and directed Gwendoline toward it. Ellie told her to stay by the car and wait for the other officers to arrive. She made to turn back to the house, but the old woman grasped Ellie by the upper arms, spinning her on the spot and pushing the officer against the vehicle.

"I have something to tell you." The old woman's hands slid down to grip Ellie's wrists, pressing them against the car as she towered over her. "You need to listen. I have to confess."

CHAPTER 46

The beams cracked and spat cinders. I cowered, turned my face from the sparks. My headache was a two-prong pitchfork. Even with the windows open, Gwendoline's bedroom was bathed in the yellow of a bad memory.

He must be here somewhere. Where would a child go to hide? Where would instinct take him? Dylan's hiding place: the priest's hole? Gwendoline had looked all around this room as though she remembered . . . *A space between the walls, somewhere in his parents' room.* This room.

Aled was hiding, like everyone else in this house. Gwendoline hid her illness. Shawna hid her son's perversion. Dylan hid from everyone. I went around the walls, kicking and slapping the wooden panels, but nothing sounded hollow. I shouted and tried to listen for a response, but the crackle of flame and the snap of timbers would drown out his little voice. "Please," I said, "show me where he is." The response was a crash above my head and a shower of flecks as plaster fell. The whole ceiling would come down soon. I shook embers off my hair like a person driven crazy by a wasp.

Please. I sank to the floor. *Please.*

A section of beam that had landed near the door burned like a torch. Its flame glinted on the wall—a reflection. I got up and kicked the torch aside. Tucked behind the door at knee height, a square of glass the size of a shoebox was embedded in the wall. It was so dirty it was almost the same color as the paneling that surrounded it, but opaque enough that I could see two pale hands pressed against it. I knelt down, reminded of the vision I'd had when I first arrived at the Grim's Holm—hands sliding down glass. That vision became reality as the two small palms slipped out of sight. Aled's hands, trapped behind glass. I'd found the priest's hole and Aled alive in it, but how had he gotten in? And how could I get him out?

I made a fist and thumped the wooden paneling, but nothing moved. I dug my nails into grooves, trying to find an edge, but nothing gave. I had no tools. I lay on my side and kicked the glass. It dislodged, and one corner dropped an inch, enough to get my fingers in and press down. It fell away into the wall cavity. But the hole was too small for me to fit through. "Aled!" I pushed my head into the gap, finding a windowless space about the width of a grave, only longer and much taller; Aled stood at the far end, holding his backpack against his chest like a shield. "Come to Mommy," I said. "You can squeeze through this hole and we'll get out."

Aled shook his head violently, and he started coughing. "I don't like the stinky stink." The priest's hole had been clear of smoke until I dislodged the glass.

"Come on," I urged him. "We need to leave now."

He shook his head again. "I found Daddy," he said. I tried to see what he was pointing at, but my head was awkwardly angled, my shoulders too wide to get through the gap. "Can you bring it here?" *I'll grab him,* I thought, *and pull him through the hole.* But instead of coming closer, Aled held up a shiny rectangle the size of a playing card. I saw a man in a soccer uniform. Aled frowned at the picture. "Is he Daddy?" I recognized a trading card. I'd collected NFL cards as a kid.

"Can I see it?" I asked. Aled shook his head and said he wanted to keep it.

"It's not Daddy, Aled," I said. "Daddy's waiting for us outside."

"It looks like Daddy."

Stanley. On the far wall stood a small table covered with soccer trophies and medals. A shrine. Dylan said he'd hidden stuff from other boys. Or maybe he tried to hide his father from them, to keep a piece of the soccer legend for himself. Either way, tears came to my eyes at the thought of my husband as a small boy, hiding in this dismal space. And more tears at the thought of losing my son to it.

"Aled, I want you to come now." As though to back me up, the house gave a deep creak, a warning from above.

"I'm scared, Mommy. Of the stinky stink. Gwen-ma said it would make me dead." He coughed. "She told me to go outside, but I couldn't find the way and I came in here. And now I'm stuck."

"How did you get in there?"

Aled turned around on the spot, hopelessly disorientated.

"Never mind, we can get you out. Bring Daddy's soccer card. Put it in your backpack—"

Behind me, the door to Gwendoline's bedroom hit my legs. Smoke rolled into the room like a gray and massive boulder. It caught in my throat, and my response was so violent, my body contracted and I banged my windpipe against the wood. I kicked the door to close it, but it sprang back as though pushed by a hand. I tried to call Aled, but my voice burned up in my mouth. Smoke rolled over me with the weight of a landslide. I reached for Aled, but my arm didn't move. It was a deadweight. *I need help.* I pulled my head out of the priest's hole and tried to move toward the open window. I imagined crawling across blissfully cool floorboards, but my limbs didn't respond. I saw my hands pressing against glass. My palms like twin hearts, one for me and one for Aled. *Poor Aled,* I thought, *and poor Dylan. Abandoned again.* I felt the warmth of his skin over my body. The lament of the dying house could have been the rumble of a voice. *Go on,* it says, *run.* But I can't run, I can't stand. I'm a pile of bones. The air turns cold. In my mind, one hand falls away from the windowpane while the other slides down the glass like England's early-setting sun.

CHAPTER 47

B ent backward over the front of the Land Rover, Ellie could hardly draw breath. It was as bad as being inside the burning house. The wind caught sparks from the roof and threw them spitefully against her face. She kicked out at the old woman's shins but only got pushed back harder; her spine creaked like the beams of the house.

"Gwendoline, I need to go back to the house, to help Rose and Aled—"

"No!" Her voice was a croak. "I take full responsibility for the death of Shawna Dourish. Listen to me—" A crash. Both women looked up to see glass raining down. Ellie tried to twist one wrist out of the old woman's grasp when she was distracted, but Gwendoline's height helped her pin the shorter woman against the car, and Ellie couldn't get any purchase. Gwendoline jabbed her chin toward the old flint barn as though tossing her words that way.

"You're a flibbertigibbet, Shawna Dourish! You know what Rhys is, and yet I get painted as the wicked one. Well, I'm going to tell the police everything, right from the start." Gwendoline twisted Ellie's wrists so tight it felt like the skin might rip. She looked between the house and the barn. "Poor Morgana . . ."

"Who's Morgana?" Ellie tried to use her weight to push the old woman backward, but Gwendoline clamped her hands to her sides.

"Morgana is a pony, just a foal." Flames reflected in Gwendoline's eyes, giving Ellie an eerie sense that the older woman was blind but could see things beyond anyone's view. "Poor Morgana—she's tied up, she can't get out of the way. And you try to drive away, Shawna, your Land Rover reverses right into her. Her leg is torn open, there's blood everywhere, and I scream for Stanley to help me, but you—" Gwendoline jerked Ellie's wrists so hard her chin snapped back. "You come over all concerned, all *let me help, let me help.* You're always sorry when it's too late. *After* Rhys did what he did. *After* Kenny killed himself. *After* you nearly kill my pony. You just keep coming back for more: drama after drama." Gwendoline looked down at Ellie's hands in her own. "Your touch is like a curse. And when you try to touch poor Morgana, I just think—no more!" Gwendoline spun Ellie away from the car, grabbing her lapels. "Get away from me, get away from my home, get away from all of us!" Gwendoline shoved Ellie with all her strength. Ellie staggered backward one . . . two . . . half a dozen steps before losing her balance and sprawling onto the ground. Gwendoline came at her again, but Ellie saw the moment she needed; staying low to catch the older woman's wrists, she pulled Gwendoline to the ground.

Ellie heard a sickening snap and Gwendoline cried out. As Ellie got to her feet, the older woman lay sprawled on the gravel, clutching her wrist. She had gone down hard. Ellie bit back a curse as she moved the keening woman into the recovery position. Slowly, the noise stopped and Ellie got her breath back. Gwendoline lay still, staring fixedly at the barn. Now Ellie swore out loud as she realized she couldn't leave an injured old woman alone and go back to the house.

"Don't curse at me, Shawna," Gwendoline said. "I didn't mean to hurt you."

The fight had gone out of the old woman. She lay fetal on the ground. Ellie squatted beside her.

"So you push Shawna away from the pony . . . ?"

"I don't know my own strength; you go flying! Right over the hatch. Stanley reaches out, tries to grab you, but it happens too fast. It must be a ten-foot drop into that cellar. Enough to break your neck. And it could have ended there, I could have called the police and explained, but of course Rhys had other ideas—"

They were distracted by a dull thudding sound. Falling masonry inside the house? No, the beat of a helicopter. Air ambulance. Ellie pulled out her flashlight and placed it on the ground to indicate where Gwendoline was lying. "Stay here," she said. She prayed she wasn't too late and started running toward the mansion, toward Rose. Toward a column of smoke above Hurtwood House that twirled like a falling woman.

CHAPTER 48

A nudge on the foot woke me. After gulping fruitlessly for a few seconds, I focused on how to breathe. Panic descended like a bag over the head. *I'm choking!* A nudge on my foot, harder. It wasn't a bag over my face; it was smoke. I forced my stinging eyes open. Bare floorboards tramlined to the window. I rolled onto hands and knees, my head a weight dragging on my shoulders, and dumbly followed the path to the open window. Oxygen washed over me. The floor seemed littered with fallen stars. I slumped down and pain shot through my hands. Not stars—glass.

Glass.

Hands on glass.

Aled.

I used the windowsill to pull myself up. Outside, voices carried on the wind. Lights streamed over gravel. Far away in the yard, a helicopter hunkered down, ready to spring into action. I tried to shout, but my voice was sand. I waved, but none of the scuttling figures looked my way. The trees bent low and the holm blew sharply into my face. I stepped back onto glass.

I drew in a deep breath. The bedroom door was open. I went through it to the hallway and—with a clap that spun me around—the door slammed shut behind me. I heard the patter of falling plaster like a sudden downpour on the other side of the door. And a chillingly understated pant of delight as the fire overhead found fresh oxygen inside the bedroom.

I only had moments before the smoke would reach me in the hallway. I faced the wall behind which Aled had to be trapped.

"Please," I whispered. There was an emphatic click, like a grandfather clock reaching midnight. The house froze in the moment before the strike. A groove had appeared in the wooden paneling. I scrabbled at the sliver of an edge with my fingernails. The floorboards above me moaned, and it seemed the whole edifice lurched. Along the hallway, the attic door slammed. But I didn't take my eyes off the wooden panel. "Please!" There was a second click. The groove became a ridge. I got my nails under it and dragged the panel aside. Aled stood there, sparks circling him like fairy dust as they streamed into his hiding place through the shoebox-sized hole in the wall.

I snatched him up, and instinct turned me the right way. My head swam; flying embers stung my face. I carried him down the stairs but missed my footing and slid down the last few steps on my backside, landing hard on the flagstones. Aled's fingers dug into my shoulders as he found his feet. I used the newel post to haul myself onto my knees. Through gray smog, the door swung open to welcome us to the kitchen. *Ellie must be here!* But the room stood empty. Aled ran ahead. The door to the outside world rattled open, and I smelled fresh air. It was so close. "Go on," I whispered to Aled, "run." I saw him sparkle in the helicopter light that streamed across the gravel. But I fell to the flagstones. One more breath. One breath too many.

ONE MONTH LATER

A moral being is one who is capable of reflecting on his past actions and their motives—of approving of some and disapproving of others.
   —Charles Darwin, born in Shropshire, 1809

—Clipping pasted in Gwendoline
Kynaston's journal

CHAPTER 49

Ellie Trevelyan arrives at the end of her row, checks her boarding pass, and eyeballs the two empty spaces between her aisle seat and the window. The cabin doors seal the passengers inside, and the aisle remains empty; no one else is coming on board. So long as none of these pinheads move, she can curl up across three seats for the next sixteen hours. She sinks into her chair. Despite dropping a dress size in the run-up to yesterday's funeral—*perhaps I could patent the guilt and shame diet?*—Ellie sags under her load. *If I'd gone back to the house sooner, I might have been in time—*

Stop!

You can't be in two places at once. She imagines her sister's words of comfort. *There was nothing more you could have done.* Tomorrow, Ellie would be with her sister again, and then she'd feel better.

But it's a sign of her bone-deep exhaustion that she's looking forward to sixteen hours sitting on her backside on a plane. A row to herself offers the added bonus of not having to chat with a neighbor who might want her life story served up in airline-meal portions. *Visiting my sister, what about you? Newly retired, what about you? Police officer, what about you? No, it's not like the movies, what about you, is your life like the movies? Thought not. That's why we watch movies.*

Ellie flips open her passport. It's not often she's the willing subject of a photograph, and this reminds her why. More baggage around the eyes than in the hold. Ms. Ellie Trevelyan, it says. Not *Mrs.*, obviously. Not *Mistress*, never mistress, no matter what people started saying about her and DI Bryan Harrow.

They only went to the pub once—*along with a bunch of other officers!*—after she was awarded a commendation. Ellie hadn't been in the mood for celebrating, not with the funeral coming up. She didn't feel like a hero, but Harrow insisted that they lift a glass to mark the occasion. So they went out once—*with other people!*—and there was no truth in the rumors about them. And what better way to prove there are no awkward feelings than by running away to the other side of the world? Out of sight, out of mind. Hopefully.

She zips the passport into her bag. Ms. Ellie Trevelyan. Not *Sergeant*; she is liberated from rank and responsibility. The hot flashes and temper tantrums are subsiding too. Her metamorphosis from one phase to the next is almost complete. And here she is, en route to Australia: another new phase.

Would I be here if it weren't for Bryan Harrow? In the car park behind the police station after their celebratory drink, Broken Arrow's farewell peck on the cheek strayed dangerously off target. No truth in the rumors, but also no smoke without fire. Rumors are like that; hot air requires a source of heat.

It was over and done with in a moment of madness. Ellie's briefest one-nighter, and yet strangely satisfying—emotionally, if not physically. After his badly aimed kiss, they enjoyed a few moments of racy eye contact while he longingly massaged the fatty mound between her thumb and index finger. Then a patrol vehicle swung into the dark car park, its blue lights throwing their shadows hard up against the wall. Harrow and Trevelyan stepped apart. Getting out of the patrol car, one of the young PCs whooped like a siren.

"I'm shaking her hand to say goodbye, you pinheads, so show some respect," said Harrow. He went home to his family, Ellie to a box set of *Luther*. Their dignity, reputation, and his marriage remain intact. On the tray table, Ellie's phone lights up. Her tummy glitches at the word *Arrow* on the screen. Ellie rolls her eyes at herself as she answers.

"Trevelyan?" He pauses long enough for her to hear the hubbub of the station. She knows exactly which room he's in from the signature squeal of the swinging door. "I wanted to catch you before you leave."

"Just in time, I've boarded."

"I thought you'd like to know, we charged Giles Hotchen with statutory rape. Robert Elks got the girl from the Nail Bar into Hurtwood nick. It took the sexual assault team a good while to gain her trust, but eventually she told us it's been going on for a year. We tracked down her family in Vietnam, who confirmed she's only fifteen. She traveled here on a false passport."

"DNA?"

"Hotchen's DNA on the girl. Fingerprints all over her room. And CCTV showing him breaking in via the fire escape on Whipping Post Lane. The same way Meredith and Dylan got into that flat years ago. The Vietnamese girl said he let himself in two or three times a week, whenever he knew she was alone. He threatened to shut down the Nail Bar if she didn't comply. The owner of the Nail Bar, Lillian Oister, is denying any knowledge, but—"

"What about Mr. Samwel?"

"The pharmacist provided records of Oister buying the morning-after pill. A sixty-six-year-old woman is going to have trouble explaining that. We'll get her too."

There's a pause, during which Ellie can smell the station. She misses the banter with the kind of pang that comes from spotting an old lover on the arm of another.

"Hotchen got away with this right under my nose," she says.

"With the aggravating factor of breaking and entering, he'll go down for ten years."

Ellie's voice is unattractively phlegmy as she thanks Harrow for letting her know. His tone drops in reply: "You okay, Ellie?"

"Not really." Outside her little window, rain shatters the flashing lights of airport vehicles. "He told me about the Nail Bar ages ago. I didn't listen."

"Your dad?"

"I got annoyed with him; he kept mentioning *Hottie*. I thought he was perving over a girl."

"You did all right, Trevelyan. On both cases. The force'll miss you."

"Can I listen for a minute?"

"To what?"

"To the station."

Harrow goes quiet while Ellie soaks it up, and when she has had enough, they ring off. She watches the ground crew retreat while the engine rumbles to life, and then she remembers something and scrambles to send a text to her new tenant before the aircraft pushes back: *Hope you're settling in. Forgot to give you the key for the back gate. It's in the drawer by the sink. —E x.*

The steward comes up the aisle, head ticking side to side: bag under seat, tray table up, phone switched to airplane mode. Ellie slides the phone into her bag and withdraws a postcard. She clips it to the back of the television screen in front of her. Sea, sun, sand. She wants all that. And she wants to see a bloody quokka. The world outside Hurtwood has been calling, and now it's time to answer. The aircraft accelerates, lengthening her spine along the curve of the seat. She imagines the pressure on her chest is the weight of the Pacific Ocean. She'll take it, predators and all. Ellie Trevelyan takes a deep breath as though she's about to jump in.

CHAPTER 50

If there's one thing I've learned from moving around the world, it's that people have an infinite capacity for adaptation. We grind ever onward, like glaciers, leaving deposits in the present while hauling the bulk of ourselves into the future.

We've adapted to a new home already. It's warmer than the cottage, so I don't need to thaw myself on the Aga like leftovers. We salvaged the pine table from the great house. It's too large for our new suburban kitchen, but Dylan needed to bring something from the Grim's Holm, and this is it. Every cup ring stained onto the wood holds a memory; all that we forget, we feel.

I leave Dylan to prepare Aled's breakfast. He's drawing at the kitchen table, coloring everything blue, and I see watery currents of confusion, eddies of trauma. Dylan says I'm overthinking; Aled's bad at drawing, that's all. "It's like me and football. Practice doesn't always make perfect, not when you're crap." The psychologist agrees, not about being crap, but about Aled being fine. None the worse for his ordeal. No evil inherent in his bloodline—I'm sure of that now—just an old head on young shoulders.

I drag myself away to make a shot list for my television documentary. Netflix wants to call it *Quest: The Real Indiana Bones*. Tomorrow, I'm going to the studios in Manchester to edit it. The name is okay, although I don't want to trivialize the lives contained within the story.

Especially the family of Kenny Bale, who bravely gave me an interview and their blessing. I've used actors to re-create the events described in Gwendoline's journal. It should be more powerful than simply reading her account.

On screen, I bring up my footage of the actors. I've already written a shot list for the part where the young actor playing Rhys sees his mother lying in the cellar and runs. Now I select shots of the actors playing Gwen and Stanley; they run after the boy, branches skitter across the ground in the wind, Rhys turns to confront them.

My shot zooms in smoothly as the actor playing Rhys waves something toward the camera. The real Rhys must have kept the item in a ziplock bag as that was how it was found, but I've allowed a little poetic license to help the audience quickly recognize the black square he holds aloft: an old-fashioned floppy disc. I let the scene play on my screen.

"What is that?" the woman posing as Gwendoline asks.

"Insurance. I have photos," says Rhys. "I don't think Cambridge University would like what Dylan's doing in these pictures."

Stanley lunges for the disc, and Rhys sprints halfway across the yard before he faces them again. The wind kneads his T-shirt against his torso.

"Dylan wouldn't do anything bad," Gwendoline says.

"It doesn't matter what he did or didn't do, I made pictures of him with that kid. Everyone will think Dylan touched Kenny and that's why he jumped off the cliff. If you tell the police, I'll show them the disc. I'll say Dylan forced both of us to pose for him."

"You'd blame Dylan? You grew up together!"

"What else am I supposed to do? It was Kenny's fault; he told you, didn't he?"

I stop the action, then select a long shot of the actor playing Gwendoline as she says: "Kenny told us you showed him dirty pictures."

A close-up of Rhys: "Is that all he told you?"

"What else is there?" She falls silent, her arms limp. I cut to a close-up of her face. I took the actor to meet the real Gwendoline, and she really nailed her expressions and body language.

I make a note to switch into voiceover at this point: *Of course, Rhys hadn't just shown Kenny pornography; he'd been making it. Kenny asked us for help, but we didn't understand there was stuff he couldn't bring himself to say. That he was so ashamed he couldn't say it out loud.*

Then I cut back to the action. Stanley holds out his hand: "Give me the disc, and we'll forget about it."

Rhys: "You won't. You're a do-gooder. You'll go to the police."

The boy runs, and the camera follows. Voiceover: *Stanley was fit once, but his bad heart slowed him down.* Rhys veers into the trees. *The boy goes to ground, with no more reason than a fox or a badger, following an instinct to hide.* The camera bursts from the tree line onto grass overlooking the Long Drop. Stanley is ahead, his arms wide as though he can catch Rhys. But the boy is out of reach. Right on the cliff edge, up on his toes with his back to the camera, body arched as though someone has punched him in the kidneys.

On the very edge of balance. Of life. He looks down at the long drop onto rocks jutting from the floodwater.

I wonder if the editor can do some wizardry so that Rhys freezes there while the actor playing Gwendoline steps into the shot to deliver her closing monologue: "As he teeters, struggling to hold himself upright, he fights forces we can't see—gravity, guilt, evil—and a part of me feels it's a fitting end for a boy who's struggled with forces that don't trouble normal people." Gwendoline turns to the camera and looks us right in the eye. "And he loses the fight—"

Behind her, the actor playing Rhys topples over the edge.

Now, Gwendoline is alone. "Gravity claims him. Or maybe evil does."

I add a shot of Stanley running toward the flooded river—it's important to make clear that they did try to save Rhys—but cut back quickly to Gwendoline peering over the edge of the Long Drop.

Voiceover: *For a few seconds, I can't see the boy, but then he surfaces, struggling as though unseen hands are catching his legs from below. After a moment, he vanishes. All night, we search. All the next day. And after the floodwater recedes, we search for his body. The disc. But we never find a thing . . .*

They say the devil's lair is close under the surface in this part of the world. Once upon a time, long ago, his roof collapsed, and he patched it up with stones that formed the holm. They say the Grim's Holm floods when the devil wants a new servant.

Gwendoline turns away from the Long Drop and walks into the trees.

I press stop. It's done. I'm pleased with it. I shut down my computer and go to the kitchen, where breakfast is in full swing. My husband glances at me as he smashes the top of a boiled egg. "How's it looking?"

"The reconstruction worked well—Gwendoline's words make it sing."

"I got a message that the contract is ready. Sure you want to commit? We can still go to Manchester or look for jobs overseas—it's not too late."

In our yard, the spaniels stare into the netted pond, quivering with the urge to get to the fish. I open the back door and the dogs stream around my legs, goofily affectionate. *What would we do with two dogs in the city?* The spaniels have chosen me to replace Gwendoline as pack leader. I settle them with a stroke.

After years of living everywhere, it finally occurred to me that I only needed to live somewhere. As I always knew he would, Dylan helped me stop running. "Let's do it," I say. "Let's sign."

"Okay, then," he says. "We can meet Robert Elks and the lawyer later today."

I pour a golden stream of tea into two mugs. Soon we'll be the directors of a media company focused on countryside affairs, leasing office space from the *Midland Post*. We're in business. My phone buzzes.

A message from Ellie Trevelyan, who's supposed to be on a plane. I scan her text, then open a drawer beside the sink. I dangle a key. "Ellie says this is for the back gate."

"Righty-o." Dylan insinuates a lump of egg between Aled's lips. "Do you think she'll come back? No job to worry about. And now her dad's gone . . ."

"Everyone at the funeral kept saying it was 'a release,' which I thought was insensitive."

"People never know what to say at funerals," Dylan says. "'He had a good innings!' That's my least favorite."

"But why 'a release'? Jim seemed fit, apart from the dementia. It was so sudden. Poor Ellie feels that if she'd gotten home sooner—"

"He was old. And it was peaceful. I can think of worse ways to go than passing away in my favorite chair while listening to cricket on the radio. There was nothing Ellie could have done; her sister will talk her round. Shame they couldn't get the same flight." He pops a piece of bread into Aled's mouth. I send a reply to Ellie, saying we found the key and wishing her a safe journey. Dylan gathers up the dishes and takes them to the sink. He lingers over the view. From Ellie's house— *our house* for a few months and maybe longer if she decides to stay in Australia—there's a long view of the Wrekin. In the middle distance, the land heaves into an unnatural shape. The holm: a place of refuge or battle, no one knows which. For Dylan, it has been both. I slip my arms around his waist.

"Do you regret selling?" I ask.

He swirls a plate under the running tap like he's panning for gold. "It's a relief."

"But your heritage—"

"Bricks and mortar. It's memories that matter. I can't tell you what a relief it is to have only good memories of my dad. And to know that my mother wasn't disappointed in me." Dylan dries his hands, then returns my hug. "The Grim's Holm is a scar we'll see every day, but a scar proves that the pain has passed." He kisses my head and goes to get his coat.

I let him go, but have the feeling he's hurting. He sold the estate so quickly; I've deliberated longer over a new hairstyle. But the sale paid for Gwendoline's hospice care, and she's settled well into the home. I hope she might even find friendship.

Our mail slot clatters, and seconds later Dylan rushes in. "Look!" He slaps a newspaper onto the table. The front page of the *Midland Post* shows Tony Thorn standing by the charred hulk of the great house: "TV Boss Fired over Sword Scam." The holm wind blows his hair so it looks like a wig. "Elks got an exclusive," Dylan says. "He'll be chuffed."

As soon as Thorn returned from his "disappearance"—which he told the press was prompted by a nervous breakdown, but which was clearly a futile attempt to avoid being arrested for fraud—he offered to buy Hurtwood House. He wants to renovate the mansion, convert the outbuildings—even the infamous leper barn—and open a hotel. It's what he'd always wanted, just as Gwendoline said. He'd clapped his hands like Willy Wonka on a sugar rush when Dylan signed the papers.

I scan a few paragraphs of the article. "The network canceled his show." I glance over the rest of the page. "And his production company declared bankruptcy. Oh shoot!"

Dylan folds up the paper. "It's one thing adding a dramatic score to a nature documentary, but another to fake an entire show. No one can touch him now. I wonder if he can still afford to renovate Hurtwood House? Or will he be lord of a burnt-out shell?"

I can't help thinking of another line from the journal: *A squire built a great house on land as had been cursed.* Dylan doesn't believe in curses, but after everything that happened on the Grim's Holm, it makes me wonder.

Aled has been standing next to us while we discuss Thorn, struggling to pull on gloves. I sink to my haunches in front of him: "Make a starfish."

He spreads his fingers, and I tug each woolen finger into place. "It was Mistress Payne," he says.

Behind me, Dylan pauses while pulling on his coat.

"Mistress Payne?" I echo.

"She doesn't like Tony Torn."

"Oh." I keep my voice level. "And why do you think that?"

"If you're mean, she takes something you love."

Thorn loved being rich and famous. Dylan ruffles Aled's hair and says there's no such thing as ghosts. Then he stamps out of the kitchen to show that the matter is closed. My son and I exchange a long look, during which nothing needs to be said. In the days after the fire, Aled explained that the hidden door to the priest's hole popped open when he was looking for somewhere to hide. He couldn't breathe. He was scared. He would have died if that panel hadn't opened. Of course, Dylan's explanation makes the most sense: shifting timbers made the panel open. It was the fire. It was luck.

It was Mistress Payne, said Aled.

"She's here, you know." His voice is light. Casual. My heart turns like the spaniels settling on their bed. I glance around and whisper, "Thank you, Mistress Payne, for saving my son."

The front door rattles, but it's only the mail. Aled shouts, "Letters!" and runs to collect them. I sit down while my pulse settles. If Mistress Payne waited hundreds of years to save a child because she wasn't able to save her own, then I'm grateful for her patience and extraordinary maternal instincts, but I can't pretend I'm comfortable with her hanging around the house like a macabre Mary Poppins. Nevertheless, "Make yourself at home, Mistress Payne," I say, wondering if a ghost can tell that your heart's not in it.

Outside, a morning sun the color of fresh tea is cupped between hills. I glance at the date on the newspaper: December 21, the solstice, the shortest day of the year. In many ways, the hardest months lie ahead, cold weeks of toil to get our business up and running. But the sky has the pearl shine of winter, and I smell snow. Aled has never seen snow. I throw open the door, looking across rooftops to the Wrekin, the ever-present breeze lifting the hair off my neck as though I'm skimming along on ice skates somewhere on a frozen lakeshore. I close my eyes and smell home. The wind blows, and I pick up speed, a propulsion that will carry me toward softer seasons. In the spaniels' sigh, I hear the past settle into a dark corner where it belongs: behind us.

Author's Note

Thank you so much for picking *The Last to Know* as your latest read. This story and its landscape are dear to my heart. The idea for the novel came in a rush, right after I relocated from Singapore to Shropshire, England. Thankfully, the town I moved to is very different to imaginary Hurtwood, and I received a much warmer welcome than poor Rose Kynaston!

When people ask what this novel is about, I could say: "Secrets! Lies! Murder!" But really, it's about home. This book will hopefully travel far and wide, into many different hands, but one thing that unites us all is an idea of home. For better or worse—whatever *home* means to you—I'm sure the concept is soaked in emotion.

So, after seventeen years of living abroad, I moved home to England. Wood pigeons and jet lag woke me on my first morning. It was January, perishing cold. Driving through the country lanes, I chanced upon a hill fort (there are loads in Shropshire) with a farm perched on top, and I stopped to read an information board that said the area used to become an island when the river flooded. I knew right away that I had to set a story in this strange landscape.

Now, I feel I should offer my apologies for making it such a dark story! I hope the beauty of Shropshire and its people shines through the fictional mire. Some readers (and friends) ask why I put my characters through such awful experiences. I have two excuses: journalism and the Victorians.

As a journalist, I often saw people fighting to protect their secrets. Sometimes, I wondered how on earth they thought they would get away with it—how they could put their head in the sand or, conversely, do something terrible in order to maintain a lie. I saw that shame is a powerful and murky motivator. And I saw that sometimes forgiveness hurts more than the original injury.

And the Victorians . . . well, I blame the literature. I share with Rose a love of Gothic tales, the way the modern world is only a heartbeat away from our most ancient and uncanny fears, as she discovers up on the holm.

I'm hoping—as you've made it this far!—that you enjoyed *The Last to Know*. A review on Amazon really helps other readers to discover my work, so if you have time to post a few words of recommendation, I'd be grateful. Think of it as dropping a tip in a busker's hat!

It's always lovely to hear from readers, so feel free to drop me a line. Connect via Facebook (/JoFurnissAuthor), Instagram (@jofurnissauthor), Twitter (@Jo_Furniss), or through my website, www.jofurniss.com. If you sign up for my (not too frequent) newsletter, I'll send you a short story in return. There's no reason to be . . . the last to know!

Warmest wishes,

Jo

Acknowledgments

As I sit down to complete my final edits, my husband is at work in another country and my kids are busy making mischief at school. The dog is asleep on a pile of clean laundry that may or may not get put away today. I'm profoundly grateful for the love and support I receive at home, and the patience required to live with a novel-in-progress. In particular, the fact that the best ideas seem to come in the moments before I fall asleep, so when that bedside lamp is switched off, you can guarantee it's coming right back on again.

Next . . . my bookish community of readers, bloggers, and writers. Like every author, I have periods of doubt, but messages and reviews from readers keep my spirits up. I'm amazed by the time and effort the book blogging community puts into supporting authors: thank you all. And my fellow criminal minds—those partners in crime—I'll see you in the bar at the next festival.

I'm grateful to Danielle Marshall, Erin Calligan Mooney, and Jodi Warshaw at Lake Union for having the faith to turn an idea into a book. Also to the brilliant developmental editor, David Downing, for cutting facets into the rough diamond of my draft; I was literally taking notes while working with him. The cover designer, Zoe Norvell, captured the mood of the book brilliantly. The whole team at Amazon Publishing make the publishing process a delight, especially production editor

Emma Reh, as well as copyeditor Lindsey Alexander and proofreader Karen Parkin, whom I can't thank enough for their attention to detail.

I'm indebted to early readers, Alice Clark-Platts, Joanne Sefton, and Imogen Clark, for tackling the toughest job of all: the dreaded first draft. Also to my friend Dr. Faye Pugh, for giving me the (missing) finger. My American colleague Bekah Graham helpfully pointed out weird English stuff. And there are many more people who've endured conversations about plot holes and problems—thanks for your indulgence.

Thank you to Shawn Dourish, who gave a generous donation at a charity ball organized by Newport (Salop) Rugby Club to have his name included in this book. Someone jokingly suggested calling one of the female characters "Shawna" and then, as you may have noticed, it stuck. I hope you don't mind the transformation into a buxom bombshell, Shawn/a.

Finally, I'm thankful to my wonderful agent, Danielle Egan-Miller, and her team, who have an uncanny knack for reaching out with ideas, insight, and encouragement just when I need them.

About the Author

Photo © 2016 Emily Newell, Littleones Photography

Jo Furniss is the author of *The Trailing Spouse* and the Amazon Charts bestseller *All the Little Children*. After spending a decade as a broadcast journalist for the BBC, Jo gave up the glamour of night shifts to become a freelance writer and serial expatriate. Originally from the United Kingdom, she spent seven years in Singapore and also lived in Switzerland and Cameroon. As a journalist, Jo worked for numerous online outlets and magazines, including *Monocle* and the *Economist*. She has edited books for a Nobel laureate and the palace of the sultan of Brunei. She has a Distinction in MA Professional Writing from Falmouth University. To keep in touch with Jo, please sign up for her newsletter at www.jofurniss. com or drop her a line at www.facebook.com/JoFurnissAuthor.